Proving Ground

Michael G. Casey

ISBN 978-1-9160264-3-8

First edition, 2019

Published by Azimuth Publishing
Dublin, Ireland

Photographic images used in the cover via Wikimedia.

Layout, cover design by iCulture

Please visit michaelgcasey.com

ABOUT THIS BOOK

Writer and TV celebrity Robert Lynskey is part of the Manhattan skyline. Despite his obvious success, he begins to doubt himself. His partner, Sarah, tries to dispel these doubts and convince him that he has earned his success. She is aware that the producer of Lynskey's TV show is also attracted to her, and she tries to keep him at bay.

Khaled Hassan, a Palestinian, is on his way to New York to free his mentor from Guantánamo Bay. To set up a hostage exchange, he and his associates kidnap Lynskey – a soft target with a high profile. They demand that his TV Network broadcast a series of propaganda tapes.

The CIA, FBI and Homeland Security become involved. Following 9 / 11 there is no question of negotiating with terrorists. There is a strong suspicion that Lynskey might be collaborating with the terrorists, especially when it is discovered that Hassan had been a student of his in Columbia in the late nineties.

Motivated by ratings, the network broadcasts the tapes, breaching the Patriot Act. Public reaction is hostile. As the network's ratings rise, Lynskey's chances of survival fall. Sarah worries that he will be killed by his abductors, and she works with the security agencies to find out where he is being held.

In captivity, Lynskey has time to review his life. He is intrigued by Hassan, who must know that the pro-Israel Administration will never free his mentor from Guantánamo Bay. What then is the real agenda?

As events move to an unexpected conclusion Lynskey finds himself in possession of the final tape which contains explosive footage that would undermine America's role in the world. The security agencies learn of its existence and Lynskey's problems really begin. With his personal life in crisis, is he in a fit mental state to bear the enormous responsibility that has been thrust upon him?

"A byword for success, Robert Lynskey is lost in the ease of his own intellectual victories. Everything he has struggled for, and achieved, now undermines its own driving logic. Potential escape arrives in the form of mortal danger. Brilliantly constructed and fluidly told, the core dilemma is very real."
—Peter FitzGerald

BOOKS PREVIOUSLY PUBLISHED
BY MICHAEL G. CASEY

Come Home, Robbie, a novel, published by The O'Brien Press, 1990

> "...page-turning urgency ... spine-tingling compulsion ... the sheer quality of the writing lends the story some of the stature of heroic tragedy."
> —The Education Times

Treadmill, an award-winning Chapbook of short stories, published by Tipperary Arts Centre and Start Magazine, 2008

> "...Casey brings to life vivid characters who captivate, amuse and engage ... (He) has a wry observation and quick wit."
> —Mike McCormack

Ireland's Malaise: The Troubled Personality of the Irish Economy, published by The Liffey Press, 2010

> "...(Casey) shows the same Confucian wisdom as his hero, T.K. Whitaker in his brilliant new book."
> —Eoghan Harris, The Sunday

Independent

The Visit, a novel, published by The Anaphora
Press, 2011

> "…a small Irish town deals with a major
> event … an interesting addition to the
> genre … clear-eyed … vivid
> description…"
> —Denis Fahey, Historian

> "…a lovely clear prose style … some
> great characters and beautifully crafted
> vignettes."
> —Stella Kane, Quartet Books Ltd

Broken Circle, a collection of poetry, due to be
published by Salmon Press in Spring 2019

> "…very powerful, intelligent poems
> made their presence known immediately
> … (Casey) uses casuistry and
> persuasiveness to rival Robert
> Browning's dramatic Monologues…"
> —Derek Selen

Michael G. Casey's most recent novels, *Smudged Mascara*, *Maura's Dance with Uncle Sam* and *The Killing of Ros Grenham*, from Azimuth Publishing, are available in Kindle and print versions through Amazon.

DEDICATION

For: Saoirse, Orlagh, Cian, Isabella and Darren.

CHAPTER 1

AFTER HIS LAST MISSION, Khaled Hassan spent a quiet three weeks in Neusiedl, a village southeast of Vienna. He prayed frequently, engaged in ritual washing, and gradually recovered his peace of mind.

From Neusiedl, after his orders came through, he made his way to Rome where his contacts furnished him with an impeccable passport on the basis of which he acquired a temporary visa to visit the US. The papers had cost him almost a third of his budget and reinforced his view that Palestinians had no real friends anywhere in the world. He had dyed his hair and lightened his complexion so that he looked like an Italian from the Calabrian region. He wore a double-breasted suit which had already begun to crumple and sag about his narrow frame. Since he carried no weapons, sharp objects or liquids there were no problems at airport security.

The Alitalia flight from Rome took off two hours late; the delay made him edgy as if it augured problems to come. This mission was the most difficult yet, his first in America. He knew the risks, especially after 9/11. Americans had come to hate the whole Arab world, and the Administration was waiting for an opportunity to crush any activists who dared go behind the lines. Many Federal agencies had taken flak and were determined never to allow a breach of homeland security again. Pre-emptive defense was the new military doctrine, backed up by full-spectrum dominance.

Over the Atlantic, which sparkled like marcasite, he consulted his watch; they might make up some time as the pilot had predicted. He couldn't eat the meal that was served and asked for a glass of water. He drank a little and ritualistically wet his hands and face, though covertly because there was an air marshal on board.

His last operation had not been successful and had led to a reprisal on a refugee camp in the West Bank, not far from the dividing wall erected by the Israelis. Eleven Palestinians had died. The Israelis had used laser-guided missiles launched from American Fl-11s. It had taken them just forty minutes and two passes to achieve their 'good hits'. Afterwards he had stood by the shattered food kitchen, a tent beside an open sewer, where they brought the mutilated bodies in the fly-ridden sunlight. What would it take for his people to be treated as human beings?

Reprisals were always swift and savagely efficient, vengeance dropping from the skies. They couldn't protect the camps from these sudden raids, which claimed victims at random and brought desolation to families already on the margin of existence. In recent years he had observed how the mourners gathered in silence to claim their dead without the chrism or ritual of tears; their mute acceptance stabbed deep.

Justice had to be achieved some other way. They had to find a way of using their weakness; that was all they had. Suicide bombing was one way. He prayed that this new mission would be blessed by Allah. He repeated the words of the Sharia: Whosoever falls in battle, his sins are forgiven.

At least the terrain would be reasonably familiar. He had been to New York before, had spent two years at Columbia to test his beliefs, and had even attended some of Robert Lynskey's classes. But his exposure to Western values in that forcing-house of easy truths served only to confirm his belief in Islam as the encompassing religion. During that two years he was friendless and isolated, except for some fortuitous meetings with Saudis and former members of the American Society of Muslims, some of whom regarded themselves as the inheritors of the Black Muslim tradition. He came to understand the hold of Zionism on the American consciousness, the unimpeachable view of Israel as the victim of history. But he also became aware of the sheer power of the Jewish lobby that extended from Wall Street to Hollywood, from newspapers to TV networks. The average American thought Palestinians were fanatical oil sheikhs using their wealth to undermine the West and oust the Jews from their own land. There was never, in all of history, such a monstrous misconception.

Khaled's thoughts turned to Jallud Fahd, a comrade and former mentor who languished in that infamous prison in Guantánamo Bay. Freeing him would be a momentous task even with help from inside. But there was no alternative. Jallud Fahd had once been a mentor to bin Laden as well as to Khaled – though that had been much later. Recent years had seen him become statesmanlike; only he had the wisdom and moral authority to lead Palestine out of chaos; only he could control Hamas and the Palestinian Islamic Jihad.

Khaled tried unsuccessfully to sleep. In the darkened interior of the plane the muscles of his pitted face twitched. He had shaved off his beard and from time to time he touched his bare face with a slender hand that could have belonged to a magician except for a livid scar that ran diagonally from knuckles to wrist. His brown eyes once held a hint of humor but not anymore; they were set deep and determined in his gaunt face. He looked older than his thirty-four years, hardened, dried; a nomad breathed beneath his skin. He dared not sleep for fear of seeing again the horror that was hidden beneath the green Hamas flag that lay on the streets of Gaza City.

The plan was a simple one and he tried to convince himself that simplicity was an asset in a complex world. To free Jallud Fahd they would have to take a hostage, not some clerk or businessman who happened to be based in the Middle East, but someone with real influence, close to the Administration. His Council had started with a list of fifteen names and finally winnowed it down to one. Though a Gentile,

Robert Lynskey was an integral part of the Jewish media establishment; there were other aspects of his background that made him fit the profile. In the jargon of the times he was a soft target with high visibility. It also seemed fitting that he had been a Professor of Political Theory at a New York University.

As they made the approach to Kennedy Airport, Khaled looked at the city winking beneath as far as the eye could see, the myriad lit buildings and avenues of Manhattan stretching to the horizon, reminding him once again of the sheer size and power of this alien country. Twenty minutes later he was inside the terminal building retrieving his bag from the carousel.

After giving his speech to the NY Film Club and finally extricating himself from the glitterati who had applauded his *grand cru* wit, Robert Lynskey left the hotel and went for a stroll in the park. It was late March and the air felt fresh on his face.

Lynskey looked fully rigged and prosperous except for a shadow of early privation and a hint of wariness in the stone-washed eyes. There was a port-wine stain, the shape of Iceland, on his left cheek. He was conservatively dressed these days but the silk handkerchief that foamed from his breast pocket was a relic from more bohemian times and a practical asset for a middle-aged man with unpredictable sinuses. He was glad to be free of the doting cloy of the Waldorf.

A shorter man with red hair like live fuse wire walked beside him. His name was Drew Hamilton and he produced the *Robert Lynskey Hour* for KNYBS. He moved with a pugilist's gait and was as ornery and hard-packed as a ball of wire wool.

"Nice speech," Drew said as they approached the ice-rink. "I liked that bit about the 'Art of the State'."

"Thanks, Drew," Robert replied. He was better at accepting compliments than he used to be, though he hadn't quite lost the habit, born of necessity, of looking for subtexts. "We do our best."

"During your talk I had a thought. You should write your memoirs."

Robert stopped by a copse of trees. It was an idea he'd toyed with recently, but dismissed. Strange that Drew should hit him with it now out of the blue. "I'm not old enough."

"You're almost sixty," Drew pointed out reasonably. Three score was old in his book. He liked having an advantage of a decade over his star performer.

"That's not memoir time. And don't tell me about Alexander the Great being in his thirties when he conquered the world..." Robert sucked his teeth and managed to dislodge the tiny piece of food that had been irritating him – a piece of quail skin, he thought.

"Seriously, though." Drew looked down at his

compact feet in the grass. "Why not give faction a shot, your facts. They're interesting." In the nine years he had produced the show for KNYBS he had come to accept Lynskey, despite feeling that he was too 'serious' to pull large audiences. Besides, since Lynskey was now so much identified with the show, an autobiography of one would give the other a shot in the arm; a sort of blood-doping. It was win-win.

Robert sampled the idea like a fine wine but resiled from it too. Memoirs suggested an end approaching, a waning of the imagination, a doyen with a back-scratcher and a wistful sigh. And what if he slipped into sentimentality? God, his critics would have a field day; he could sense them out there in the long grass waiting for such an opportunity to winkle him out of his protective, faintly cynical shell.

"The show's been running for almost a decade now," Drew said passing a hand through his red hair. "You must have interviewed every celeb in the cosmos."

"Oh, so it's not me. It's my contacts you're after." Robert knew Drew's tabloid tendencies only too well.

"Well, there's nothing wrong with a splash of glamour. It sugar-coats the serious stuff."

"Which is what?" Robert asked suspiciously.

"You know. The lurch to the right, with The Donald. The new American Empire. Fear as an instrument of oppression. The rise of China ... All that." They walked on.

Robert reflected on how he'd started out as a socialist, then slid into cultural Marxism. Now he wasn't sure where he was positioned on the spectrum. Maybe it was better to analyze things on a case-by-case basis without the baggage of ideology. It would be a relief to get away from fiction for a while. It had become such a struggle and a strain to walk that wire between credibility and imagination. Who believed in fiction any more – unless the consumers of same could see on stage or screen the characters cavort in living color before their very eyes? It was a mug's game and one which had begun to seem downright silly for a man of his years. At this time in his life he was developing a yen for the easy luxury of fact.

Drew moved aside to let a jogger struggle past, wired for sound, the ultimate in alienation. Both men watched the ample runner lumber past the bleachers being erected for some 10K or mindless marathon, and harbored rueful thoughts about the march of the nation.

"All you have to do," Drew suggested, "is feed all the biographical stuff to your research team and let them pump out a first draft on your computer."

Robert took another peek at him. Was Drew criticizing his Warhol-like production set-up, his electronic cottage over there in Brooklyn Heights? Well, that was how it was done these hi-tech days; he wouldn't apologize for it. It had taken him some time to get used to having his own research team working an office routine in the lower part of his brownstone. Some mornings as he wandered among his staff, having just left his apartment on the upper floor, he was struck by the change. Long gone was the bedsit in Columbus Avenue – when a pad in the Village was beyond him – and the manual typewriter that wore its wounds with pride: the yellowing keys like organ stops, the broken spacer bar grooved from a trillion thumb taps. Now, he could work online; floppy disks had long since being consigned to the geriatric ward.

Drew shrugged. "It's just a thought. You have expenses too."

"You're not wrong." Robert's ex had a witch's instinct for knowing when to go to court for an increase in her alimony. Maybe she looked at his reviews and ratings in the same way that day-traders looked at the Dow Jones Index, but he suspected it was something more psychic. Entrails perhaps, but whose? Anyway she never failed. Probably cried in court too. He never challenged her. It was a lien on the past, the cost of poor judgment. Like the woman Schopenhauer pushed down the library steps, Nita would take her dollar revenge for the rest of her life and there wasn't a damn thing he could do about it. He was her personal ATM. What he regretted most was that Nita refused to give him a child even after six years of marriage and it was abundantly clear that her career wasn't going anywhere special.

The growing frequency of wired-up dudes on roller skates suggested that they'd reached a rougher section of the park, but the two large egos strolled on oblivious of danger, as though fame conferred immunity. And maybe it did, because such surly glances as came their way brightened with recognition. Robert gave some autographs, signing cigarette packs and bus tickets with a flourish.

Robert looked at the buildings that rose above the treetops of the park in this town which once, in a moment of infantile ambition, he had sworn would be his. Now even his most implacable critics had to admit he was part of the Manhattan skyline. The adjective 'Lynskeyesque' had currency in this realm, a smoky-bacon-flavored way of looking at things. As one rather gushing Times columnist put it, he had moxie and street cred. He was on all the important guest lists, including those of the White House and the Governor's Mansion in Albany. It went without saying that on his infrequent trips to the west coast he was automatically placed on the Hollywood A list. It sometimes worried him that he might be above criticism. Maybe memoirs would evoke some honest reviews. But could he take reasonable criticism anymore?

It really was odd that Drew should have mentioned memoirs. That very morning Robert had woken in a curious trance-like state, the waking sequel of a dream in which he had re-lived part of his life. He couldn't shrug off the clinging tendrils of the dream, so he went with the mood like a worried grocer taking stock of his remaindered fruit. He had looked in the mirror more than usual; his rubbled face looked older than the mug shot on the dust jackets of his books and he wondered how it got to be like that. Each line and crinkle no doubt told a story but one in which the plot was hard to follow.

Fluffy vague thoughts opened him up to guilt, those he had harmed on the way up, his self-promotion. Christ, he was fixated on himself. In the seventies he'd walked out on Hollywood to get away from the stables of booze-hound, fawning writers. 'Integrity!' the press screamed, and were kind to his next book; New York took him back to its real tinsel heart. But had it been integrity or simply a subtle marketing ploy?

The corpuscles of guilt formed a pus that morning which he couldn't draw out. He was slick and droll, could strike a match against his teeth with one deft movement, but what exactly was it that the flickering light revealed? What had he really done with his three score years – apart from becoming an institution?

Then, all that talk of memoirs … What goes around comes around. He glanced at Drew; producer or promoter? He gave an involuntary shudder as if some strange ugly insect had landed on his skin. It would not end well; something was going to catch up on him.

CHAPTER 2

AT IMMIGRATION KHALED'S PAPERS held up under scrutiny; there was no record of his iris or fingerprints in any data bank, nor was he on any watch-list. The screen apparently had nothing good or bad to reveal about his fabricated identity; he was safely under the radar. The immigration officer asked him how long he was going to stay and what his business was. Khaled answered well, feigning poor English and an Italian accent. A ten-day visit with his brother in little Italy, even less than the span indicated on the visa. The official waved him through with a bored gesture.

As arranged, Khaled waited by the Hertz counter until his contact arrived. He recognized him immediately, a tall black man with a patchy tight-curled beard. He wore designer jeans and a bomber jacket that accentuated his narrow waist. His hair was slick and the dark glasses were in the shape of a narrow band that fitted the contours of his face.

"It's good to meet you again, Richard." Khaled extended his hand.

"Same here, man." Having shaken hands Richard took his bag and led him to the electronic doors. "Had a good trip?" he asked over his shoulder.

"Yes, thank you." Khaled followed him to the satellite car park. Dusk was condensing into night, the dark air was thick with the smell of jet fuel.

Several aircraft circled overhead waiting for clearance from some unseen presence in the blue-lit control tower. Once inside the old Buick, Richard said, "As-salamu alaykum."

The greeting was just barely recognizable to Khaled who responded, "Wa alaykumu s-salam." They embraced briefly, awkwardly.

Richard slipped the car into gear and drove round the loop of road leading to the exit. They picked up the Van Wyck Expressway and merged into the fast-moving traffic.

"Any problems?" Richard asked, taking off the dark glasses and giving his eyes a brief massage with thumb and forefinger.

"No. It went smoothly." Khaled stared straight ahead, leaning forward slightly as if urging on the car.

Richard took one hand off the wheel, opened the glove compartment and pushed a revolver and shoulder holster across the bench seat. Khaled removed his jacket, put on the harness and tested the magazine with deft fingers.

"How long has it been?" Richard asked.

"Ten, eleven years."

"A lot has changed."

"Yes." Khaled knew what he meant. The Nation of Islam was long gone and the American Society of Muslims was in disarray; many of its members had been forced underground since 9/11. Some indeed had fought in the Iraq war, others now worked for Homeland Security. Only a hard core remained faithful, one of them Richard.

While Khaled was drawn to him as one dispossessed to another, he wondered about the depth of Richard's commitment to Islam; perhaps he saw it as a means of achieving some kind of identity, separateness. Belonging to the lost-found tribe of Islam seemed to offer reassurance to some black people. Like the Palestinians they were homeless in their own land. That's why so many had rallied to the Black Muslim cause all those years ago.

"Bush didn't help." Richard grinned ruefully at the understatement. "And Trump is off the wall. Well, you know that too." There was no limit to the vengeance the US wanted for 9/11. The wars in Iraq, Afghanistan and Syria were not enough. Khaled wondered if there was a deeper agenda, some overall strategy aimed at the heart of Islam. Richard drove through Queens and crossed the East river into the Bronx.

"Justice is a slow process." Khaled said. "Sometimes it's hard not to despair. But it will come if we believe." His voice was quiet with an edge of ice. Through the corner of his eye he saw Richard shrug slightly. His thoughts went back to the refugee camp after the last Israeli reprisal. They were outsmarted and beaten on every front, tied down like a beast being slaughtered; all that was left was faith. And action. This time it would be different.

Richard drove over the Whiteside Bridge and paid the toll, flinging the money into the exact-change basket. The tugs on the East river moved slowly, leaving in their wake white chevrons cresting on the gray water. Passing through a run-down area due for demolition, Richard nodded in the direction of a deserted warehouse as if pointing out a tourist attraction. "We got some weapons stashed there, AK-47s mostly."

Soon afterwards they entered a building in Harlem that was once the central mosque in the days of Malcolm X; the cramped living quarters used to serve as a meeting place for the Fruit of Islam. Most of the painted tiles had fallen off the walls and the structure of the building seemed dangerous.

Richard introduced him to Anna, a striking woman in her mid-thirties. Khaled concealed his surprise during the formal low-voiced greeting. He also met Daniel X, a committed Black Muslim who was devoting his life to perpetuating the work of Malcolm X, his boyhood hero. Daniel would not be taking part in the mission but was responsible for provisions and would be contactable at any time day or night.

"You probably want to wash up." Anna showed him to a small room which had a camp bed, a sink and little else. He opened his bag and spread his doshak on the floor, then he shaved and washed his face and hands.

They sat together later around a wooden table in the main room. A third man, Bart, appeared from the kitchen and served food: bread, salad and yoghurt. A heavy-set black man, formerly a Fruit of Islam guard, he looked as if a weight pressed on his head, forming a ridge across his forehead, compressing his neck into a solid plinth.

"You must be hungry, man," he said, pushing the bread towards Khaled, staring at him with wide-eyed intensity.

They made small talk for a while as if propriety demanded a measured approach to the real agenda. Finally Anna said, "I was sorry to hear about the reprisals..." Her voice carried a faint Mid-European accent; it was deeper than her porcelain face would have suggested.

Khaled nodded, accepting the sympathy but also indicating that he didn't want to talk about it. The green Hamas flag flashed before his eyes, then, fortunately disappeared.

"This will go better," she said grimly. Her mouth seemed viperish and out of place beneath the vivid blue eyes and straight hair that framed a flawless icon-like face. Behind the smooth skin glazed in cellophane was a sense of implacability. Khaled knew immediately that she wasn't just a rich kid indulging herself in revolution but he also sensed that she could be dangerous.

"Have you been to Mecca?" Bart asked suddenly as if he couldn't contain himself any longer.

"Yes," Khaled replied.

"I bet it's fantastic," Bart boomed. His sudden smile showed a crooked tooth that somehow undermined the tough exterior.

"The Hajj changes everyone," Khaled answered. "Once Allah shows you the light you must walk in it."

"I bet, I bet..." Bart kneaded his big hands enthusiastically.

"I think you can clear away now," Anna said abruptly, watching Bart until he'd gathered up the dishes; her eyes escorted him out of the room, through the kitchen door.

"He means well," Richard said. "Tries too hard."

"Maybe he's right," Khaled replied.

After a passage of silence Anna laid down her coffee cup with deliberation and asked who the target was.

"Robert Lynskey."

She frowned and looked at Richard who made a token gesture of distancing himself from this decision. Daniel X had no comment to make; this wasn't his concern.

"He's not Jewish."

"Well, he has supported Zionism in the past. In one his TV programs he claimed Israel had followed the Camp David Accord and the so-called Road Map. He has criticized the Holy War as fanaticism. Besides, he symbolizes Western values." Khaled opened his hands; the case rested.

Anna was silent, reserving judgment on this first and critical aspect of the plan. Lynskey would not have been her first choice but he was high profile. That much she could concede. She changed tack,

"How important is Jallud Fahd to you?"

"The future rests with him." Khaled spoke

slowly and with authority. "Without his leadership America will divide and conquer the Arab world and extend the unlawful State of Israel. We had hoped that President Obama would have freed him ... but that has not happened. It is unlikely that the current President will do anything. Jallud Fahd must be released."

Richard whistled softly. He glanced at Anna who nodded. A strand of fair hair fell forward across her face and she stroked it back, looping it behind her ear. But the languid gesture did not conceal the excitement that quickened her skin. This was enough for now, more than enough. She needed time to absorb it into herself, to realize that the waiting was over. She made her excuses and went out through the kitchen. Daniel X asked to be excused and wished them well, making sure they had his contact numbers. The two men stayed behind for a while, still seated at the table. Judging by the swishing sounds of traffic that drifted up from the street below, it had been raining for some time. Spring was slow to establish itself.

"You must be tired," Richard said.

"A little. Tomorrow we will discuss the details." Khaled hesitated then added, "May I ask where ... Anna fits in?"

"She's worked with us for seven years," Richard said. He smiled. "She's not black and she's not a Muslim but she's OK."

"What motivates her?" Khaled had to know for the sake of the mission. He had sensed her strength but didn't know how it was directed. Women that powerful were beyond his experience and made him uneasy.

"She's Austrian, man, her grandfather was hounded by Wiesenthal for twenty years and finally killed himself..." Richard didn't have to say more, though he sometimes wondered if there was more to it than that.

"And you? Do you hate Jews?"

Richard thought for a while rubbing his dusty beard. "They're white." He shrugged. "The Jew is the man in New York. We don't owe them any favors." He paused as if to rehearse the next thought. "Maybe they've taught us a lesson..."

"Which is?" Khaled leant forward, the overhead light shading the hollows of his face.

"How dumb it is to want integration with the whites. The Germans didn't buy it." The understatement left the shape of a sneer on his mouth.

"Is your ... movement as strong as it was?"

"No." A flicker of weariness passed over his face. "But there are enough left. If this job goes well it might strengthen us." His father and Daniel often told him about the heady days of Malcolm X and Louis Farrakhan when everything seemed possible. But that era was followed by sickening dissension, infighting and the final inevitable split. Those who stayed loyal lacked mass support and were driven underground. But their day would come, maybe sooner than he'd ever allowed himself to imagine. The rise of Islam was inevitable.

"And Bart?" Khaled pressed.

"Not playing with a full deck but he's OK."

"I could sense that." Khaled nodded. Partly to reassure himself he added, "It will be a holy alliance. If you take one step towards Allah he will take two to you."

"Let's hope." Richard looked down at his hands.

Khaled touched him on the shoulder and went to his room. He washed again and prayed, then he lay on the doshak listening to the strange sounds of the city, and tried to sleep.

————————

Anna reached for him when Richard got into bed; her movements were urgent, uncontrolled. Something had set her normally strong urge for sex at an even higher pitch.

"I'm bushed." He faced the wall from which plaster and paint were peeling. Strident sounds from the street echoed around the small room. Harlem never slept. He wondered if Khaled would get any rest.

"You hypocrite," she grated.

"Wha...?"

"OK, so it's going to be a big week. But don't lay that Sharia shit on me. He's not the Prophet. Don't snow yourself with that Islam stuff."

This was more than he expected and less than he deserved. Confused, he said, "At least I try to believe."

"We've been fucking for two years. Now suddenly because the precious Imam is here you get religion. I preferred you when you were a pimp. Don't kid yourself, you want power just like everyone else." Anger, sudden and inexplicable, clawed at her throat and face, mottling her fair skin.

"What do you want, bitch?" He wondered if she'd taken crack when she went into the kitchen; he knew how bad she was in withdrawal. But that was hardly twenty minutes ago. It didn't figure.

"An end to how this fucking country is run. An end to Jewish power."

"Then what?" He lay on his back and stared at the ceiling, knowing the answer. It was always the same.

"Then anything." She reached for him again, this time with greater insistence and laughed abruptly when he mounted her: an ancient resolution, though not a permanent one.

Maybe she was right. He had lost his older brother in Baghdad towards the end of the war. Missing in action; it was doubtful if the military even looked for him. What was one black kid more or less? Uncle Sam got the oil; that was all that mattered. After his brother's death their father became a bum wandering from shelter to shelter until he just gave up and died on a deserted platform in Grand Central Station. He was buried by convicts from the city jail in a mass grave on Hart's Island. Anna was right: anything different had to be better. Almost anything.

CHAPTER 3

THEY WAIT IN THE BUICK across the street from the KNYBS building that reflects the spring sunshine in its glass panels. People come and go through the cantilevered entrance above which a gold eagle in bas relief presides over a fluttering stars and stripes. The movement of people gradually solidifies into a queue behind a lollipop sign which reads, 'The Robert Lynskey Hour, Studio 5'. Within minutes a ragged saxophonist appears from nowhere and begins to work the queue with a groaning downbeat version of 'Nights in Tunisia'. Many of the people standing in line are eating breakfast out of polystyrene boxes, others fumble for coins for the busker. They are coralled and cajoled by uniformed attendants.

At nine-thirty sharp Richard draws Khaled's attention to a Cadillac that cruises to a stop outside the building. They see Robert Lynskey shoe-horn himself out of the car, have a quick word with his driver and scamper up the steps with the earnestness of a man taking his only exercise for the day. The commissionaire tips his cap in greeting; Lynskey gives a brief nod of acknowledgment and disappears into the building through the revolving door.

His brief appearance causes a belated stir in the line of people which now stretches around the corner of the block. The teasing glimpse causes a satisfied buzz of talk among the pensioners and housewives who form the nucleus of every daytime studio audience. Having seen the star they are reassured, and accept with equanimity the long wait.

These are the people Stephen Colbert ribs about waiting in the rain or blistering heat, and they must punch in another hour at least before they shuffle in to take their seats and be warmed up for the recording of the 'RL Hour'. The tickets are free; in return they will give applause when asked and, taken as peers for a day, bring in a kind and generous verdict.

"He's punctual," Khaled observes from the passenger seat of the car parked across the street.

"Not more than two minutes either way," Richard confirms, looking at his watch then pushing the dark glasses up his forehead so that they nest in his hair. "There's tight security inside the building, mainly in the atrium. But his driver shouldn't be a problem." He begins to see the merit of the plan; Lynskey is as near a perfect choice as makes no difference, despite what Anna might think.

"How long does he spend in that building?" Khaled asks.

"He'll be in there shooting for the rest of the morning. He goes to lunch at one sharp."

"Outside?"

"Yeah, he goes to one of those ritzy places in Midtown. Bart's been tailing him there." Richard takes a pack of Marlboro Lights from his shirt pocket and flips it until a cigarette pops up. Lowering his head, he extracts it with his lips but hesitates about lighting it in front of Khaled. He puts it behind his ear for the time being.

Khaled doesn't answer but sits pensively in the passenger seat, his eyes narrowed in concentration, the collar of his Italian suit up around his ears.

Drawing some additional intelligence from the tabloids, Richard begins to digress. "He has a neat place in the Heights with another bunch of staff. His wife left him about four years ago. He's got a regular girlfriend now but makes the scene as well. The sonofabitch has it made…"

"Oh?"

"Celebrities can do what they like in this country," Richard felt obliged to explain.

"Only for a time."

"Yeah … maybe," Richard says almost sadly. He lights up and lets smoke out through his nostrils, waving it away from Khaled. Maybe Anna was right; the man is a killjoy. But still, there is something straight about him that draws Richard's respect.

"What about weekends?"

"I don't know for sure. He probably goes out of town. Daniel X says he has a brother somewhere in New Jersey." Seeing a patrol car cruising the far side of the street, Richard instinctively turns his head aside and lets the glasses fall visor-like over his eyes.

"That might have possibilities," Khaled says

when the danger passes. It is his turn to digress. "Have you ever read any of Lynskey's books?"

"No. But I've seen his show a few times. It's a cut above Oprah and Jerry Springer."

"It's strange how an intelligent man can be so wrong." Khaled doesn't elaborate but the paradox demands an answer. Rather than mark Lynskey down as a propagandist, which somehow seems too easy, Khaled tends to regard him as an apologist for the soft, venal life that conditioned him. The characters of his books are flawed, undisciplined, and he makes allowances for them on grounds of 'humanity'. His lectures at Columbia, some of which Khaled had attended several years ago, though radical by today's standards, were marred by the same indulgent latitude and the gift of easy virtue. Self-interest was his theme – and the rock he would perish on.

"You don't have to be right to make it here," Richard says, slipping the car into gear.

As they drive away Khaled asks out of the blue, "Are you and Anna ... sleeping together?"

"Yeah," Richard answers warily, and when Khaled makes no response, continues defensively, "Look, it's different over here, man. Different rules. OK, so we can't uphold the Five Principles." He takes his hands off the wheel and splays them out in extenuation. Then he opens the window and spits out the cigarette butt. "Times change. It's a different scene. What the hell, it's not going to affect the operation." He hits the steering wheel with the heel of his hand as a familiar sense of exclusion crawls over him.

In the hospitality room Robert meets his guests and briefs them again on the format of the show. Both stellar protagonists are surprisingly nervous. Robert tries to put them at ease, knowing how difficult it is for actors to go on without scripts. It had taken Robert himself a good five years to relax in front of the camera; now he treats it as a friendly, if rather curious, neighbor peering over the garden wall, or some harmless, long-snouted quadruped, snuffling for insects.

"So you see, we can edit all we like. There's no live pressure."

The pre-show conversation continues for a while in that halting, diffident way that Robert is so used to; it's as if the protagonists are saving their energy and adrenalin for the moment when the cameras begin to turn. The audience had been seated for half an hour eating popcorn and listening to the floor manager when the stars begin to process into the studio. The split second required to confirm recognition – and possibly one's own existence – is followed by a burst of applause for which no cue is required.

At his console Chaim gives the instructions, "Go tape and fade up one. Turn over ... Running ... Action..." At the floor manager's signal he says briskly, "Move in on Robert, one. Lights up and angled. OK, we're off..."

The cameras quietly stalk the bodies in the Kleig-lit clearing. Robert introduces his guests and the subject matter, making minimal use of the autocue. As the debate gets under way the colonial history of the US gets a good run; so too the recent adventures in foreign parts, the rise of the Neocons, the question of whether a Globocop can stop at peace-keeping without having at some stage to take over and run sovereign states. The guests argue well but the issues are put, and dealt with, simply – pablum being gummed by an infant. One of the stars is inclined to sweat, and needs frequent applications of the make-up girl's powder puff during the ad breaks.

Robert chips in a comment or two but the *longueurs* are mercifully few and he relaxes into his preferred role as facilitator. Sensing that the audience is rapt, he wonders, not for the first time, what it is about the luster of the famous that commands such trust. The answer somehow is too close to be seen.

In the final segment he opens up the discussion to the audience. Questions come thick and fast, addressed respectfully to the panel. The debate takes a turn towards America's hidden agenda regarding oil stocks, and they bat the breeze for a while on that. Until one irate rooster of a man bursts through the polite commonplaces to swear vengeance on all the Looney Tunes who try to jerk Uncle Sam around. He uses appalling language about Arabs. It will of course be cut out but Robert is again struck by the fear and hatred that seem to be building up in so many ordinary Americans. The man, bristling and unrepentant – Robert sees him as a loner, maybe a survivalist who lives in a cellar growing mushrooms under the stairs – shouts into the fish-pole mike dangling over his head, "Where do all these Mideast countries get off? They're just flyspecks getting their rocks off yanking our chain. Forget about shock and awe. Just nuke the towel-heads."

The security men move in and Robert adroitly changes the subject; he doesn't need other so-called deplorables emerging from the basket. The wind-up signal doesn't come soon enough. In his dry gnomic style he thanks everyone on the panel, in the studio audience and those watching at home. He disdains the teleprompter, the first line of which reads, "Well, there you have it…"

Another show, another dollar, putting the world to rights, and somehow missing the point. It wasn't even particularly good entertainment. Before McLuhan faded into obscurity he had once told Robert that TV, by regressing to a tribal acoustic tradition, was placing individualism at risk. Charisma, he argued, meant being a lot like others. Robert disagreed at the time but now he's not so sure.

After the audience filed out of the studio, Chaim insists on doing some master close-ups and cut-aways to satisfy the film editor; then he wraps it up.

After a little more 'hospitality' the stars fly out to new galaxies and a brief postmortem ensues in Drew's office.

"It was a little heavy but I think it'll just about fly," Drew comments. "How did it look from your end, Chaim?"

"Talking heads are always static but with these mega types I think we'll get away with it. In the future though I think we should try to loosen up the format. More audience participation maybe." Joining his hands behind his head, Chaim leans back in his chair. He always gives the impression of being a little less than fully involved and this, Drew surmises, is because gays have to put most of their energy into their often fraught relationships. But Drew knows that Chaim will always go along with him because, as director of the RL Hour, he is right up there in the fishbowl of the gay community. Such a cachet gives Drew a neat whammy over him.

"Speaking of which," Drew says, "we'll have to lose that racist fruitcake in the final segment."

Robert agrees but with reservations. "It was real. The man unburdened himself. Other people were nodding as he spoke. We mightn't agree with what he said but unfortunately there's a growing constituency for the line he took..."

"He was off concept," Drew answers with a shrug, filling his pipe with phantom tobacco. He hasn't smoked it in years but likes to fiddle with it.

"Since when is theme so important to you?"

Robert is genuinely confused. It's not like Drew to reject an exotic incident, especially when it goes in the direction of his own rightist views. "Come on, what's the real reason?"

"Well, he just wasn't credible, was he? What did you think, Chaim?"

"He looked pretty wild about the eyes in close-up," Chaim loyally replies.

"I see. So if it had been some well-heeled yuppy who expressed the same thoughts, you'd keep him in?" In the indifferent silence which follows, Robert takes his leave. Political correctness is also beginning to grate on his nerves. He will have to get the thoughtful Jordan Peterson on his show sometime, despite the reservations of his colleagues.

As the elevator takes him down, he sees his face in the surrounding mirrors, profiles extending to infinity, challenging him with a strange reproachful mien. Maybe it's just self-pity, he thinks, but that seems ridiculous since no one else in the world could possibly sympathize with him. Here I am, he berates himself, as 'glitterate' as they come, in rude good health, close on twenty million in liquid assets, my own show and research team, not without talent and not having to live by the side of the road. I've lunched on capon and Montrechet today, rubbed shoulders with the great and good and am shortly to be collected by my chauffeur. And yet, dear Lord, and yet … If only he could be more like his brother, Gary, whose remedy for all forms of self-pity came from the old country: a good kick up the arse.

His staff would have left the brownstone by now and he hates the prospect of going into his empty apartment. There is this Writers Guild reception he could go to but somehow he doesn't feel up to it. He tries to rally his spirit by planning out his evening. He would open a bottle of that good Burgundy regardless of what his 'daily' left in the oven. Then a little TV with a book in his hand to fill the inevitable lapses of interest. Maybe a modicum of writing but only if something comes – he will not use the cattle prod. Then a hot bath and bed. Then what? And then? His plan fizzles out and leaves him with a maundering listlessness. Wondering if he might be coming down with something, he feels, as his mother used to do, the glands of his throat, but discontinues the diagnosis as the mirrors throw back an image of self-strangulation. By the time he's ensconced in the back of the car he has decided to revise his skimpy plan.

Sarah didn't need too much persuading. She had learnt not to complain about being at his beck and call. When you dated part of the Manhattan landscape you didn't have to be so proud. It was, she supposed, as she put the finishing touches to her make-up, a question of valuation. Anyway she adored him in her way while keeping her options open. Prudence demanded that she hold a second string of assets in the portfolio of the heart.

She smoothed a little rouge into the hollows of her cheeks to accentuate the bone structure. Sitting upright on a furry stool so that her slender back curved inward from black bra strap to neat, smug rump, she was the picture of self-satisfied accomplishment. With pins held between her teeth and white arms arched above her head, she reinforced her hair which was piled high in a cottage loaf with little, carefully arranged, straggles escaping at the nape of her neck. A strikingly handsome woman, not yet forty, her movements had the brisk assurance of a princess doing good deeds. It was her movements – ballet was still her love – that first caught Robert's attention; those tapering gestures, graceful as silent prayer, put out tendrils that enveloped him and drew him close.

This evening at her suggestion – she liked to try new places – they went to a recently-opened Thai restaurant. He liked the stares she drew but was conscious of how they gradually drifted towards him. The sheer elegance of the Versace silk jacket accentuated her model walk as she moved between the tables. The head waiter put them in a booth with bamboo curtains optional. Sarah placed her sequined purse on the table and gracefully lowered herself to the chair held by the waiter who was got up in those rooster-leg pants last worn by the King of Siam. Across from the booth a waterfall played over a ledge of blue vitreous mosaic into a lily pond.

"I'm glad you called," Sarah said. "It was a draining week. Wouk's galleys came back a mess. If this week were a fish I'd have thrown it back." Her hand fluttered to her throat, then adjusted her pearls.

"I know what you mean." But he wasn't absolutely sure that he did. She had taken her late husband's place on the board of a publishing firm and always seemed to Robert to be a little vague as to the nature of her duties. Still, her plaint was as charming as it was mysterious.

While she continued to settle herself at the table and take her bearings, Robert used the opportunity to appraise her on the sly. He was always taken by her handsomeness, that integral quality of countenance and figure which imposed an elegant unity. He recalled standing before a life-sized statue of Aphrodite in the British Museum and felt that same sensual awe in the face of perfect form. The fact that it was made of stone didn't seem to matter. While there was something formal about Sarah it was just one of her three countenances. She could also be girlish, especially when she brought her small hands together in a clasp of delight. And then there was her sensual side which was an entirely different matter.

As she finished her reconnaissance of the restaurant she turned to him and said, "You're quiet," as if he had been guilty of some social gaffe.

"Just noticing how well you look," he said honestly.

"Thank you." Her smile produced two dimples on her second, girlish face. "How was your week?"

"Oh, full." He left it at that in case elaboration would bring on that spiritual fatigue he'd experienced in the elevator when he didn't know which if any of his repeated reflections was the real one.

"How did your talk to the Film Society go? I heard good reports."

"Yes, it went well enough, thanks." He dropped a few names for her to chew on. He looked around the restaurant which seemed more French than Thai and probably given to miserly 'nouvelle'. He'd been to a restaurant once in Phuket where the Thai clientele did their own cooking on little gas stoves plumbed into the tables; poor people ate out a lot because their own wharf-side shacks lacked kitchens. He'd watched them brew up great steaming stews of cabbage, fat pork and chunks of fish, blotches of yellow grease floating like lozenges on the surface of the juice. He had admired the easy grace of the people who sometimes ate in the temples, too, right under the golden benevolence of Buddha. In Bangkok he had seen a woman throw Chinese dice and pray to the reclining Buddha. This was wrong, the chain-smoking monk told him, because Buddha was not

God. But the woman had happily invented him.

"I ran into Drew on Wednesday," Sarah said, chafing her fingers free of atomistic crumbs and dipping them in the lemon bowl.

"He never mentioned that." He wanted to try something out. "I think I should start writing again." He paused as if to gather strength. "Maybe even memoirs."

"Oh relax, you workaholic. You don't ever have to work again. When are you going to learn to enjoy the moment?" She gave him a fleeting smile, then buried her head in the menu so that he could only see the whimsy of her hair that seemed to ruffle slightly like the tail feathers of a duck drinking. The expertly applied mascara on her lowered eyelids seemed magenta in the candlelight.

"I'm insecure," he said, a little stung by her reaction. But in a way he meant it. She knew nothing of the years of rejections and rebuffs and the early reviews that almost battered him into submission, those rancid years of devilling in silence like a starving animal on the scent of raw meat. Looking back on it now he could hardly believe the dream had come to pass. The odd thing about it was that the shock of success was almost as painful as the despair of failure. No, Sarah had no experience of his dismal lineage; she'd taken him at the flood, dripping with honors and credentials. Neither did she know of the corners he'd cut, the people he'd avoided, if not quite trampled on, and the fine-grained calculations that went into his self-promotion, all of which he was now beginning to regret.

"You, insecure? Don't make me laugh." She did anyway, a sort of crystal tinkle that ended abruptly as she plumped for the great prawns in fennel.

During the meal he dwelt on her absorbed face, glad that he had changed his plans. Self-pity melted away in the heat of anticipation and the sauce of spit-roasted duckling. It was good to be alone with Sarah. Their date the previous week was at a publishers' reception where he was fawned over and button-holed under the shadow of a giant ice sculpture on the buffet table. That marked the beginning of his disenchantment with the beau monde; he began to see himself as a cartoon in the New Yorker. This was better. His relationship with Sarah might not be of the gut-wrenching variety; he'd had enough of that with Nita, at least in the early days, and it ended as dramatically as it had begun. No, this was a mature covenant that served the interests of both parties and, in the small print of the heart, guarded against profligacy. In this mood of gratitude and anticipation he complimented her again.

"You're not so bad yourself," she responded, dabbing the corners of her mouth with a napkin. "But why don't you get that birthmark removed? It's so easy nowadays."

"It might change my personality," he answered. Sarah wasn't the first woman in his life to make that particular suggestion but so far he had successfully defended his slightly embossed crest which tended to take on a purple hue when he was excited or angry. "Remember Gorbachev? He had one on his forehead. Mind you, the Soviet press used to touch up his photographs."

"How do you know that?"

"Twenty odd years ago I was doing some research in the Hermitage in Leningrad ... Petersburg now..."

"That was for 'The Georgian'?"

"Yes. And I went into this restaurant one evening with a copy of 'Time' that Beth sent out to me. It had a picture of Gorbachev on the cover. In no time I was surrounded by waiters and other people. Even the chef came out of the kitchen to have a look. They'd never seen the birthmark before. They thought the Western press had added it in as some sort of insult."

"I rest my case," Sarah said, showing her neat teeth. "You should get it removed."

"But you mightn't love me anymore."

"Trust me." She pushed her glass forward towards the neck of the bottle he proffered, then she raised it in affirmation, looking steadily at him over the crimson wine. "You know, you really should let us handle your next book, if you insist on doing one."

"That's a thought." He ordered another bottle of wine, murmuring, "What the hell, it's the end of the week." There was something about Fridays he had to admit, a promise of freedom. A gypsy-styled vendor in a gingham apron offered a basket of posies. He bought a nosegay of violets and handed it to Sarah.

"How sweet!" She treasured it with her small hands and laid it beside her purse while she finished the prawns. Then came the self-flagellation over the dessert trolley after which, with much expression of guilt, she chose a small wedge of chocolate cake which she ate with amazing delicacy. Noticing the double prong at the edge of the cake fork, Robert was put in mind of a prediction that, in three thousand years, the little toe would merge with the one beside it. Jaws would disappear too, because of soft food. What a race we are, he thought a little drunkenly, adaptable to a fault. For some reason Drew came to mind, and Chaim, who was once nicknamed 'Castor Man' because he went in whatever direction he was pushed. What kind of principles would you like me to have? Was that Woody Allen? Robert ordered brandy with his coffee.

Sarah nibbled at the cake, and alternated with sips of coffee. He liked the way she pampered herself. They were two softies, a pair of puffed sparrows in sun-patches. If she was epicurean, he was greedy and since the only difference lay in quantity, he couldn't afford to be judgmental. He wondered if he had any capacity left for real pain.

This was one reason he valued his relationship with Sarah; it was light and fluffy – his mother's description of good pastry. Since Nita turned sour on him he tended to walk on eggshells where women were concerned. He was in favor of feminism though he did find some of the 'third-wavers' a little OTT at times and inclined to toss off moral imperatives at the drop of a hat. On the whole though he saw it as a legitimate cause as long as it was seen for what it was, a distributional coalition like any other, aimed at carving up the usufruct.

Drew, on the other hand, was a dyed-in-the-wool male chauvinist. He once told Robert that more men would be critical of women except they were afraid their hostility would be construed as fear of women's superior capacity for sex. This superiority, he added, which took the form of unremitting pelvic activity, was nature's way of preparing the female for childbirth. It followed, therefore, that any man who could keep up with a woman all night in bed was not a stud at all, but in fact had an excess supply of female hormones. Robert immediately concluded that Drew was no good in bed.

Chaim of course was a different proposition altogether and it never ceased to amaze Robert how naturally he – and other gays – related to women. It wasn't just that there was no need to fence; it had more to do with shared interests and simple comradeship without the complication of sexual desire.

All these thoughts unsettled Robert and made him hasten for the bill. Sarah rose with a smile as he held her chair. The scent from her neck was jasmine.

Back in his apartment which was still fussed

up with Nita's chintzes and brocades – she developed a fabric fetish in their last year – he mixed a couple of nightcaps which they brought up to the roof where he used to sit in isolation like a lightening conductor, waiting for inspiration to strike. The roof garden was in reasonable order and the scent of ampelopsis and fuchsia filled the night air.

"It's so peaceful here," Sarah sighed, making herself as comfortable as she could in the director-style chair. She put her feet up on a copper-fastened chest that served as a coffee table, and crossed her ankles. Her brown eyes took in a row of bonsai trees in ceramic pots then, looking upwards, the dark sky frosted with stars. City sounds drifted up from the street below but were not so strident as to dispel her lazy, lofty mood.

"Stay the night, Sarah?" He kissed the nape of her neck.

"If you want me to."

"I do."

"Then I will."

In the bedroom they fell to with a will, muscling in with an abandon that might have surprised their friends. Then came the inevitable: "Be back in a minute, darling", the blown kiss and the sound of the bathroom door closing. Lying back in exasperation on the four-poster bed amid white *broderie anglaise* cushions, Robert wondered what exactly went on in bathrooms at these moments, but decided finally that he didn't really want to know. These breaks, however, were not good for his nerves and at his age ran the risk of losing the momentum that had miraculously produced tumescence. These days, despite pharmaceutical advances, erections had a scarcity value and were not to be treated cavalierly. This particular one was well up to par, standing there in all its purple embarrassment, like some freshly hatched creature wondering if this was the life it expected. Robert, like a good woodsman, gave it a few strokes to encourage it to hold on for just a little longer.

A lot of Nita was still in this bedroom, from the gilt-wood rococo furniture and French Provençal armoire to the flock wallpaper and swagged drapes. At least it was better than the bedroom she designed in her Japanese period, when he had to sleep on nothing more than a palette with tatami mats and futons, and kept bumping into delicate screens painted in *bois de rose*. It seemed to him that all his pads had been designed by women.

Leaning towards the bed table for his brandy, he accidentally bumped his member with an elbow. It recoiled in shock; this was not the sensation it expected. Robert hoped Sarah would return soon to put that idiotic thing out of its misery, before he had another accident or his ardor cooled.

She returned glowing in a negligee and descended on him slowly with the calibrated movements of a swan, covering him with her plumage under which she was gloriously naked.

Beneath this erotic caravan she took his erection quite firmly in her hand and guided it into her vagina. From that moment on the image became more equestrian and, as she spurred on her mount, he let her romp. Being younger and wildly enthusiastic – her third face magnificently revealed – she was happy to take the initiative though still seemed to appreciate his occasional encouraging thrust. Holding with her knees she shimmied up his trunk and plunged from tip to hilt, both moaning now, surprise piled on surprise as further treasures of feeling unfolded. He was only good for one these days, but age had its compensations; it would be some time coming and the interval would be good for both. Her excited commentaries began to get to him but the old maestro paced the finale – age was a good synchronizer too – and he choreographed the eager procession until all the brass bands struck up together.

They lay sweating and breathless after their mutual triumph. In the roseate silence Robert watched the traffic lights play on the ceiling as his heart slowed to a more normal rhythm. Sarah placed her arm across his chest and asked with a sleepy smile, "*Il t'a plu?*"

"Oh yes." He kissed her gratefully on the nose as she snuggled against him in preparation for sleep. The clock said one. He rummaged quietly in the drawer of the night table and palmed a Dalmane, hoping she wouldn't notice. Perversely, the release she had given his body did not calm his mind, which renewed its attempt to find an algorithm to steer by, for whatever years remained. Maybe his soft life of recent years and his doyen role made him incapable of the effort needed to go back to first principles. Would memoirs solve that? Had he been down this road himself and chosen magic as an out? Keep busy, Robert thought, or go to sleep, for the dreaming was over.

More immediately, he had to plan his weekend; he felt threatened by the emptiness of two long days that loomed ahead of him, and he resolved to visit his brother, Gary. They had always been close, and Gary was much more rooted; for Robert he was the ultimate reality check, and was singularly unimpressed by his brother's fame.

"Fancy a trip to New Jersey tomorrow?" he said into Sarah's ear. The words reinforced the decision.

"To see Gary? Yes, absolutely." She spoke without opening her eyes. They drifted into sleep together.

CHAPTER 4

BY THE TIME they'd reached Port Chester and were crossing the State line into Connecticut, Richard had figured it out.

"He must be going to visit with his brother." He had dispensed with the dark glasses and his eyes were bleary with a tinge of redness in the whites. Now that the traffic had thinned out he was finding it hard to keep up with the Cadillac which Robert was driving.

"And the woman?" Khaled asked.

"Sarah somebody. She lives with him on and off." He didn't know that much about her; the tabloids mentioned her only when she appeared at functions on Lynskey's arm. But she was a fine-looking woman, Richard thought a little wistfully. That cracker had the pick of the bunch. Richard put the pedal to the floor and made up some of the distance; he kept his thoughts to himself.

Although no longer surprised by it, Khaled still found it difficult to understand how Americans could live, apparently at ease, without any code. Financial markets could still do as they pleased after horrific errors that destroyed economies. And it was abundantly clear that large corporations ran the political system. What really confounded him was that such license seemed to go hand in hand with a strange sort of incorrigible innocence as though the country was still wet behind the ears and, for that reason, could not be held to account. Maybe this fledgling nation hadn't reached the age of reason yet so the question of corruptibility didn't arise. In those lonely years at Columbia he had been struck by the *L'il Abner* cartoon, which came up in Culture Studies. How perfect a symbol it was: a big young farm boy, energetic and dumb. But the excuse of youthful ignorance could not be sustained indefinitely, nor did it guarantee immunity. The future of the world was in the hands of spoiled brats, trying to be men. 'Lord of the Flies' was the story of America.

More than anything else it struck him that the highways illustrated the sheer power of this country. Nuclear arsenals, missile silos, financial markets, factories, skyscrapers were hidden or intermittent. But the highways were everywhere visible, scything through the huge continent, going up and over, curving back on themselves; these equators of concrete proved in every flyover and clover leaf a complete and epidemic mastery of the environment. There was no need for Shock and Awe to make the peons feel inferior. Read these roads and weep. The men who financed these roads – and the railroads – had wiped out over twenty million indigenous people without a thought. It was no coincidence that the current President was an ignoble builder.

He noticed the perfectly legible green and white road signs that left nothing to chance and he was intrigued by the Indian place names: Saugatuck, Winnipauk, Manasquan.

Dispossession was nothing new. The forked tongue was replaced by empty rhetoric about freedom, independence, peace at any price. But peace without justice meant nothing.

Near Bridge Port the highway was skirted by trees, many already in bloom, tulip, chestnut, maple and those strange eucalyptus trees with bark patterned like damask. Another irony forced itself on Khaled: the natural beauty of the country despite everything. Beauty like that should have brought out the best in people, instead of the worst. Were they blind?

Route 95 continued on stilts like a bridge thrown over the whole town, and it gave glimpses of Long Island Sound on the right. Following the Cadillac, they cut off at a turnpike and followed a smaller road into a modest suburbia.

At a safe distance they watched Robert park in front of a timber-frame house with painted wooden siding and a white stoop. They observed the greeting, genuine and jovial, as the visitors were made welcome, ushered into the porch and served with iced tea. Children played with a baseball in the front yard which also had a basketball hoop over the garage door. The asphalt driveway was marked out in white for some other sport like badminton.

"Looks like the brother has a bunch of kids," Richard remarked, switching off the engine.

"Yes," Khaled said. "It's surprising he would come here to spend the weekend." These people somehow managed to cover the whole spectrum of pleasures, including the innocent ones.

Richard looked up and down the quiet neighborhood; no other house in sight showed much sign of activity. At that time on a Saturday morning people were probably still in bed or at the shopping malls. It was an opportunity that might not recur. His heart began to beat faster. "We should ... do it now."

On the porch Robert greeted his nephew, John, a brown-eyed boy with a shy smile. What he felt for this boy was pure and unalloyed; there was no need to question it. The youngster, corralled between his knees, offered him M & Ms and answered all the questions about school, subjects and games that his smiling uncle put to him. When Robert finally released him, John went running back to resume his play with the older kids but from time to time he returned to offer more of the grimy sweets to Robert.

"Where does he get such looks and charm from?" Robert asked in a parody of puzzlement.

"From me of course," Gary replied with a sidelong glance at his wife, Sue, who said to Sarah, "The Lynskey brothers are noted for their modesty. I'm sure you've noticed." Sue was a teacher who became so disenchanted with the low standards in the education system that she decided to home-school her children.

"Now that you mention it..." Sarah replied with a laugh. She'd enjoyed the drive down and knew already that her positive anticipation was not misplaced.

Gary went into the house and returned with a bottle of Southern Comfort. "Iced tea won't do for my brother, the celebrity. You know," he said to Sarah as he filled her glass, "I should be the embarrassing brother hidden away in the sticks. Hell, maybe I am."

"I doubt if you could embarrass him," Sarah replied, giving the impression that she knew Robert inside out. Feeling overdressed by comparison with Sue who made do in jeans and sweater, Sarah removed the jacket of her linen suit and hung it over the back of the chair.

"Whatever you do," Sue told Sarah, "don't let him get too pompous or serious. He can be a real buzz-kill when he gets on his soapbox."

Having filled the glasses, Gary sat in his wicker chair and contemplated his family and few paternal acres with a large grin on his face. Six years younger than Robert, he was leaner and fitter. Less mileage, Robert thought ruefully, looking at his own podgy hands, fewer fraught nights worrying about the next step in the grand design. Gary seemed to have everything because he wanted so little. It had taken Robert years to discover just how remarkable his brother was. But where did he get that simple acceptance? Of two brothers one was given ambition and a self-surmounting urge, the other was given peace.

Whenever Robert tried to compliment him, Gary would put himself down, saying he was just a bore who had no talent for anything.

"Except living," Robert had said on one occasion when they visited the old country together.

"Yeah, but that's easy. Any fool can do that." Gary replied.

But Robert never found it so; he dwelt mainly in the future, hardly even knowing what year it actually was.

Sue stood up abruptly and shaded her eyes. "John," she called out, " Don't go on the road. Stay in the yard, that's a good boy. William, will you please keep an eye on him." She sat down stroking back a wisp of hair. "The Lawson's must have visitors too."

"Oh?" Gary looked down the street. "No contest. That old Buick isn't a patch on our visitors' Caddy."

"Lay off." Robert squinted at a shimmering cobweb that was slung like a hammock between two balusters of the porch; it acted like a prism, splitting the sunlight into radiances of purple and green. He hadn't felt so relaxed in a long time. There was no pressure, no impression to create, no audience to please or appease. They were just hanging out together; there was no purpose other than being there.

"What was that show you did with what's-is-name?" Gary snapped his fingers trying to ignite a spark of memory. "You know, the one that got a bit out of hand?" He looked for help to Sue. "That radical guy?"

"Chris Hedges," Sue offered.

Gary shook his head. "Not as smart as him … He made 'Bowling for Columbine'.

"Michael Moore." They all spoke at once.

"Yeah, him. What a live wire."

"Is that all?" Robert bent to retrieve the baseball that rolled on to the stoop and threw it gently back to John, who fumbled the catch and giggled as he ran down the elusive ball.

"It was a yell," Gary said. "He really put you in your place. What did he call you? A 'pseudo-intellectual'? Yeah, that was it."

A slithering pain inserted itself between Robert's ribs; he tended to take Gary seriously because he had no axe to grind. He knew he was reading too much into the remark but, nevertheless, a disturbing thought installed itself in his mind: just suppose his popularity came from his pomposity and the promise of this being punctured on screen? Was he being set up every week, a cock-shot for all those regular guys guzzling beer in front of the tube? Was this the unwitting secret of his success? Getting to his feet with a mumbled excuse, he brought this worrying thought with him to the bathroom, where he peered at himself in the mirror. He didn't look pompous but how could he be sure? If he was, he wouldn't recognize it in himself. He urinated briefly out of habit and washed and dried his hands. As he straightened his tie, he began to feel more composed. Of course it was nonsense; there was no conspiracy of derision. But he was annoyed with himself for worrying about his goddamn image. He was still a superficial sonovabitch when all was said and done. It wouldn't even have crossed Gary's mind that he had hurt his brother with such a harmless remark. And Robert had no intention of making him any the wiser.

When he returned, he found the others, children included, grouped together on the lawn looking up at the sky. With a few quick strides he joined them in their heavenward gaze.

"Must be Air Force drills," Gary suggested, keeping his eyes trained on the spectacle.

Some thirty thousand feet up skydivers in freefall seemed to hang in the air like sycamore seeds held in place by a confused wind. The sight of parachutes opening on some unheard command, was followed by delayed popping sounds as the pods filled with air. Noticing John's upturned face and rapt brown eyes, Robert put his arm around the boy's shoulder out of deep affection but also to touch something that would never be his.

"Glad to see our boys in action," Gary said. "And to know we're being protected."

"Maybe we're being invaded," Sue suggested.

Robert wondered vaguely if the troops weren't being trained to strengthen the US presence in Afghanistan or Syria. It hardly bore thinking about. They never learnt a damn thing from the pointless tragedy of Vietnam, and they had no one else to blame but themselves.

The diversion palled, the kids went back to play and the adults returned to their drinks and lazy chat, forming a cosy tableau between the painted pillars of the porch.

"You know it's a funny thing," Gary mused in his patriarchal chair, lacking only a back-scratcher. "About genes, I mean. There's Robert oozing with talent and here's me as thick as a plank."

Before Robert had a chance to rebut – he wondered if Gary wasn't laying it on deliberately – Sue followed up with interest. "What's your secret?"

"Clean living," Robert answered uncomfortably. He wasn't sure whether talent entered the equation at all. It was more a matter of persistence; doing and producing and coming back like a pest even when – especially when – kicked in the teeth. Eventually there's a tipping point – if one lives long enough – where the damn work imposes itself on the consciousness and becomes a style, its own style. No, it wasn't talent; just willpower born out of desperation and a yen to get even. No doubt his former colleagues in Academia now regarded him as a popularizer … or even an entertainer. The thought didn't bother him as much as it used to.

"It's a question of putting in the effort," he said.

"Even if that were true," Sue persisted.

"Where do you get the drive from?" It was clear from her tone that her own dear husband was lacking in the drive department.

Robert loosened his collar hoping they would soon get off the subject of him. "It's a form of compensating, I suppose…" He broke off; it was all so trite.

"Oh come on…" Sarah's laugh started with a peal and diminished to her hallmark tinkle.

"Well," Robert shifted in his seat, "I was once a young immigrant with a patch in my trousers. Hunger is a good sauce. Maybe that's why America is so achievement-driven." But how, he wondered, not for the first time, had Gary managed to avoid that impulse?

"Compensation," Sue mused. "I find that hard to believe."

"I think it explains a lot of things," Robert said, relieved that the conversation was widening out; he pushed it further away from himself, the self he was becoming heartily sick of. "It may even explain the difference between the sexes…"

"I must hear this," Sue said, leaning forward.

"Let me take you back half a million years…" Robert began in a feigned academic manner.

"Oh Christ he's off," Gary said accusingly to Sue. "Look what you've done."

"Ignore him. Carry on, Robert."

"Before the agricultural revolution men were still hunters, right? OK, then it follows that they probably didn't understand how children were made, at least their own part in it…"

"You mean," Gary put in, "they never saw a bull with a cow. Oh right, I saw this on the 'Discovery Channel'. Men thought women were miracle-workers or goddesses because they could produce life. So the guys tried to compensate by painting the walls of the cave."

"There you go."

"I always knew it," Gary said, deliberately missing the point, "Women were responsible for putting men down from the word go. They gave us the inferiority complex."

"No sale," Sarah said. "You can't explain away male chauvinism that easily."

"I can," Gary countered, "Because I'm a member of the toxic patriarchy."

"Only a junior member," Sue ribbed him.

"Speaking of kids," Gary said, "times-a-passing, Robert, old son."

"Hey, don't rub it in." Robert glanced at his hands still stained from the M&Ms John kept giving him. "I'm envious enough as it is."

"Ours came late," Gary said. "I had a motility problem ... you know, the little guys didn't swim very well..."

"Too much information..." Sue laughed.

"We know," Robert added with a grin.

"Yep, had to wear baggy pants for a couple of years ... But I think you enjoy kids more when they come late." He patted his wife's hand; the gesture didn't go unnoticed.

"It's not too late," Sue said.

"Oh, now. I'm nearly sixty." Robert was

conscious of using this excuse for something else recently. Was it an excuse? What was the occasion?

"You mean, you can't...?" Gary started to laugh.

"He can, he can." Sarah laughed, placing her hand on Robert's shoulder and teasing the short hairs on his neck.

"Glad to hear it," Gary said.

Kids, Robert thought, hadn't been in the grand design. He had six good books behind him, not counting the 'entertainment', some of which won prizes, including the Pulitzer on one occasion. Two PhDs had already been written on his work and another was in train in some Midwestern University. He'd seen most of the world, rubbed shoulders with the great and the good of three continents. But, god, how soon was eaten bread forgotten? There was no flesh of his flesh, only a few cave drawings. For the first half of his life he was afraid of death, now he was afraid of being found dead, having died alone.

CHAPTER 5

THE BUICK RATTLED a lot and every imperfection in the road was instantly transmitted by inadequate shock-absorbers to the driver and passenger.

"Why not?" Richard inquired as they picked up Route 95 South.

"It was not how we planned it," Khaled said.

"Yeah, but it was a good opportunity." Richard stroked his beard between thumb and forefinger, forming a tight nub of hair at the point of his chin. He had wanted to get it over with, this job that was bigger than anything he had ever been involved in. Back there outside the house he was ready, primed. Now dread crawled over him, thinking of the days of endless waiting that lay ahead. He wondered if Khaled really understood the extent to which Americans hated Arabs. They called them 'sand niggers' and even worse. The conquest of Iraq and the execution of Saddam Hussein and bin Laden had done nothing to lessen that hatred. If the mission went wrong it would be torture and life imprisonment for all of them, including Anna.

"The arrangements haven't been finalized," Khaled said. "You've spoken with Daniel X as well. He's still working on that place in Metuchen."

Now that he had the choice, Richard observed the speed limit; his mugshot was in Post Offices all over the State and caution had become a habit, now more than ever. But there was an upside; if the plan went well he and Anna would be able to put life back into the Nation of Islam – maybe even the Black Muslim movement. The Jihad would work for them; the time was right. Anna was in no doubt about that and he trusted her judgment. Besides, it was payback time – for his brother and his father.

During the journey Khaled prayed for a while as the shadows of foliage played on the windscreen of the car. As open country gave way to high-rise concrete, he felt that the light enveloping the streets had a special sepia quality as if it came from another age and stilled all movement; yet it could have been the film of his eyes that so transformed it. He had no way of knowing. But he recognized the same sun that presided over his own land and he was suddenly overcome by the happenstance of things and of time. How did he come to be here with this African American who burned with a mission of his own? There were two answers to everything; the reasonable one and the one that is not given to man to understand. The first answer was simple enough...

A Palestinian by birth, Khaled lost his parents when his village was bulldozed out of existence by the Israeli tank corps. He spent the next two years in a refugee camp with nothing to live for except the sustaining energy of hatred. In the Spring of 1986 Jallud Fahd paid a surprise visit to the camp and met Khaled who was ten at the time. Seeing the blight in the eyes of the urchin, Fahd took him under his wing and brought him to the shrine city of Qom where he became a pupil in the Shia seminary near the Shrine of Fatimeh Masumeh.

Although it took several months to adapt, Khaled's life changed completely. He threw himself into the study of the trivium of which logic was his favorite discipline, and he came to love the beauty of the Koran and of the walled gardens where he dwelt among the jasmine bushes, the quince and pomegranate trees. In those cloisters he walked with the Imam and the Mullahs wearing the green robes of the Prophet.

During those years of study he was not very aware politically but this changed gradually as he delved into the history of the region. Jallud Fahd described some of his own experiences to him, including the overthrow of the Shah of Iran who had been a puppet of the West. Revolutionary forces in their thousands had moved up Kakh Avenue to seize the office of the Shah's Prime Minister. Jallud quoted from memory the announcement which followed: "The ill-omened regime of the Pahlevis is finished and an Islamic Government has been established under the Ayatollah Khomeini. The blood of martyrs has prevailed over the sword." It was a momentous turning point and Jallud, caught up in the fervor, left the seminary where he too had studied, and joined the swelling crowds in the streets and bazaars, wearing his turban and black aba with pride. Even the hated secret police, Savak, bowed to him whereas previously they pushed him aside or beat him. He listened to the chanting in the streets. "Through the blessings of Allah we are saved ... Great God, never let the shadows of the Mullahs grow less ... From this moment the Jihad begins..."

Jallud Fahd told this story with such passion that Khaled began to understand the enormity of the change. True believers were no longer the outcasts and ignorant nomads of whom the Westernized Pahlevis were so ashamed. It was a change so complete, a change of heart no less than leadership, that nothing would ever seem so hopeless again. What had started in Iran must surely spread to his beloved Palestine.

"At last we were free," Jallud Fahd had said. "Allah humbled to the depths the unbelievers. God does not guide an unjust people. We have seen justice return and are blessed for having witnessed it in our time. Khomeini prepared the way," Jallud explained, realizing that Khaled was too young to have experienced any of it. "Working through Allah, the tapes he sent from exile, the i'ilamiyahs, influenced the people who were ready to listen. Wealthy merchants gave charcoal and money to the people. The radicals assimilated the spirit of Imam Hosein, especially after the month of fasting. The Pahlevis were ashamed of us which meant they shamed Allah. They thought of us as primitive, we who regard the touch of a non-Muslim as impure, requiring a ritual washing. The Shah preferred the America of Watergate and even the atheism of Russia. So to the people he became the Taghuti incarnate. The Mustazafin had to bring him down. He wandered the earth homeless with his cancer. The Americans didn't want him after all his fawning and *folie de grandeur*. When the blessed Khomeini returned to Iran, the people who had listened to his tapes rose to meet him."

"Through Allah's servant justice came upon the land. But, my friend, we Iranians had to spread the Word throughout the whole of Arabdom." He put his hand on Khaled's arm. "And above all we must seek justice for Palestine, your people. That is your calling."

"But I am just a student, a juriconsult..." Khaled had said, conscious of his youth, all his inadequacies.

"We must all now become active," Jallud said. "This is the Jihad. The prophesy is fulfilled."

After a light meal of honeyed bread and boiled meat they went into the mosque where the sessions of Hawza were held. Khaled's skin began to tingle. This was where the young Khomeini slept on his doshak after the Savak murdered his children. Unable to penetrate the mosque, the police could not touch him and so he prevailed, right in their midst.

When the ceremony was over Jallud Fahd continued the account. "Khomeini reunited church and state as was always the purpose of Islam. On one of his tapes he said, 'Let every mosque be made a Komitay for the Revolution'. And the people reacted to him as leader when the revolution was complete. 'The soul of Hussein is returning', they cried, 'The doors of Paradise have been opened.' Jallud added that the Sharia was the literal word of God and should not be interpreted in any other way. The Imam would eventually return and fill the world with justice. The Palestinian people would live again. Khaled did not question the words of his mentor; they moved his heart.

But his sense of wondering was to recur, making him feel unworthy. He had to put his faith to the test, to see if the rest of the infidel world was so steeped in perfidy. Selling his few belongings, he went to the US on a student visa in the mid-nineties and discovered a way of life he could not have imagined. The campuses were quiet; gone was the student revolt and the drive for justice that he had read about. A selfish mindset prevailed at all levels of society. The disparity between rich and poor was even greater than had existed in Iran under the Pahlevi regime. In the wasteland evil took root and flourished; reason was separated from reality. When he wasn't ignored he was treated with contempt as if he had been responsible for raising oil prices. Americans, like bulldogs protecting their food, had developed a hatred for the whole Arab world and dared to see them as infidels! And this was before 9/11 happened.

After eighteen months Khaled had seen enough, felt an even greater pull towards the religious certainty of Islam and the incontrovertible justness of the Palestinian cause. These two aims became wedded in his mind. So he returned to Gaza City more convinced than ever and ready to join the Jihad for the benefit of his beloved Palestine. There was no point in trifling with justice; it was all or nothing. Consecrating himself to the spread of Islam and the fight for Palestine, he undertook commando training with the PLO and al Qaeda. Gone were the walled gardens and long periods of reflection. This was the battle for the hearts of men. The powerless had to fight, not just for survival, but for identity. The Prophet had said, "I swear to God in whose hands is my life, that to fight for religion is better than the world and the prayers of six years."

CHAPTER 6

DUSK CAME ON, illumined by fireflies, and hoarse with the semi-tropical sounds of cicadas and tree frogs. Gary rounded up the children and put the two youngest to bed; the older two went to the lounge to play a popular video game. The adults all chipped in preparing dinner, making forays into the crowded kitchen to lend a hand. There was no fuss or standing on ceremony. As she set the table, Sarah noticed that the crockery didn't match; hardly any two pieces were the same.

They sat down together at the oval table in the dining area and Gary carved the lamb with intense concentration. Behind him a grandfather clock ticked resonantly inside its teak casing and gave a whirring prelude to eight limpid chimes.

Sarah sipped her wine and sighed, "It's great to get out of the city." Here was an image of the kind of home she would have liked to grow up in, instead of that bleak apartment in Queens with a brutish father and neurotic mother who, by her incessant complaints, made Sarah resolve never to be trapped by a man without substance. She liked the disarray of this house, the cross-fertilization of objects, toys among the plates on the Welsh dresser, a catcher's mitt on the drinks trolley, hanks of knitting wool on chairs. There was no evidence of style or wealth, indeed the house exulted in its modesty and proved that just enough was better than too much.

Robert passed down the plates laden with lamb, mint sauce and natural juices. He watched Gary stand to carve an awkward piece near the bone; his head was bent to the task and the overhanging light placed his face in a deep repose of shadow. For Robert a lot of feelings and memories intersected on that momentary image of his brother.

"Grub's up," Sue called into the lounge. The older boys drifted in, accepted their plates and made for the door to go back to the TV.

"Mind the rug, and bed at ten sharp," Gary cautioned them.

"They're great kids," Sarah remarked when they'd left.

"Did I tell you," Gary asked, sitting down, "that I'm retiring in a few months?"

"But you're only fifty-two," Robert protested, laying down his silverware. "You're crazy." The thought of retirement horrified him.

"Yeah, but it's time to walk the plank. That food-store can manage itself anyway. Besides, there's a lot Sue and I want to do. Ourselves, and with the kids." His temples rippled slightly as he chewed, his head tilted to one side.

"I think that's a marvelous idea." Sarah reached for the pepper mill, ground it over her plate, then offered it to the others.

"You mean you're going to give up work?" Robert asked. "Everything?"

"Work isn't everything," Sue pointed out

calmly and slowly because it was like reasoning with a child. There were times like this when her brother-in-law appealed greatly to her.

"We've been looking forward to this for years," Gary said, still chewing with maddening concentration.

Robert rushed to fill a perceived pause, "Travel then," he said. "Go on a cruise, see the world. Egypt..." He'd read Mailer's *Ancient Evenings* years ago and couldn't help wondering if the Pharaohs' leanings towards sodomy were in accord with history. Norm rarely let facts get in the way of a good yarn.

"We don't want to be too organized," Gary said, reaching for the sweet corn.

"I want you to do this. A round-the-world-cruise. On me." Robert's eyebrows sat high on his forehead, earnest, almost pleading.

Gary raised a hand. "Thanks, but no thanks, Bob. You've done enough for the kids."

"Look, I've more dough than I can shake a stick at. What've I got to spend it on? I'd enjoy it if you did this. For me. Do it for me."

"No thanks."

"But..." Robert had depressing visions of Gary whittling on the porch, knee-deep in shavings in the ineffectual twilight of his years.

"No 'buts'. We just want to hang out. Here, have some sweet potato." Gary passed the dish down the table, as imperturbable as the Sphinx he would never see.

Robert wasn't sure why the prospect of

idleness bothered him so much. Maybe *enforced* idleness wouldn't be so bad because there would be no need to feel guilty. He envisioned a small jail cell with no distractions except the mice scurrying across the floor at night; he could really get down to some serious writing then. But to *opt* for inactivity, no, that was beyond him.

"You can't just waste your best years," he said. It was his final shot; he knew he couldn't dissuade Gary once he had made up his mind. He also knew that there was no point in appealing to Sue, who rarely disagreed with Gary, except over the question of home-schooling – and she had been proved right in that respect.

"Who said anything about waste?" Sarah put in with a look that ridiculed the suggestion. "Just because *you* can't stand still for a minute doesn't mean everyone should follow your lead."

"Oh, I suppose you're right," Robert said humbly. It was a lost cause.

Close to midnight the women went to bed, leaving the brothers to their reminiscences. Gary lit a fire in the grate more for mood than warmth. As he looked at the photographs on the mantelpiece, Robert asked, "You remember Dad, don't you?"

"A little," Gary said. "I was about five when he died."

"What was your impression of him?" Robert had his own recollection of him but wondered how accurate it was.

"I don't remember all that much." Gary

scooped up some peanuts from a bowl on the coffee table and popped them one by one into his mouth. "A big kind man with a loud laugh. He often carried me on his shoulders. Uncle Dave told me some stories later on about Dad's exploits in the reservists who paraded up and down the town, determined to keep Hitler from invading Ireland. Dad used to say that Churchill never forgave De Valera for keeping Ireland neutral during the war, so the reservists kept an eagle eye on the British too. Uncle Dave used to rib Dad about what his little toy army would do if Hitler did invade and Dad used to reply, 'Mr. Hitler would have his hands full, and he might get more than he bargained for.'"

"You must be a chip off the old block," Robert said, thinking of Gary's stubborn streak.

"No, I don't think so. They used to say you were more like him."

"Me?"

"Yeah, he couldn't stand still either." Gary leant back in the recliner, bringing up the footrest, as if to *prove* that he was the easy-going one.

Robert smiled. It was as if he'd just been handed a gift. It was true about his Dad and it was strange he had not made the connection himself.

"Why bring it up now?" Gary put another log on the fire and watched it spit and hiss until the lichen turned to cinder.

"I like to compare notes."

Gary lit a cigar, one that he'd been saving for a special occasion, and watched the smoke curl up towards the ceiling. "You and Sarah. Anything happening there? She's nice."

"We get on well together…"

"Maybe you should get married."

"You're a good ad for it but I don't think it's for me, not at my age." A new thought occurred: was there, beneath it all, a fear of leaving orphans behind? Age was not on his side.

"Come on," Gary chivvied him, "you said you could still rise to the occasion."

"When the flesh is willing." Robert laughed. He became aware of a loose spring sticking in his rump and moved further down the lived-in sofa. As he watched the fire he thought of heretics being burned at the stake. If they had money they could bribe the executioner to put some green wood on the fire; that would allow the smoke to kill them before the flames. We were all so much more enlightened now, the Dark Ages well behind us. He wondered if that were true.

"Of course you're not stuck for choice," Gary said, "though I guess you have to be careful nowadays."

"Have you ever cheated on Sue?"

"You probably won't believe this," Gary said. "I haven't." His face crinkled into a smile.

"I'd kill you if you had. She's an extraordinary woman. I don't know how you got so lucky."

"Mind you I've sometimes wondered what it's like to play the field."

"To tell you the truth," Robert said, sitting

forward his hands lashed around his knees, "I've become a bit scared of women." He doubted if he would have admitted this to another soul.

"That's because Nita is bleeding you dry. And your divorce was a bitch of a brawl."

"Maybe." Robert looked into the fire again, as if an augury might be found in the flames that feasted on the crackling wood and struck sparkles from the andirons.

"Of course you can't blame women for looking after their own interests," Gary went on. "They were kept down for long enough."

As Robert was absorbing this with a preliminary nod, he happened to spy their two graying heads in the mirror over the mantelpiece. It was a droll discovery to happen upon this brace of elderly white-plumed birds taking themselves rather seriously in front of the fire. He tried to get the image back again, as if to lock it into his memory, but whatever way he turned his eyes he could only get one face at a time; maybe Gary had moved, but the pictures of both were irretrievably lost. He gave up and sipped his drink. "I'm such a selfish bastard," he said suddenly. "Sometimes I can't face myself in the morning."

"Come on, Bob, look what you've achieved."

Robert resisted this blandishment. "I did it for me." He prodded his sternum with a contrite finger. "Mea culpa..."

"Your books are valuable. The shows..."

"Entertainment, Gary. One notch above Gerry Springer." No notch if Drew got his way.

"That's important. People need to be entertained. You can't change the world."

"Still, I wonder about my motives." Those he had shouldered aside in his grandstand play came into his mind like figures on a frieze, thrown into sharp relief by the knowledge that Gary and their father had never hurt anybody or tried to get the upper hand on perceived rivals. By comparison Robert was a shit.

"Everyone's got mixed motives." Gary rushed to his defense. "Like me. I want to retire 'cause I'm selfish. But it'll also be good for the family, see? Bad *and* good. Go easy on yourself. Sometimes I think you're not so smart." He stretched out his legs and studied the toe-caps of his worn slippers. "In the Gulf War I did some things I'm not proud of but I also did some things right. And it wasn't bravery. I was scared of being a coward, if that makes any sense."

"I funked the war." Robert stared dolefully into his glass.

"Oh Christ, you did no such thing. You were exempt." A trace of irritation crept into Gary's voice. Being cast in the role of confessor was awkward enough but having his absolution thrown back in his face by a stubborn penitent called the entire sacrament into question. "Look," he laughed abruptly, "who the hell knows why we do what we do? And does it matter? We're not axe-murders. If we mean well, maybe that's enough."

"Hmmm." Robert took it under advisement.

He appreciated Gary's sympathy but he wondered if you could really be forgiven by a man who temperamentally found it impossible to accuse anyone of anything. One thing was certain though, he would never be as well-meaning as his brother, not in a million years.

He looked again for their joint reflection in the mirror and, missing it, thought of a parable. Two brothers started out as pioneers and came across a gold green valley with woodland and streams. One brother settled and made his home, but the other went on, and on, over the next ridge and the one after that, and eventually couldn't stop until he reached the eternal ocean, and even that he wanted to cross. Since the universe was curved, and certainly the planet, maybe the wanderer would eventually come back to where he started from. It might be true that you can never go back, but maybe you come back the other way without knowing it.

Robert had stayed on in Dublin to finish his degree in Trinity where he had a scholarship. Then, at twenty-two, he had followed Gary and their mother to America, choosing, for sentimental and economic reasons, to travel by ship. As he came sailing up the Hudson past Ellis Island his heart jumped; so many others had come down this shining channel. The view of Manhattan was a legend come alive; it was a homecoming. Gary with his wild hair had rushed through the crowds to meet him at the dock. His shy, wonderful, mother wasn't far behind. They all embraced and wept in full view. It was a moment he would not forget. Thinking about it now made him more emotional than he wanted to be.

He loved the vast wild freedom of America. Closeness to England had been suffocating, like being pressed up against the face of a cliff with no perspective on anything else. That sense of relief and release never left him and, though the country of his adoption had many faults, he was always glad that the power necessary for world peace had been given to America, and not to those old skulking European war-mongers. And it was the anonymity of America that allowed him to make his name; it was a country that allowed you to try anything and not be laughed at.

Once, sitting in a fast-food place, unable to control his nervous fingers, he fashioned a toy airplane out of a polystyrene hash-brown container.

"That's a great idea," a passer-by said. "Send it in to the company." Robert laughed but the man didn't see the joke. "Send it in. They could really go for that gimmick." He did, and made a thousand dollars. He couldn't believe it. He walked around for days with the check in his pocket, laughing till his face hurt.

The Kennedy brothers, no longer alive, had done a huge amount for the Irish in America. Robert had felt welcome from the very beginning; being Irish gave him a head start that he made full use of.

He wrote speeches for Reagan, who had been a decent man, and some of his words were now inscribed on public buildings in Washington. In his early forties he'd accompanied Bill Clinton on a visit to Ireland and couldn't resist the sentimental thought that his parents were looking down on them, their boy with the President of the United States. It was a magical experience. In the pubs it seemed as if Beckett and Behan and Kavanagh, Joyce, Yeats and Synge, Swift, Shaw and Wilde were in the back room, talking up a storm. Although it was captivating, he had to remind himself that most of those writers had done their best work abroad. So he had to extricate himself from the black velvet trap and return with the fire of a pioneer to the prairies...

———————————

As they drove back to the city the mood in the car was one of muted satisfaction; the weekend had renewed them both in different ways. Robert didn't feel like talking about it in case words would reduce the experience; he was still European to that degree – so he was a little disappointed when Sarah sighed, "They've got something so real there."

"Yep." He kept his eyes on the road that streamed under the smooth prow of the car.

She ploughed deeper. "You can feel the closeness, the partnership."

"It's very rare," he said, hoping this concession would suffice. It didn't.

"No it's not. Plenty of couples have that. Why do you think it's rare?" She turned sideways in the passenger seat to study his profile.

"I meant special." He was caught in an undertow of confused feelings and somehow found himself on the defensive.

"It's not that special either. Just because we each have one bad marriage behind us doesn't mean the whole institution is down the Swanee." She thought fleetingly of her ex-husband whose brashness she mistook for accomplishment and who, layer by layer over a dismaying three years, was finally stripped to a mediocre pelt. With him there was never any possibility of domestic bliss *and* success. Was it asking too much, she wondered, to want both?

"Still," he went on, vaguely aware of digging himself deeper in, "Gary and Sue are kind of selfless. That makes it easier, I think. No big egos to get in the way…"

"Look, Robert," she interrupted him, "We're not kids. Why don't we give it a shot … and move in together?"

"That's a thought," he said brightly, wondering what the well-meaning Gary had said or done to push her in that direction. At sixty he still wasn't ready, or had he lost the habit of intimacy? He saw himself turning into a bitter old bachelor set in the privacy of his ways, regretting the loss of this fine young woman; maybe the souring process was already under way because, for the life of him, he couldn't give her the answer she wanted.

In the wounded silence Sarah considered her options.

CHAPTER 7

HAVING SWITCHED ON the wave machine, he swam in his cello-shaped pool lined with postcard-blue mosaic tiles. Then he hauled himself out, had a brisk rub down and did some token running on the spot, until the bouncing of his chest and gut made him stop from embarrassment.

In his hooded terrycloth robe he breakfasted in the lounge among Nita's patterned silks, paisleys and Aubusson tapestries. The woman had a lot to answer for. Fortunately, she'd taken with her all that idiotic Italian stuff, anorexic chairs, Spluga barstools, halogen lamps on stalks – but still her posturing mark remained too much in evidence, reminding him of her fussy, grandiose soul. Now that he was descending into final bachelorhood he would have to get a grip on this apartment and make it his own. His ideas were vague; leather, he thought, and some of his bright Thai paintings that Nita had stored in a closet. Yes, it was time for him to put his own stamp on his immediate surroundings, as he had on more distant fronts. Past time.

Downstairs in the 'ideas factory', Beth, the den mother, took him aside by the elbow to discuss a proposal made recently by a large publishing firm.

"They want you to do a book," Beth informed him, sitting on a desk and swinging a shapely middle-aged leg, "on that recent family murder in the Midwest."

"Where the father shot his wife and three kids?" The father, Robert recalled from newspaper reports, had belonged to a cult and was, conceivably, brainwashed. There was certainly plenty of psychic meat in that story but somehow it would be too easy to do and he didn't particularly want to be a carbon copy of the late Mr. Capote or the late Mr. Mailer. It occurred to him that faction wasn't real at all. Perhaps fact wasn't either.

"Well, how do you see it?" Beth asked, sipping coffee from a plastic cup.

"It doesn't sound right," he admitted honestly. The proposal wasn't just commercial; it was exploitative and voyeuristic. And he just plain disliked the downgrading of fiction.

"Big bucks," Beth pointed out with a rueful cast in her eyes which peeped questioningly over the top of her half-glasses. "An advance of two-fifty k, plus a good deal on movie rights. I could put Liz and Jerry on it. They could finish the interviews and research in about three months, I reckon." The way she hung on his reply showed how keen she was.

A compromise came to him. "Why not do it yourselves?"

"It's your name they want," Beth replied with a small smile, mocking his innocence. "The team is a little underemployed at present." The pressure she was exerting was calm and light but well aimed nonetheless. Drew by contrast would have made a meal of it. His name, Robert thought, a designer label. It had taken him years to establish it and now he wasn't sure he wanted to use it. He finally gave much the same answer as he'd given Sarah. "Let's think about it, Beth. I'll get back to you." Thank god he could afford to be indecisive.

"Right." Beth knew when to ease off. She lowered herself down from the desk and straightened her tweed skirt. "By the way, your piece on *Media, Myth and Metaphor* is just about finished. We can get you a hard copy this afternoon."

"Thanks, Beth. Maybe you could copy-edit it for me and I'll give it a final polish tonight." It occurred to him that he depended on her almost as much as Gary depended on Sue.

———————————

At the studio they were ready to shoot next week's show. He had finally persuaded Drew to do something reasonably decent on human potential and the various cults and therapies that purported to deliver the goods in that growth area. The guests included Christina Hoff Summers, a heavyweight academic well known for her TED talks, and a mature character actor who had turned his talents to sexual dysfunction. He it was who, to Robert's growing dismay, dominated the discussion, speaking straight to camera as if involved in foreplay with the lens, and used the final segment to plug his book. Robert fought a losing battle trying to buy time for Christina, whom he admired greatly. Within the hour the patchy program was in the can, the lights went down, the audience filed out. It was always a little death; this one littler than most.

Afterwards Sarah called and they agreed to meet at a new restaurant she'd discovered on sixty-fifth street.

"I'll go straight from the office," Robert said, matching with some relief her light tone. "Should make it about seven-thirty."

"See you then. Ummmmah." She blew him a kiss over the phone.

As he was leaving he met Drew coming out of the cutting room with Chaim in tow.

"There's a lot of it on the floor," Drew told him with a provocative smile.

"If you've chopped Christina I'll sue you for having no soul," Robert said. That was it. No book about the murder of a family either, no commercial faction. The decision came down clean and fast. It probably wasn't a moral stance at all; he just couldn't do it anymore.

"Anyway," Chaim put in, "We won't have a big audience on Friday. The Mayor is appearing on PBS to deny the transport scam in Queens."

"Thanks a lot," Robert said, "for that vote of confidence." He walked out.

"I wonder," Drew mused aloud when he'd left, "if he isn't losing it?"

"Maybe it's just a passing phase." Chaim wasn't moved to sedition. And he appreciated Robert's high profile which had opened many doors for him in the gay community. "We all have our moody blues. Maybe Sarah is causing him some grief?" He shrugged his narrow shoulders to show he was merely speculating.

"I wonder..." Drew tailed off into silent reflection as he padded along the well-carpeted corridor.

"Could be," Chaim said more positively, encouraged by Drew's non-dismissal of the idea. "And that sort of thing can be rough."

"How would you know?" Drew queried, clutching the pipe with his teeth as he smiled. "A man of your ... persuasion."

"Hey, I'm Jewish. Don't tell me about pain." Chaim made light of it because there was no way of convincing Drew that gays had any feelings. The man's forcefulness came as much from his fixed and certain mind-set as from his electric orange pigmentation.

Drew slapped him on the back. "Come on, I'll buy you a bacon sandwich." As they waited for the elevator he wondered about the Sarah connection. Robert didn't deserve one hair of her head. He had no real appreciation of her qualities.

On the way out Robert returned the glances of recognition with his practiced smile, carefully modulated so as to be pleasant but not inviting. He was hurrying to meet his broker, Simkin, for their weekly financial chat. After that he would, he decided, cancel his talk at Columbia, go home and think. Without prejudging the outcome of that promised think-in, he felt sure he would want to review all the easy options and sleight of hand that had cushioned and quilted his recent years; a sabbatical from the show might be one possibility.

In his small room in the abandoned mosque the sun cast a lozenge of light near Khaled's feet. He had fasted for two days and now prayed for the mission and the release of Jallud Fahd, who languished in that appalling prison at Guantanamo Bay, a man who loved freedom almost as much as justice. As he prayed he thought of his comrades in Hamas and in the Palestine Islamic Jihad, most of whom were hunted and dispersed across Europe. He needed this victory to raise their hearts. He needed Americans to discount stereotypes and propaganda and to embrace the truth.

In the adjoining room Richard paced up and down, fingering his cropped beard. During the first couple of weeks tailing Lynskey he had at least the distraction of activity, but the last few days of planning, cooped up in these bleak rooms, had made him edgy. Five years ago when he was really committed to Islam, in the way Bart still was, he would have had less fear, or the fear would have been suppressed by belief. Now, however, he was wide open to the undermining imagery of failure and its consequences. Though he had spent many years as a small-time hood he had never fully lost his innate sense of the power of religion. As a child he used to go with his grandmother to Gospel meetings in Atlanta and lose himself in the music and ringing sermons that filled the wooden church with swaying, relentless energy. He would probably never have become a political activist if it hadn't been associated in his mind with the compelling call of religion, that urgent mission of Jesus and Mohammed to change the old order and give back to the people what was rightfully theirs.

But with the passage of time and after many failures and disenchantments, his former certainties eroded to the point of despair, he wanted one last opportunity to recapture all that was lost and taken. Anna fed his desire.

The phone rang; it was Bart, who was sent ahead earlier that morning with detailed instructions.

"I followed the man," Bart said.

"Did he go into the office of Simkin and Heller?" Anna asked.

"Yes."

"And you got parked outside the building as we told you?"

"Right outside. At a meter…"

"OK, move out when you see us. Then go straight to the place in Metuchen and wait for us. Have you got that?"

"Sure, I remember the plan."

Anna replaced the receiver and took a deep breath. "It's on." Nothing else needed to be said.

Richard had never seen her look so intense; he tried to borrow from her strength of purpose. Everything about her quickened. She went to the fridge and using both hands took out a phial of scopalamine. She wrapped it in tissue paper and put it in her purse. "Where's Khaled?" she asked tersely.

"In there." Richard jerked his thumb towards the bedroom.

"Go and get him."

"He's ... not ready just yet."

"What?" Her glance of disbelief was like the pass of a blade.

"He's praying."

"Christ Almighty." She looked at her watch. "Can't he stick to his own plan? We've got less than an hour. Get him out here."

Richard hesitated; the moment had come too soon for him. His stomach was a mess. If only they'd done it last weekend when he was ready, when it would have been far easier.

"You OK?" She looked into his face.

"Sure, what do you mean?" He turned aside in case his eyes gave him away. With relief he saw Khaled emerge from the bedroom; his aura of quietness, almost of holiness, helped Richard's confidence.

"It's time," Khaled said, pulling on the jacket of his suit. As if he sensed the mood, he put his hand on Richard's shoulder and said, "Takbir, Insha Allah. We will succeed, bi-smi-LLahi."

"Insha Allah," Richard mumbled in reply.

"Let's do it," Anna said.

Khaled double-checked the weapons as Richard drove; he put a fresh clip in the AK-47 and replaced it under the bench seat. Anna took from her bag a tiny syringe, like a toy in a child's doctor kit, and filled it with scopolamine. Then she put on a specially made glove and concealed the syringe inside it.

It was twelve-thirty when they turned off River Drive and headed into the financial center. Past Wall Street they drove into Exchange Place and continued at a slow pace until they came to the office of Simkin and Heller. Richard flashed the lights and Bart moved out, leaving the space for them.

Khaled checked his watch. "He should appear in that doorway in five or ten minutes." He nodded to Anna, who put on the gray jacket of her business suit, a black wig and dark glasses. She gathered up the purse containing the syringe and got out of the car. She walked up the steps of the building and waited in the lobby.

"So you see, Robert, since the financial collapse we have to be like Caesar's wife." Simkin, the senior partner, refilled the sherry glasses from a

Waterford decanter and sat beside Robert on the leather-backed settee. "We'd hoped to set up an office in London but there were so many skeletons falling out of cupboards over there too, we thought it best to keep our heads down for the time being. It's murder out there. And Brexit is the last thing we need." He waved his hand over the city, indeed, the whole financial cosmos.

Robert sipped his sherry with a smile. Simkin's hurts were always grievous and his plaints prodigious, yet he was as rich as Croesus (or Soros) and had the reputation of a guru in the markets. Robert had once based a character on him, a man whose life was so bland and comfortable that he had to spice it up with imagined calamities and conspiracy theories. Yet he was a likeable old fraud with his striated face and glum eyes. Listening to him one might almost believe the myth of stockbrokers enmeshed in tragic ticker tape, perched on window sills ready to take the plunge.

Robert once told him that according to Galbraith, no one had ever jumped, not even in the great crash. There was no evidence whatsoever of any jumpers in Wall Street. Not in the thirties or, for that matter, in the noughties.

"What does he know?" Simkin had replied, implacable, fighting to sustain the legend, "That ivory-tower *chuchem*. Listen to me; they jumped."

Robert enjoyed his weekly visit to his broker; it had become a routine like Sunday mass used to be, to pay his respects to Mammon and the high priest. He had given Simkin full power of attorney over his financial affairs.

"That's a good move," Simkin had told him at the time. "You are an artist." He placed his thin arm about his shoulders. "You shouldn't have to worry about financial matters. Leave the worrying to me. I'm used to it." And he gave him his worn, woebegone smile, showing how much a martyr he was to the punishing vagaries of the market.

An aide entered the office and handed Simkin a folder. For clients above a certain age, hard copy was *de rigueur*.

"This is your portfolio, Robert. Let's have a look at it." He laid it on an inlaid Regency table and gestured Robert to a chair. They pored over it together but Robert didn't understand any of the figures that ran up and down in rows and columns. Money was weird, he thought; how could it beget money? Yet somehow it was fecund stuff, self-propagating in city soil. He knew that Muslims still clung to the Aristotelian notion that money was barren and that interest was therefore unnatural. What then did the Arabs do with all their petro-dollars? He would have to ask Simkin some time. Gold and silver he could almost understand, pork bellies and soya beans, maybe, but money left him mystified, especially when it was just an entry in a ledger. What if someone erased it or the computer went bananas and added on a row of zeros? And then why did he always feel a little guilty spending it on himself?

Simkin had once tried to explain money to

him. "Money is a claim," he'd said, "on someone else."

"But I don't want a claim on anyone else," Robert had replied.

"What are you, a saint? Do you want to give it all away?"

"No, I just don't want to have a hold over anyone else. Why can't I just have my own money?"

"Because," Simkin replied with a sigh, "there isn't enough to go round and if there was, it wouldn't be worth anything. You couldn't be in credit unless someone else was in debt." The old broker watched in faint amusement as Robert wrestled with this. Then he relented, "Why do you like having money?"

"Oh, for what it buys ... and for the security it offers..."

"Wrong," Simkin said. "The right answer is 'identity'. And for that you must have a claim over others." And that was his last word on the subject.

Simkin scanned the pages of the portfolio eagerly, giving an odd grunt and sigh as the story behind the ciphers unfolded. "The money market funds are doing all right. We should stay fairly liquid until the economy recovers."

"When will that be?"

"When we stop borrowing from the Chinese ... Now, I do think we should clear out the high coupon bonds. You've had the cream on those. You could re-invest in some high-cap shares;

they're a good buy at present…"

"Whatever you say," Robert mumbled weakly. He didn't want to ask what universal calamities underlay these decisions. When AIDs first came on the scene Drew had gone into condoms and made a packet, bemoaning the fact that he withdrew too soon. After the property meltdown in 2008 he bought distressed homes at twenty cents on the dollar.

"…and maybe a call option on copper futures…"

"OK." At this point Robert's mind began to wander. He thought of inviting Simkin to be a guest on his show at some stage but how would he be able to sneak him past Drew and how on earth would he interview him, this weary sad-sack who had substantial cards to play but exulted in keeping them flat against his vest? He worried these problems for a while and then his mind turned towards Gary. He could take the initiative and present him with cruise tickets, but this idea too began to wilt as he realized that his stubborn brother would thank him kindly for the gesture and return the tickets. The thought prompted him to ask, "How are my nephews' trusts doing?"

Simkin turned a page. "We're going for long-term growth there. Let's see … they've made fourteen percent, over the last four years, not bad in the current market, if I may say so. Your nephews are going to be pretty well-heeled sophomores. I hope they appreciate what their uncle is doing for them."

"It's not that much." Robert didn't like being cast in the role of some Victorian patriarch or family-centered godfather, but he was glad the trusts were doing well. His attention wandered over the Adam's fireplace, book-lined walls – who read those huge leather-bound tomes? – and the ornate stucco of the ceiling with its swags and garlands, reminders of spacious days. The room was a sanctuary in the marzipan layer of the organization, but he knew that somewhere else in the building, dealers were going mad, hacking at the coalface, yelling into three phones at a time, punching up their PC screens. Here, however, in this cosy, embellished room, safely behind the lines, the senior partners gave indefinite time to their important clients of which Robert was, amazingly, one.

There were so many different worlds, Robert thought, and this particular one seemed to epitomize his present comfortable status, his doyen role. And yet it didn't quite fit. He'd been an outsider for maybe half of his working life and somehow that had a stronger pull – claim? – on him. Maybe Simkin too, whose father had survived pogroms and purges, felt the call of tougher times and could only accept his present success by imagining, or recalling, the opposite. Drew had a point: success was difficult to handle – unless you were third generation at least and had wiped the slate of memory clean.

Some years ago in this same office Robert had asked Simkin how he felt about the trial of the last

Nazi war criminal who had been brought to justice by the Wiesenthal Foundation.

"We can't afford to forget," Simkin had said. "But who likes remembering'?"

Despite their different orbits they had a lot in common. But on that occasion Robert wanted to push it further. He acquainted Simkin with Canetti's theory that the hyperinflation in Germany had destroyed all values, not just material ones. With prices doubling every hour, six million did not seem to mean much. When numbers were lost, values were lost.

Simkin was not convinced. "What was really destroyed was identity. Without that a man will do anything. The Nazis were butchers because they had no identity. But the Jews had, so they had to be destroyed."

Simkin closed the file with a contented sigh as if he had just finished a story with a good ending. "I think we have a good balance here between risk and reward."

"Good." Robert felt he had to make some comment to this savant who inspired the same respect as a family doctor who braved storms to deliver one's children. Robert accepted another half glass of sherry to keep his old friend company.

Having surreptitiously fed the parking meter,

Richard returned quickly to the car and sat into the passenger seat.

"Something's wrong," he said nervously. "He normally leaves at one sharp." His hands instinctively grasped the steering wheel as if he wanted to take off.

"Bart did see him go in?" Khaled queried.

"He said so ... But he could've made a mistake."

"We wait." Khaled's face was impassive, his eyes narrowed slightly in the strong light that streamed through the windscreen.

Ill at ease, Richard looked out at the busy street, even more thronged now at lunchtime with well-dressed bankers and brokers and slick Ivy League types. Not far away was Ground Zero, where the twin towers had been replaced by an even taller structure called 'Freedom Tower'. Khaled had not seemed to notice as they drove by some minutes earlier. The plan to snatch Lynskey suddenly seemed unreal, hopeless. To add to his consternation he noticed that Anna had come out of the lobby and was waiting on the steps of the building.

"Christ," he groaned. "We can't leave her there. The pigs cruise this street. She'll be made..."

"No," Khaled insisted. "She won't be recognized. Give it another ten minutes."

CHAPTER 8

ROBERT SAID GOODBYE to Simkin with some reluctance, though he looked forward to the afternoon he'd promised himself. He laid down his glass on the walnut coffee table and stood up, straightening out the folds of his pants.

"It's reassuring to know the old affairs are in order," he quipped.

"We aim to please," Simkin said. "You don't have to worry about a thing; you're in good shape, which in this market is a miracle. See you next week, same time, same place." They shook hands and Simkin walked him to the elevator which, in a smooth whoosh, quickly deposited him in the lobby.

As he went through the revolving door, Robert bumped into a woman wearing dark glasses. She seemed confused in her movements. Her purse was between them and her gloved hand came up as if to protect herself.

"I'm sorry," she said moving to the left, blocking his path.

"That's OK..." He felt something sharp on the back of his hand. He moved away, instinctively bringing his hand to his lips. Outside, as he walked down the steps, he felt the ground going away from him. By the time he reached street level he could hardly breathe and his vision was clouded. He panicked. Good god, a stroke. He clutched his chest. But there wasn't any pain. His legs buckled. Someone was helping him, easing him into a car. But he hadn't arranged for his driver … An ambulance? How much time had passed? His fear of passing out gave way…

Breathing hard, Richard switched on the ignition and moved out into the traffic.

"He's out cold," Anna said in a terse whisper.

"Were we made?" Richard met her eyes briefly in the rear-view mirror.

"Drive around for a while just to make sure." Anna was wary; this was her weak moment, being so close to success.

Fifteen minutes later they picked up the West Side Highway and crossed through the Holland tunnel.

"We've done it," Richard cried, rubbing the back of his neck. "It was so easy. And right in Wall Street as we planned it. Christ, I can't believe it…"

"That was the easy part," Anna reminded him. She looked at the slumped form between her and Khaled. His mouth hung open but his breathing was regular. She hadn't been sure about the dosage of that twilight drug, first developed by the CIA, and now took pride in the fact that she'd gauged it about right.

They skirted Jersey City, crossed Newark Bay and went by the south of Elizabeth until they reached open country and eventually farmland. Past the village of Metuchen they drove for about five miles, then turned up a rutted drive of baked mud and wild meadow grass to an abandoned farmhouse.

Anna went ahead and opened up. Bart, who was there already, came out and helped carry Robert inside. They manhandled him down a wooden staircase to the cellar and laid him on a makeshift bed.

"He'll be out for a while," Anna said when they came upstairs.

"How much of that stuff did you give him?" Richard asked.

"Enough." She turned to Bart. "Put the car in the barn at the back and bring in the weapons."

Khaled looked out the window. The isolation was perfect. The unused track leading to the road was easily a half mile long and almost completely overgrown. A belt of trees and high hedges almost hid the house from view. He walked to the back of the house. Two of the windows were bricked up and Bart had blacked out the other one with cardboard. Behind the house was a large deserted field and beyond that a tree-covered hill that provided adequate cover. The bare, must-smelling room in which he stood, originally the kitchen, would be their living quarters; from it the stairs led down to the cellar. There were two smaller rooms off the kitchen which they would use for sleeping; Daniel X had equipped them with rudimentary bedding. He had also laid in tinned food, a tank of fresh water and a primus stove.

Khaled looked at the others and smiled, "Now it begins."

Once in LA Robert had been woken at five in the morning by an earthquake. Having registered the tremor in some dormant part of his mind, he opened one eye and saw the water slop in the glass on the night table. He said to himself immediately, "That's an earthquake," rolled over and went back to sleep.

When he came to from the scopalamine his recall was, surprisingly, just as lucid. "I've been kidnapped," he said. Remembering the brush with the woman, he raised his hand and in the gloom detected a speck of dried blood. "And they're pros," he said with the same clarity. He checked his pockets; his cell phone was missing.

The earth-floored cellar gave off an overpowering smell of rotting vegetation. There was only one door, as far as he could make out, a solid timber one which was locked. Fading light came from a semicircular window high up in the wall opposite his bed. The light that came through the bars had that leaden quality of dawn or dusk, he couldn't tell which.

In the middle of the cellar there were two large wooden joists, from the top of which the adze-marked rafters radiated, some with rusted tenterhooks embedded in the split timber. By one wall there were old rotting meal and grain sacks, a log box and rough wooden shelves which bore the imprint of rotted and petrified fruits.

At the foot of the trestle on which he'd been lying was a bucket that he didn't find in time. He vomited on the floor. Then a fuller realization hit.

He lay back in shock on the bed which was covered with two army blankets. And listened. There were no sounds, except his heart – not even livestock.

He didn't know how long he'd been unconscious. His watch said eight-fifteen. My god, that meant almost three hours. Assuming it was the same day...

Who are they? He wanted to call out, but couldn't.

He fought the urge to shit; the smell of vomit was bad enough. He sat on the edge of the bed, holding his face. Who were they?

He thought he heard the distant sound of a plane and felt grateful. Where was this place?

Hearing a key turning in a lock, he spun around in fear. To see a splinter of light widening. A sudden torch-light blinded him.

"Who ... are you...?" There was no answer. The figure went out and a dead bolt shot home. "Tell me..." Heavy footsteps on a creaking stairs faded into silence.

Eyes still blinded, he fell back, his stomach sick with fear. His mind raced against the slow tide of silence. Why?

He saw two stars appear at the black window but couldn't recognize them. Don't abandon me. Oh, my father...

CHAPTER 9

POLITE TO A FAULT though with an eye to business, the Vietnamese waiter asked for the second time, "Are you ready to order yet, Madame?"

"No, I'm not," Sarah snapped, grabbed her purse and flounced out, her face burning. Robert could be a bastard at times but he'd never stood her up before. Not even a phone call. And to think she was ready to recant their last conversation, to mellow him out. She hailed a cab and went home fuming.

She phoned him from her apartment and texted him. Then she tried his land line and got his voicemail.

"What the hell is going on?" she spat into the dumb recorder. She went for a shower and sublimated some of her anger in vigorous scrubbing and scalding water. Then she made herself a double-decker sandwich of corned beef and lettuce on rye, got into bed and switched on the TV. And there he was in living color, putting a bunch of half-assed intellectuals through their paces, showing how smart he was, how he could match their wit. She punched the remote control and got a re-run of 'Curb Your Enthusiasm'. When that was over she methodically popped a pill and fell fast asleep.

In the morning, using the wall phone in the kitchen, she called KNYBS. Peggy answered and said Robert hadn't shown.

In no mood to deal with secretaries, Sarah asked to be put on to Drew. She laid down her coffee cup and lit a Black Russian cigarette while she waited.

"Hi, Sarah." Drew's voice was breezy though muffled by the empty and ubiquitous pipe.

"I'm looking for Robert. Have you seen him?"

"He did the show yesterday," Drew explained. "He doesn't often come in the day after. Sorry, Sarah, no can help. Have you tried his apartment?"

"Yes, of course." She suspected a conspiracy of men. Maybe she couldn't even count on Drew any more.

"Well, you know him," Drew said in a maddening lilt.

"What do you mean by that?" She drew heavily on the cigarette and expelled the smoke from the side of her mouth, away from the phone.

"Oh, you know ... He's his own man." A canny note crept into his voice, wafting a tiny seed of subtle meaning that found its mark in her delicately tuned ear.

She was no wiser but was inclined to reject the conspiracy theory; indeed, she detected a split in the ranks. Was this a thought to pursue further? "You're being deliberately oblique, Drew." Her sharp tone was designed to draw him out.

"Sorry, didn't mean to be. It's just that you and Robert ... well, I mean..."

"What do you mean?"

"It's not exactly ... happening, is it?"

"Christ, you're doing it again. What's not happening?" She had his drift now but it was a trickle that needed to be flushed out more fully.

"Do I have to draw you a picture, for god's sake? You and me, Sarah. We were a better proposition ... We were going somewhere." His voice was hushed and intense, almost croaking.

"We were?"

"You know we were." His voice slid to an even lower register. She guessed he'd removed the damn pipe, as he usually did when conversations took a serious turn. It occurred to her that Drew had no pride, but this criticism was outweighed by the comforting realization that he was still there for her; it was a compensation of sorts. But she wanted to test him further.

"It's a bit late in the day now."

"No, it's not." His voice had an ardent hush, a monk at vespers. "Robert's too old for you, Sarah. And he's a loner, set in his ways, scared shitless of commitment..." He was going to add his recent view that Robert was becoming distinctly odd, and that whatever the inner conflict was about, it would not involve her. But on reflection he thought better of it, not wishing to use all his ammunition at once. Anyway that was something she would have to find out for herself. Maybe Robert's 'disappearance' was the next step in his descent into oddity; he might well have spent the night on his roof, baying at the moon. Drew had already discussed his weird behavior with the network VP.

"That's not very loyal." Sarah inserted another probe, as delicate as a fiber-optic catheter.

Drew didn't feel a thing. "All's fair in love and war," he answered quickly.

"Where's the war?"

"Maybe it's the other thing."

"Humph."

"What's 'humph'?" Drew asked with a cautious laugh.

"I'm keeping my powder dry." She smiled, unable to fend off a roguish fellow-feeling, or deny that they'd had their moments. That week in Atlantic City on Drew's expense account had been a blast; they drank, ate, swam, gambled and fucked twenty hours a day and returned to civilization with secret, unrepentant memories. She never expected high principles in a man – indeed, was a little wary of them in anyone. The only problem with Drew was that, despite his pragmatism, he was essentially second-rate, having reached the level of his incompetence, perhaps exceeded it; still, despite all that he was good collateral.

"Don't keep it dry too long," he said softly. "It may go off."

"Maybe we should end this conversation," Sarah said. It was enough for now.

"Defer it," he corrected hoarsely. "Remember, I know you, honey…"

She made herself another cup of coffee slightly laced with cinnamon and brought it into the bedroom. Her mind was fully occupied as she finished dressing. She appraised her elegant, business-suited frame in the full-length mirror and decided to add a necklace. There was no sign yet of wattles so she could afford to highlight her slender neck.

She took a cab to the office on Third Avenue and spent part of the morning on a tedious copyright suit. One of 'her' authors, James H. Henfy, who had made them a lot of money with his 'How To' books, had been sued by another author claiming plagiarism of his work on *Indoor Gardening*. Sarah's defense, following Ladbroke versus Hill, 1984, was that although the portion appearing similar – the watering of ferns – was extensive, it was not important to the work as a whole. It was an international suit and she had to delve into the Berne Convention of 1886 and the Universal Copyright Convention of 1952. With dusty tomes piled high on her desk and a broken fingernail to show for her efforts, she was not favorably disposed to her money-making author, James H. Henfy, who could have, for all she knew, plagiarized everything he'd ever done for them. Any damages, she knew, would be based on an assessment of 'infringer's profits' and to firm up a definition of that, she had to wade through The Royalty Agreement of 1897. By coffee time she'd given up in despair and passed the whole lot over to one of her assistants, consoling herself with the thought that delegation was good for morale.

She called Robert's apartment again and still got his voicemail. She tried his second number and got through to Beth.

"I haven't seen him this morning," Beth said.

"Don't you normally have a conference around eleven?"

"Yes, but he didn't show this morning." Beth's voice was flat, factual.

Sarah wasn't quite sure how to put the next question and finally decided to plunge, "Did he come home last night?"

"I have no idea." The tone of Beth's response was somewhere between glacial and contemptuous.

"But you could check. I mean his apartment is just above you."

"I don't really think..."

"Please. It's most important." Sarah hated having to plead with this woman who, like Peggy, protected Robert as if it were a sacred trust. What did he have that made all these vestal virgins do handsprings for him?

Beth left her hanging on for almost ten minutes even though the apartment was only one flight up. Then her verdict was brittle and unhelpful, "I don't think he came in last night."

"Did he have a late appointment?" Sarah inquired.

"I thought he was seeing you." The *coup de grace* was delivered with a swish of fine steel.

"Bitch," Sarah thought, signing off. Where the hell had he been? There was so much of his life that was still a mystery to her. Those occasional glimpses, like the visit with Gary and Sue, were strictly rationed – and hence more tantalizing – by the cautious, inward sonofabitch. Drew was right; it wasn't happening. Maybe she should cut her losses while she had most of her emotional capital intact.

She spent the rest of the morning on the phone to an agent who bled into her ear about a young author he was representing. "All right, he's not Tolstoy," the agent conceded, "but he's got a strong voice, a resonance…"

"The hero is a wimp," Sarah said. "In chapter five he walks away from the high stakes table in the casino."

"But that's the whole point," the agent said despairingly. "He has to consider his family. He's a three-dimensional, feeling sort of guy."

"Then it's a fantasy not a thriller. Anyway," Sarah went on, "the author is unpublished. Who ever heard of him?"

"They all have to start somewhere. This guy will make it, believe me."

"We're not in the gambling business. Come back to me when he's a name … and a name that's associated with a definite genre."

She checked with her secretary for messages, then went to the Ladies to touch up her face, before going to lunch with the company lawyer to discuss a damage limitation strategy for dealing with the mess made by the DIY maestro, James H. Henfy. This on top of everything else, she thought, applying a touch of hair spray.

That afternoon Drew and Chaim worked together on building a show around a recent pronouncement from the *American Medical Association* that promiscuous people should not be allowed donate blood. Drew paced around the office pulling ideas out of the air, skewering them with the stem of a French briar pipe, while Peggy sat quietly in the eye of the creative storm, taking conscientious notes in her expert shorthand.

"We've done AIDs before. It's old hat." Chaim pointed out, passing a hand through his tousled mop of hair as he often did when tendering a diffident opinion or trying – usually without success – to avoid being sucked into Drew's slipstream. "People are now worrying about a new 'flu virus. There are doomsday-preppers laying in supplies of…

"Ah yes, but this will be a new angle," Drew interrupted. "What we're going for here are the social and sexual implications. Is fidelity-stroke-romance back in town? Are the high-risk groups being discriminated against? We've all heard of cases of gay chefs and airline stewards being fired from their jobs for no good reason. Some of them were not even antibody positive. We could salt the studio audience with them to generate a heated debate." As he paced by the noticeboard behind his desk, he made the pinned papers flutter. The conversation with Sarah had quickened his spirits. This fabulous woman who had tested his mettle some three years ago and then, without explanation, threw him over for Robert, might, just might be his again. To Robert she was just an adornment but to Drew, though he couldn't quite explain it, she was a challenge as compelling as any he'd ever experienced. She was the only person who could see right into him and recognize, with a faintly mocking air, his Chinese box of secrets. It could be infuriating at times and it kept him off balance but, god damn, it was exciting, even magical.

Chaim decided he would have to take a stand. He didn't know for sure whether Drew was homophobic or not, but he was definitely years behind the times.

"Well," Chaim began a little diffidently, "the gay community is now fairly well established and the AIDs scare is … really … a thing of the past." He and his partner had a clean bill of health and no longer harbored fears. "The LGBTI movement has achieved an enormous amount of good legislation over the past decade … Though maybe the rights of transgender people have not been fully recognized yet … Maybe that would make an interesting show … We could invite people like Caitlyn Jenner…"

"No," Drew said. He sat with the ankle of one leg resting on the other knee, showing a length of nylon sock. His good humor following the phone conversation with Sarah quickly evaporated. "I'm not getting drawn into all that mullarkey about seventy-eight different genders ... and sex being a social construct. It's all bullshit." He eyed his assistant. He had often wondered if he was active or passive, a pitcher or catcher, and sometimes sneaked a peek at him in the John, but the jury was still out. On balance though, given the way he draped himself over the furniture, passivity could probably be inferred.

Peggy politely intervened, "I know it's not my place ... at these meetings ... but..."

"Go ahead, Peggy." Drew gave her permission.

"Well, I mean, there is one aspect ... I think it's wrong for parents to encourage young children to make a definite choice ... about gender reassignment..."

"My god, that's an excellent point, Peggy. There are a lot of so-called liberal parents out there who completely screw up their kids because they believe, or pretend to believe, in this social construct stuff. They may pressurize the kids to change genders ... They should be exposed. I like it. Yes, I do."

"We would need to achieve ... balance though," Chaim ventured. He knew how cynical Drew could be about a topic like that, testing people, playing one off against the other, going for friction rather than issues. He had some deep urge which sometimes unnerved Chaim of pushing things to the limit and studying reactions from a safe distance behind the camera. He just loved it when rows broke out, just so long as he avoided the flak.

"That goes without saying," Drew said almost as an aside. He went into creative mode, looking up at the ceiling. "Parents and children and a couple of so-called experts ... I see it as a sort of collage, each protagonist a detail in the whole ... Think of the long shots, the close-ups."

"It's a ... serious subject." Chaim entered a heartfelt caveat. It was at times like this that he needed Robert to counterbalance the tendency to trivialize. "I wonder what Robert will think of it?" He passed the buck to the absent star, appealing by proxy to better judgment.

"I'm glad you mentioned that." Drew's crooked finger came up, indicating he was about to share a confidence. "Between ourselves, I think Robert is becoming more and more out of touch. He's like some John the Baptist out there in the wilderness looking for converts. Wherever he is, it's not here. Or now. He's just not..." he was going to say 'happening' but changed to... "with it any more. I've had a word with the VP..."

"You're not suggesting..." Chaim sat bolt upright.

"Not immediately. We've decided on a phased approach, using a guest host every second week. In fact, I put out some feelers this very morning."

Chaim was lost for words; the bell had tolled too suddenly. Without Robert's restraining

---

influence on Drew, the show could degenerate into burlesque; he had a flash vision of blond lady jugglers in fishnet tights. Maybe Robert had contributed to his own downfall but in Chaim's view there was no one else to touch him for style. All his friends thought so too. Whereas Drew, oh god, thought real style began and ended in those tacky prewar Berlin nightclubs, brought so well to life by Lisa Minnelli. For the first time Chaim felt that he would soon have to declare himself; it was an ominous thought. He didn't like upsets or disagreements of any kind. They made him queasy.

Having asked Peggy to read back his last thoughts, Drew resumed his flow but was interrupted by a gum-chewing messenger who thrust an envelope into his hands. "Urgent delivery for Mr. Hamilton." The messenger winked at Peggy on his way out and helped himself to some candy she had put in a bowl on the credenza.

Drew tore open the envelope and read the note with impatience. Suddenly his red, pocket-battleship frame went rigid.

"I don't believe it." He passed the note to Chaim. "It says Robert's been kidnapped."

CHAPTER 10

AT THE MIDTOWN PRECINCT Lieutenant Mahon had just left an interrogation room where a crack-pusher was negotiating with his brief to cop a plea. With a mixture of weariness and disgust Mahon crossed the busy main floor and escaped into his glass-box office. He was locking up his arraignment folder and books of evidence in the institutional green filing cabinet when the phone beat a tattoo on his metal desk.

Mahon was a run-of–the-mill cop who had pounded a beat for so long he could do drum-major tricks with his night-stick. He got his sergeant's exam on the twelfth attempt and was considered lucky, even by himself, to make Lieutenant eight years later. Not a Pandora's box of credentials and *cum laudes*, he nevertheless did the job the best way he knew how, and over the years he had acquired a foxy instinct, even a slight wisdom. As far as his career was concerned he was content; he had no desire to make Captain because of the political shenanigans that went on at that level.

But he was sickened by the way the police force had been undermined and foiled at every turn by shyster lawyers, lenient judges and bed-wetting liberals over the previous two decades. He himself was tough on hoods, tougher still on bad cops, and he admitted to some racial prejudice – it was difficult for working cops to disentangle poverty from color. Loyal to his friends, he had once dropped a piece to save a rookie partner who panicked and shot an unarmed drug dealer. It had nearly cost him his badge at the time but he never regretted it and his colleagues remembered him for it.

He wore a lightweight suit, the jacket of which didn't quite reach round his gut. Although he wore strong elastic suspenders, his pants ballooned comfortably around the crotch. Since he'd started putting on the pounds he dispensed with his shoulder harness and carried his weapon in a holster fixed to the left suspender. His eyebrows were heavy and raised on deposits of scar tissue, a legacy of his boxing days. His face was a clone of his body, heavy and knuckled, yet quick at times with the memory of youthful strength.

After taking the call patched through by the desk sergeant, he moved with unaccustomed speed, rattling the glass stud partition of his office. He picked up a patrolman and raced across town, using the siren to get through the evening rush-hour traffic.

"Do you know this guy, Lynskey?" he asked the driver.

"Sure Lieutenant. He's on TV a lot. The Robert Lynskey Hour…"

"Oh yeah. I've seen it. Funny, they'd snatch him." Mahon didn't much like Lynskey's manner but he respected what he stood for. And Mahon's folks had come through Ellis Island too. If there were Arab terrorists behind this he wouldn't give much for Lynskey's chances.

———————————

After brief introductions in KNYBS, Mahon studied the note. It was tightly printed in ballpoint on a sheet of notepaper that could be bought in any Drugstore. The message was as stark as the printing: the release of Jallud Fahd for the life of Robert Lynskey. Mahon didn't have to be a *wunderkind* to know how serious this was, how deep it would stab into the heart of the political world. The Administration would see this as another Arab attack on the US. Although he knew the matter would soon be out of his hands, he went about his job in a workmanlike way, assembling the basic facts.

"When was the last time you saw Mr. Lynskey?" he asked, handing the note to the patrolman who put it in a plastic bag.

"About noon yesterday," Drew said. "He was as regular as clockwork. He always went to his stockbroker on Exchange Street at that time on Wednesdays." Now that the two policemen had materialized in his office, Drew was almost ready to believe the truth of what had happened.

"Which broker?" Mahon asked, a pencil poised over his notebook.

Drew looked for help to Peggy who answered in a shaking voice, "Simkin and Heller."

"OK, we'll pay them a call later. And Mr. Lynskey didn't show up here today?"

"No," Drew said. "I think he probably … went missing yesterday…"

"Why do you say that, Sir?"

Drew mentioned the call he'd had from Sarah. "She was waiting for him yesterday evening and he didn't show."

Mahon asked for Sarah's address which, after a quick search through her contacts app, Peggy supplied. "I'll also need a list of Mr. Lynskey's other friends and associates."

Drew nodded to Peggy, who got unsteadily to her feet and went out to her own desk to print off a list.

Mahon sat in the chair she'd vacated and balanced the spiral-bound notebook on an ample knee which strained against the flimsy material of his pants. It was quite a while since he'd eaten lunch – a snatched pastrami sandwich in the maelstrom of the situation room – and his capacious stomach rumbled with the helpless plaints of a dog scratching at a kitchen door. He asked how the note had been delivered.

"I've checked that out," Drew said. "It was handed to the receptionist in the lobby by some kid in sneakers."

"We'll talk to the receptionist later." Mahon was silent for a while, figuring out the calls he would have to make and the questions that would be asked of him. He wasn't absolutely sure yet how to handle it. The only thing he was certain of was that it was way above his pay grade.

Drew used the silence to form a question of his own. "What do you make of it, Lieutenant?" His eyes seemed scalded under the peaked brows as he waited for the reply.

"It's much too early to give an opinion," Mahon said, not quite evasively but giving the impression of the law taking its ponderous course, of volumes of painstaking work remaining to be done and written up in triplicate.

"But his life must be in real danger," Drew pressed. "I mean this guy, Jallud Fahd, is public enemy number one ... since bin Laden was ... taken care of."

"Yes, sir, it's a serious matter." Mahon didn't want to say more. He knew that the foreign intelligence aspect would put it in the CIA's jurisdiction and those guys wouldn't even talk about the weather.

"It's obviously some Arab terrorist group..." Drew forged on, undaunted.

"It certainly looks that way," Mahon conceded unhelpfully. But which one, he wondered. What if it was al Qaeda?

Chaim, who had been sitting quietly in a corner of the room, said in a low voice, "There are over sixty known terrorist groups in the Middle East. New ones spring up every day. Then there are sleeper cells..."

Mahon didn't answer, because he didn't have these facts and he didn't particularly want to be shown up by these media types who liked to take pot shots at the Police Department whenever they got the chance. He stood up slowly. "If there's any further news or communication of any sort, please contact me immediately." He left his card on the desk and made to leave.

"But..." Drew blocked his path.

"Yes sir?"

"Is that it...? I mean..."

"For the moment. They haven't given any instructions about the hostage exchange, so this is just the first contact. There'll be more messages and they'll probably come through here." By now Mahon had decided on the people he should call and he reckoned they would get on the stick immediately, so he added, "It would be helpful if you could remain here for another hour or so. Other officers" – he didn't want to say 'agents' – "will want to talk to you."

"I don't understand..."

Mahon didn't enlighten him; it occurred to him that maybe these TV guys weren't all that clued in after all. "Now, I want to talk to the receptionist." On the way out he collected the list of names from Peggy, who apologized for the fact that it was far from complete. With a trembling hand she pointed to Beth's name and address and suggested that she would be able to add to the list.

"Thank you, miss," Mahon said kindly.

After they'd left Drew fell into a brown study, gently massaging his closed eyelids, trying to bring his ambling mind up to speed. The departure of Mahon and the patrolman left a void which was even more difficult to cope with. Still holding his head, he said at length, "I often warned him about walking around in public without protection but he wouldn't listen. He liked … likes … his freedom. Jesus, freedom. How ironic is that?"

"I can't believe any of this," Chaim said.

They stood around, balked by the enormity, feeling a great need to go beyond platitudes – who was comforting whom? – but unable to, so the silence which followed was natural, though awkward and a little redolent of guilt.

"Mr. Plod doesn't exactly inspire confidence," Drew said at length.

"Well, he's just an ordinary cop."

"God, I just realized," Drew said, smiting his forehead. "He's going to bring in the Company. "

"I guess so." Chaim wasn't so startled by the thought. "I think you'd better send Peggy home."

"Why?"

"She's shaky." Chaim nodded towards the glass door through which Peggy's bowed head could be seen in frosted shadow.

"Right." Drew was abstracted by events and what they set off inside him. The limit he'd been pushing towards all his life had come suddenly without any intervention by him. That part was disappointing. Justice would be rough and seek no quarter; he would have to make sure he was standing under the lintel when the house caved in.

———————

"They must've used some kid off the street," Mahon said to the uniformed officer after he'd finished questioning the receptionist. He sat into the patrol car, made his calls and waited. After years of stake-outs he had almost mastered the art of waiting.

In a little over an hour, Captain Leo Limon, Assistant Chief of Foreign Intelligence, joined him in the lobby of the KNYBS building. Limon was lean and rangy with a sharp canny face, made sharper by an isthmus of dark hair brushed forward to a point between the two balding temples. Everything about him seemed stretched and angular, in contrast to Mahon's easy-going amplitude. He listened in strained silence, intelligent nostrils dilating slightly, as Mahon briefed him.

"I'll need a sitrep in writing," Limon said. "But for now you work in your normal way. I'll send the ransom note to forensic in Langley." Extending his hand for the plastic bag, he noticed Mahon's hesitation. "I'll take full responsibility. I've already had a word with your Chief in Midtown."

Mahon shrugged and surrendered the evidence. He didn't care much for the Agency or its M.O. but Limon at least was one of the old guard; he could be abrupt and demanding – a product of his military service – but, unlike many of the younger spooks, he didn't patronize the Police Department. Mahon knew he was ambitious but that was no skin off his nose. Indeed, knowing his own limitations and recognizing legitimate inter-agency demarcations, Mahon was happy enough for Limon to get out front in this case which was, in any event, likely to be a bitch.

They rode up in the elevator and assembled in Drew's office. For Limon's benefit Drew had to go over the ground again. This time the questioning was sharper, more layered, but it didn't seem to add much to the sum of knowledge.

"They're probably going to use you as an intermediary," Limon said after he'd completed his own notes. "We'll have to set up a communications center here. Some people from Special Services will call first thing tomorrow. In the meantime if anything breaks, call me or," he added as an afterthought, "Lieutenant Mahon."

A question formed itself on Drew's lips as he walked the two officers to the door. "Incidentally, we've got a show in the can, scheduled to go out on Friday night…"

"So?" Limon queried.

"It doesn't seem … appropriate," Chaim intervened, "to air the *Robert Lynskey Hour*… in the circumstances."

Limon thought for a while, his head tilted to one side. "I understand your concern. But it's important to proceed as if nothing has happened, at least for the time being."

"OK." Drew seemed satisfied. "You're right."

On the way down in the elevator, Mahon grunted half to himself, "Fucking Arabs." He had seen documentaries dealing with the gas queues in the seventies, the panic and disbelief of Americans suddenly awoken from the dream of plenty, their seven-liter wagons beached and helpless, on the verge of extinction. Queue-jumpers had been beaten up and even shot at gas stations throughout the State. Conmen, posing as pump attendants, had worked the queues for payment in advance. Though only a teenager in the sweltering summer of seventy-four, Mahon had felt the rage in the air; it burned his lungs. The anger that followed the capture of American hostages in Iran was subtler but more deep-seated. Whatever people thought of Carter, they saw their President sweating blood for one whole year in the Rose Garden, being ground down and finally humiliated. Over the years there had been wars in the Gulf, Iraq, Afghanistan and Syria. The unbelievable assault on the Twin Towers had shaken him to the core. He had been involved with the firefighters at ground zero and had lost many good friends there. Now this. He couldn't understand how a bunch of half-assed nomads could cause such havoc in the most powerful country on earth.

Deep in his own thoughts, Limon let the comment pass. He knew with sudden clarity that he was finally in a high-stakes game. Years ago he'd been caught up in a CIA bloodletting, was 'wrung out', assessed, polygraphed. He'd survived. Just about. But younger men with Harvard law degrees and IT training had gained the inside track in the Company.

After the putsch Limon had been assigned – some said semi-retired – to a CIA Station in Germany. He worked his ass off to prove himself and was eventually brought back to the Middle East Desk in Foreign Intelligence where he had to compete with the new, bushy-tailed breed of electronics experts and quants. Since 9/11, however, the Ivy Leaguers had come under the spotlight. Why had there not been more warnings, better intelligence? What had happened to the much-vaunted electronic chatter? There was just the faintest indication of a reversion to older, less clean-cut methods of operation. If the Lynskey case turned this into a trend it could only work to Limon's advantage. But it was an all-or-nothing play.

One problem would be the FBI and Homeland Security. They would want in. But Limon had a head start and he would have to hold the high ground as the investigation got under way and all the glory boys flocked to the scene.

When they talked to Simkin they didn't tell him the full story, only that Lynskey was missing.

"Missing?" Simkin, who was about to offer the inevitable sherry, straightened his willowy back, real concern in his face. "Officially missing?"

"Oh, it's probably a false alarm," Limon said with his all-seasons smile. "You know how people fuss about celebrities. We thought we'd just make a routine inquiry as we were passing."

Simkin's narrow frame returned to its easier, curved scholar's stoop. "With him you never know. He could be just staying out of the limelight for a while. Maybe he went to visit with his brother in New Jersey. He did seem a bit down when he was here."

"Financial pressures I suppose?" Limon prompted with a dry chuckle. "After the bail-out of Wall Street."

"My dear sir, this is Simkin and Heller." The old broker straightened his gleaming shirt cuffs and flicked a fleck of lint from a fine mohair sleeve. He had put down his marker without breaching client confidentiality.

"Well then, why 'down'?" Limon asked lightly as Mahon silently gazed upon the riches of the room.

"Who knows?" Simkin spread his quick sparrow-hawk hands in a plea for wisdom, then loosened the starched collar of his shirt. "Writers must be allowed their moods. So must we all." He pointed to a richly draped window. "If you were to look out there you'd see a lot of well-dressed people. You might be forgiven for thinking they were happily making money. But you'd be wrong. They're unhappily trying to make *themselves*. So, yes, we all have moods. You can tell me nothing about moods."

With a covert glance in Mahon's direction, Limon turned to specifics, the time Lynskey arrived and left the premises, and the broker's answers were as precise as an auditor's report. Simkin was either crystal clear or hopelessly cryptic; he shot from one pole to the other with nothing in between. Limon wondered if he wasn't a little mad or at an early stage of senility.

"Thank you," Limon said. "I'm sure there's nothing to worry about. We'll see ourselves out."

Simkin shuffled towards the door with them anyway and handed Limon his card, asking him to let him know when Robert turned up. "If you give me your number I'll call you if I see him first."

Limon hesitated for a second. "It would be better if you contacted Lieutenant Mahon."

When they left Simkin had an uneasy feeling that started, as usual, in his sinuses but would soon move to the pit of his stomach. Despite his lapses into vacuity he was no fool. He had only seen Mahon's I.D. and *he* hadn't opened his mouth. Who was Limon? And there was something else. They hadn't asked for the address of Robert's brother. Simkin was on his home ground now: worried.

As they drove back to his office Limon reviewed the information. "That means Lynskey was snatched sometime between one and about seven-thirty."

"It's a fairly wide window," Mahon said.

"My guess is it was shortly after one."

"In broad daylight, right in the financial district?" Mahon let his jowls drop in a skeptical moue as his stomach started to grumble again.

Limon didn't rise to the bait and remained silent until he dropped him off at the precinct. Mahon was about to go in when he changed his mind and headed for a nearby Pizza Hut where he ordered the large pan with kaleidoscopic topping, anchovies, ham, black olives, mozzarella cheese, the works. As he wolfed into it wedge by wedge he remembered with dismay that he still had his report to type up.

Back in his office Limon called the Chief of Special Operations at his home in McLean and arranged for technicians to install the necessary equipment in Drew's office the next morning. They also decided that a female operative would take over from the receptionist at KNYBS.

Then, using the protected line, Limon called his own Chief in Manhattan and gave him a full report. To almost every question put to him, Limon was able to say, "That's been arranged."

"It seems like you've done everything you can do, for the moment," his Chief said.

"Yes sir." Limon felt he had bought in.

"This is going to go all the way."

"I realize that."

"Leave it with me. I'll get back to you within the hour."

Apart from the security men who ambled silently in the corridors, the building was deserted at this hour; even the cleaning staff had left.

Except for the green desk lamp which cast a confined aureole of light, Limon's office was in darkness. The apparent peace was in contrast to the events that had just been put in motion.

As he waited in a state of nervous expectancy, Limon took a huge sheet of drawing paper and spread it on his desk. Using a finely pointed pencil he began to jot down in telegraphic form the facts of the case that had so far emerged. He underlined some key words and circled others. Then, looking for interrelationships, he penciled in connecting lines, some hatched, others with arrows. Not being computer-literate he had to work this way and he was glad that none of the egg-heads were looking over his shoulder as he slogged through his pseudo algorithm. When he'd finished he sat back and studied the chart from a greater distance, as if the changed perspective might offer something new. It didn't. But it would serve as his master plan and he would add to it every day.

He used his computer to access everything he had on terrorist organizations in the Middle East. The list was long and complex. Known terrorists regularly changed from one group to another or went to ground; the organizations themselves often changed their names or split up into factions and splinter groups. He tried to make a short list of those which had the resources and temerity to conduct an operation in the US. But he couldn't keep track of the almost daily ebb and flow of names and acronyms; cryptography wasn't his strong suit and his own files were not completely up to date. He could not, however, rule out al Qaeda or one of its newer cells.

He would have to get one of the quants to access the more comprehensive databank on the central mainframe in HQ and to do the cross tabs he needed. It galled him but there was no other way. Without a full analysis at his fingertips he would not be able to keep that one essential step ahead. It had to be *his* investigation from start to finish.

It was ten-thirty when the Chief came through on the private line.

"I spoke with the Director. There's to be an emergency meeting of the Intelligence Council at 1100 hours tomorrow."

"That means the FBI … and HS?"

"Of course. We'll need a crash estimate for the meeting. Can you send it to HQ tonight on a secure line?"

"Yes sir."

"Meet me on the chopper pad at 900 hours tomorrow. HQ wants a briefing session before the Intelligence Board assembles."

Sustaining himself with black coffee that percolated consolingly as he wrote, Limon worked steadily into the small hours. Using his chart he typed out the facts simply and in chronological order. That part went well. But when he came to the required evaluation he had pause for thought. In normal cases there would be no question of a deal. The Administration had made it clear that Americans taken hostage in the Middle East were on their own, but Lynskey wasn't in that category. He was also close to the White House, how close Limon wasn't exactly sure, but he had interviewed President Obama twice, and Trump once. The problem was to make his evaluation authoritative without being too specific.

It was two when he sent the report to Langley. He brought extra copies with him as he drove home. Not wishing to wake his wife, he crashed on the settee and had four hours uneasy sleep before joining his Chief in the helicopter the next morning.

Limon himself did not attend the meeting of the Intelligence Board. He kicked his heels in the waiting room, looking periodically at the silent and locked double oak doors. A few military aides and civilians – probably FBI – also waited in the ante room, sitting with their backs to the wall under the stern gazes of heavy oil portraits. They briefly acknowledged each other's presence and thereby at least partially shared the angst of waiting and the ambivalence of service loyalty.

At noon the word came down. No hostage exchange, no negotiations of any sort, a doubling of security on Jallud Fahd. To his relief, Limon was formally put in charge of the investigation; he was to work to a special steering committee representing the different agencies. He was given the widest mandate: all necessary action.

CHAPTER 11

SUMMER CAME ON like a brass band, the sultry heat radiating in shock waves. The city burned, its asphalt melted to a rubber solder that clung to shoes and tires, tower blocks became solar panels, steam rose from vents in the street as the metro hurtled and roared beneath, exhaust fumes blended into the sulfurous heat haze which lay like a poultice over the feverish city. People used their last ounce of energy to get a fix of recycled air in the nearest department store.

As he crossed the street with sinking heart and boiling blood, sweat stinging his eyes, Drew wondered why they'd bothered to con the Indians out of this stinking island. Yet, despite it all, he couldn't live anywhere else. It was a proving ground, a fiery gauntlet that had to be run by the truly ambitious.

Robert alone was cool, an egg in aspic, in his stone and earthen cellar.

A pall hung over the office. Drew sat quietly behind his desk stabbing at unread papers with a bamboo letter knife. He found it hard to work, not least because of the presence of two agents setting up the communications equipment, special recording devices, a phone-tracer and a voice-recognition machine. He also had a decision to make.

"I'll leave you to it for a while," he said to the two young spooks in business suits, in whose smooth faces the conferring-day bloom still shone. Were they from Black Ops, he wondered as he went next door to Chaim's office.

He helped himself to a drink from the water cooler and threw the paper cone in the waste basket. Chaim's office lacked authority; it was done out in colorful molded plastic, the better for bouncing ideas off. Drew perched himself on a yellow stool in this adult crèche which lacked only a tub of Lego and assorted building blocks.

Chaim stood at a drawing board, studying set layouts and camera angles; over his head there was a square panel of neon light set into the false ceiling, like a trapdoor opening onto eternity. Since he hadn't been concentrating very well he didn't mind the interruption.

"I think we should tell the news desk," Drew said.

"Is that wise?" Chaim removed his glasses and pinched the upper bridge of his nose, smoothing out the pink lug marks. Without his specs his face looked bald and fleshy, almost indecent. "From what Limon said I don't think they want it broadcast yet."

"He didn't *say* that," Drew pointed out, waving his pipe like a baton.

"Not in so many words. Maybe we should call Limon and ask his advice."

"No." Drew shied away from that, holding up two freckled hands. "It's a media matter. This is our responsibility. Our judgement call." He made it sound heroic. Oddly, Chaim's reservation helped him reach this decision. He slid off the stool and picked up the phone. "Peggy, get me the news editor."

Chaim wasn't sure how to read Drew's expression as he spoke to the editor, though he had the vaguest impression of a tampering and illicit curiosity which could well have repercussions. He had seen Drew in this guise once or twice before, a producer who from the depths of some foiled instinct, wanted to produce the ultimate show, regardless of consequences. He had, however, no sense of Drew's infatuation with Sarah and, therefore, could not foresee any possible conflict of interest.

Following a conference with the news editor and the president of the company, Drew's view carried the day. The item was headlined in the lunchtime newscast:

"Robert Lynskey, author and TV personality, has been kidnapped by a terrorist organization demanding the release of Jallud Fahd. The demand note was sent to this network late yesterday evening. The authorities have been notified. Further details will be provided by this station as they become available."

Watching from behind camera Drew said, "It's in the lap of the gods now." The broadcast put the final seal on reality.

Shortly afterwards Limon called to KNYBS to check on the work of the special services. He explained to Drew that the equipment would be manned by agents around the clock and that another agent had been installed in the main reception area in the lobby. With that out of the way he said coldly, "It wasn't very bright to broadcast the news without checking with us." He knew, however, that it could be construed as *his* error in that he should have warned them in advance and so pre-empted the broadcast.

"We have a responsibility to the public," Drew answered.

"You may have put Mr. Lynskey's life in greater danger."

"How? Why would the kidnappers object?" Drew kept his voice light but he hated Limon's moral tone; it was like being lectured to by a traffic warden. He smiled over the simple logic of his question.

"It may make negotiations more difficult," Limon replied in his calm superior way, folding his arms as he looked down at the shorter man.

"I doubt that," Drew said, fixing him with a basilisk stare. "In fact I doubt if you're going to negotiate at all." The silent reception of this probe gave him the victory, at least for the moment.

Limon made a mental note to keep a close eye on Drew. It wasn't just that he was a shit-disturber; he recognized in him something of his own instinct for bringing things to a head, and it was clear that the recognition was mutual.

"I have to ask you one final question."

"Go ahead," Drew said graciously.

"Is there any possibility, however remote, that Mr. Lynskey might not be ... an unwilling victim?"

The double negative threw Drew for a moment then he snorted, "For god's sake! I've heard everything now." He turned away from Limon as if to avoid mocking the afflicted, but there was something false about the protestation.

Chaim rushed to Robert's defense, "His views are a matter of public record. He ... loves this country." It was preposterous. He turned away and looked out the window.

Limon wasn't fazed by the eulogy. In his business you looked under every stone: nothing could be taken at face value. There were mavericks in high positions, especially among the so-called intelligentsia. Even Britain had its share of traitors, all of them in the top echelons of the establishment, who had sold out for unfathomable reasons. Simkin had sown a seed in his mind.

"Let me put it this way. Has his behavior changed in any way?"

Drew was about to bluster a denial but ran into a sudden silence.

Limon sensed it. "Think about it," he coaxed. "Anything unusual?"

"I guess, a sort of ... general questioning." Drew looked down at his hands, hating having to make even that modest concession.

"Like what?"

"About the show, his life, I suppose." He flapped his arms. "It happens to us all once in a while. Male menopause ... whatever."

"I see," Limon said in a flat voice.

"That has no significance whatever," Chaim cut in. "Absolutely none." He felt weakened by the declaration; it was a small reminder of that other pronouncement he'd made several years ago. New York was probably the easiest place in the world to emerge from the closet but it had been tough nevertheless. It had taken months of rehearsing, anticipating the reactions of parents and close friends. Having made his statement he fell back into his natural mode of living behind the scenes and letting live. Now, however, he was being called again and it heaved up memories of naked hurt. Limon's manner of questioning grated on his nerves. Did these people, he wondered, study ways of putting others on the defensive? He had once seen a documentary about the social behavior of apes in which the self-proclaimed leader of the tribe used low peripheral movement to keep the others on edge. Limon had that same calm commanding quality. Even Drew seemed slightly intimidated by it.

"I looked at his *Collected Essays*. Some fairly subversive stuff in there."

"Harmless by today's standards." Chaim hardly realized that it was he who had spoken.

"You're probably right." Limon smiled at them and after the usual exhortations to keep in touch, he had a final word with the communications people, and left, closing the door behind him with hardly a sound.

Chaim threw a questioning look in Drew's direction. Was it his imagination, or had Drew been deliberately lukewarm in his defense of Lynskey?

———————————

On Friday the *RL Hour* went out at the usual time. Before the logo and theme music came on Drew did an introduction to camera using a head-up device: "The program you are about to see was recorded before Robert Lynskey was kidnapped. We at KNYBS thought carefully about the propriety of broadcasting the show in present circumstances. On balance, however, and given our interpretation of Robert's own preferences, we decided to go ahead. The theme of this show is one that Robert is particularly interested in and it is ironic to think that he would regard personal freedom as being the essential prerequisite for realizing our potential as human beings. Needless to say, we all hope and pray that he will be freed and returned to us in safety."

"How was it?" Drew asked later, referring to his own performance, as he removed his make-up in the director's booth.

"Fine," Chaim answered neutrally, wondering what the question meant; it had just been a standard head and shoulders shot. They went to the commissary for coffee. It was quieter than usual. People nodded sympathetically as if Drew had experienced a personal loss. His regular waitress put an unsolicited plate of cakes and cookies in front of them. A bit player from a daytime soap patted Chaim's shoulder as he passed.

"Let's hope," he said.

Chaim nodded.

Exactly half an hour later, when the program finished, the calls began to come in. Within five minutes the switch was jammed and Drew requested every spare secretary and research assistant to man the lines. Emails and text messages flooded in. Apart from the inevitable few cranks, the messages resounded with sympathy for Lynskey and many of them – a surprising number -- were quite explicit about what should be done to the perpetrators of the crime. Was it love of Lynskey that evoked such hostility, Drew wondered, or was it that such an act, right smack on Main Street, USA, was the last straw, especially after 9/11? The authorities should, as one of the more irate fans put it, "break the camel-fuckers' backs."

"It's extraordinary," Drew mused aloud as he pored over the station's website. As if on cue, he got a call from Audience Research, which predicted colossal mail on Monday, probably an all-time record. They'd just opened a book on it and the big money said the 9/11 record for audience feedback would be smashed.

"I'll go with that," Drew said. "Put me down for a hundred. It's a pity we don't have another program in the can." He hung up on that note, which replayed itself in his mind. What was he going to do for next week? He could contact Letterman, who was keen to make a comeback, and some of the other show hosts; there would just be enough time to set something up. But still, in the circumstances … Jesus, it was a tough call.

―――――――――

Next morning the *Times* carried the following leader:

"Lynskey for Fahd: No Deal

"The kidnapping of Robert Lynskey by as yet unidentified Arab terrorists, operating for the second time inside the United States, poses the greatest imaginable threat to National Security and marks a sinister and unacceptable turning point in the so-called Holy War. While Mr. Lynskey is politically connected at the highest level he is not a political figure as such. Indeed his abduction contains a cruel irony in that he is one of the leading exponents in this country of the sovereignty of the individual. He has, moreover, contributed enormously, through his writings and broadcasts, to cultural and religious freedom in America. He is an innocent victim in the truest sense of that term and all possible efforts must be made to rescue him and return him to safety.

"However, the authorities must not give in to the hostage demands. To do so would invite other barbarous acts and bring violence and disorder right into the streets of our towns and cities. The Administration must stand firm on its recent policy of dealing with terrorists. Jallud Fahd must remain in prison; there can be no question of release or of extradition, which would amount to the same thing. We believe that Robert Lynskey would agree."

"Much the same sentiment was repeated with slight stylistic differences in the other dailies, one of which quoted from one of Lynskey's recent essays:

"...a policy that deals solely with institutions and structures and ignores the deep-seated wishes of individuals is procrustean and deeply flawed. That recently derided notion of frontier spirit is still the driving force of this society, precisely because it permits the possibility of individual greatness. But there have to be constraints on license; this is the function of the lawmaker. *Force majeure* or the tyranny of the few can never be acceptable in a free society..." The anonymous editor had omitted the last sentence, "A balance must be struck; that is the function of the Statesman."

Later in the day the Intelligence Board went public via a statement issued through the State Department, and a White House spokesman held a special press conference. The utterances were well coordinated. No effort would be spared to save

Robert Lynskey but there could be no deal with terrorist kidnappers. Lynskey wouldn't want it any other way.

Sitting in his study late that night, Limon was a little surprised that not even the more liberal papers had entered a plea for Lynskey who was, after all, one of their own. Sipping a much-needed drink of bourbon, he thought, not unsympathetically, "He's in deep shit." But he had no quarrel with the verdict, which indeed was strengthened by the almost unprecedented unanimity between the media and the authorities. What did bother him was not that the ball was now completely in his court, but that he was expected to save Lynskey without a shot in his locker, not even a compromise deal. That meant the end game had to result in deadly force; in a worst case scenario Lynskey himself would be killed, and Limon would have to carry the can while his bosses would run for cover.

Flicking through a batch of computer output which his assistant had provided, he had a moment of doubt. Was he mad to have bought into this slugfest? It could destroy him. On the other hand, if he could somehow, against all the odds, crack it ... Jesus. He went into the children's room and kissed two downy faces.

The Audience Research department was right. A new feedback record was established, one that would probably last a decade. On top of this the *RL Hour* went up seven Nielson points which meant an extra six million viewing households in just one week. The people had spoken in more ways than one. It occurred to Chaim that as KNYBS's ratings went up Lynskey's chances of survival went down.

CHAPTER 12

ON THE FRIDAY before the kidnapping, Sarah nibbled away at the James H. Henfy lawsuit with growing unease. A final strongly worded writ had been issued to her and, like most non-lawyers, she blanched in the face of the latinised legal imperatives. If they went to court god only knew what might happen. Henfy was a strange man with a twinkle and offbeat charm which, for all she knew, could be symptoms of madness. Suppose he had plagiarized everything and it came out in open court? There would be no end to the litigation; her firm, which had little reserves, would be driven into bankruptcy. She could make an offer to settle out of court but that would cost money, and damage the reputation of the company.

His 'How To' books were well written with a nice reassuring turn of phrase implying, 'If I can do it so can you', but suppose he had cannibalized other works for facts and ideas, and merely added a veneer of style? They had promoted him actively too, using a professional publicist who had taken Henfy in tow up and down the Eastern Seaboard, signing in bookstores, doing radio spots and the blue-rinse circuit. She had accompanied him on a few trips and seen him in action with his rather winning apologetic smile that could, god forbid, have concealed a multitude of quiet lunacies.

She rang the publicist and told him about her worries, about other skeletons that might be waiting to tumble out of Henfy's closet. The publicist didn't add much except to say that Henfy was quirky like many authors. He did, however, come up with one good suggestion: that she could drop into Henfy's house, sound him out diplomatically, and look at his bookshelves to see if there were 'How To' books by other authors. If there were a lot, it *could* mean that Henfy was a serial plagiarist.

Sarah ruminated on it for a while and decided to call on Henfy. Her mood improved later, in the salon as the blow drier, expertly wielded by Octave, her regular stylist, fluffed out her freshly cut hair which then fell back in remembered layers. As she sipped her coffee she read the news on her cell phone.

When she got through Queens she switched off the air conditioner and let the hood down, protecting her new coiffure with a silk headscarf. She decided to stay on Route 27 which went right out to the tip of Long Island and gave glimpses of the fine homes in Patchogue and Suffolk County. She wondered if she was doing the right thing. Robert might well be trying to reach her. Well, too bad for him; she had never been stood up before. Let him sweat it for a change.

She slipped off her high heels, and pressed her stockinged foot hard on the gas pedal; the car, which she didn't use much around the city, responded well, like a stabled horse suddenly let loose in a field. The trees and hedges that lined the road were heavy and lustrous with blossom and foliage, but when she reached the Shinnecock Hills the terrain grew sparse and sandy. She overshot the turn-off for Montauk Beach but, since the traffic was light at this remote spot, she managed to do a U-turn.

Henfy's house was off the beaten track, close to a deserted stretch of stony beach which nobody used. It was a weather-board Cape Cod-style house that had seen better days; the siding was in need of paint and the brickwork was moldering. Not even the elastic tag of 'faded charm' would be appropriate as a description, and it certainly didn't look like the house of a DIY expert who had written a book on how to maintain a house. The battle-weary clunker that sat in the driveway didn't inspire confidence either. Had he written anything on how to service a car? She couldn't recall.

James H. Henfy's smile was all-embracing as he waved her regally into the gloomy interior where she sat in a sagging chair and looked at the disarray of the room, at his torn jeans and sweater.

"This is a surprise." He grinned on all cylinders, sitting opposite, one leg curled under him.

"I was passing and I saw your mail box." She patted her new hair-do and delicately shook her head as if to loosen the tight inlaid structure of her coiffure. She looked around the room for evidence of other 'How To' books and didn't find any. So far so good.

"Can I get you something to drink?"

"White wine if you have it." She remembered his book on home brew; it was the first to get into the drugstores.

The wine, however, was a cheap Californian red which, in her anxious mood, she drank rather quickly.

"I hope I'm not interrupting." She stole a quick look at a stuffed magazine rack and caught a glimpse of glossy pink flesh and red car-bodies. Nothing incriminating there.

"Not at all." He filled his own glass and left the bottle on an end table beside his chair. "Writing is a lonely business, you know. I enjoy having beautiful publishers call on me." His unwavering look seemed to stalk her reaction.

A spaniel pup appeared from nowhere, jumped on to her lap and began to shed long curly hairs. A salty rancid smell drifted up from him, originating, she suspected from the floppy tangled ears. *How To Care For Your Dog* had done well too, especially in pet stores on the West Coast. It was doubtful however if it was this particular pooch that featured on the dust jacket.

"I think I can guess why you're here." Henfy's weather-beaten face lit up with gnomic pride, spreading lines across his crab-apple cheeks.

"Oh?"

"It's about that pesky law-suit. You probably want to know the extent of the damage. Was it just the watering of ferns, etcetera?" He clapped his hands and rubbed them briskly together, knowing he'd scored a hit.

"Well, was there more?" She asked straight out, glad in a way that the masquerade was over.

"That's our little secret." He gave a maddening wink and re-filled her glass, twisting the neck of the bottle to catch the last drop.

"But Mr. Henfy, it's important..."

"James, please call me James. May I call you Sarah?"

"Yes, of course." She felt a little ill at ease in this remote crooked house with this strange man eyeing her steadily through the grainy gloom and outwitting her in some cryptic game of his own invention. For some reason the house didn't seem to be his. It wasn't just the absence of photographs or personal accoutrements; there was no sympathy between him and his ambience; the furniture didn't even bear his imprint. She had the impression of a man who used his surroundings without any compunction about maintaining or replenishing them. Although it was she who had sought him out, she couldn't resist the image of a butterfly ending up in a spider's web. There seemed to be a sort of fuzzy haze veiling his canny features.

"Tell me," he asked. "What is original? Was Flaubert original or Tolstoy? They all did research, used the facts of the time. Robert Lynskey uses a *team* of researchers..."

"Mr. Henfy ... James ... we're talking about 'How To' books..." Not wanting to confront him too directly, she tailed off.

"What's the difference? If you ask me, only God is truly original. Einstein didn't invent mathematics, did he?"

"The law defines it in more practical terms." She felt it important to enter that caveat at least.

"Oh bugger the law," he said with a toss of his head that scattered sparse strands of sandy hair and dismantled his comb-over.

"I'm very much afraid," Sarah thought of saying, "that you've done that already."

"Do you know how to comb your hair?" he asked suddenly, letting his eyes roam over her glossy chignon.

"Of course…"

"So, if I wrote a book about hair-care would that be original? How about all those diet books cobbled together? Take the Atkins Diet…"

Outside, the clouds were louring over the Atlantic and the wind was getting up, rattling the loose window frames and shingles of the Henfy house. Sarah couldn't afford to humor him anymore; she had to bite the bullet. "James, I have to know about your sources, the unattributed ones."

"Who was it who said, 'if you steal from one author it's plagiarism but if you steal from several it's research'? You think I've transcribed everything, don't you?" His eyes looked out from their tight enclosures on a bizarre world, safe in their own amused asylum. He reminded her in a way of some old farmer who silently mocks the posturing of city folk. But he lacked the farmer's tolerance; indeed, James H. Henfy might look askance at the world but he was well able to bend it to his own purposes and have a joke at its expense. She really had serious doubts about him but she needed proof.

"Well, have you?" She smoothed her skirt over her knees; her slim legs tapered downwards at a slant towards the dun-colored rug. She sensed that Henfy was admiring her and sending her compliments from his microdot eyes.

"I'm not saying." A small satyr perched on rust and ochre cushions, he replayed his infuriating grin. Watching her take in the room again with a furtive glance, he said, "I work in the bedroom."

"I see."

"Yes, I do my *best* work in there. In the bedroom."

"Mmmnn, I'm sure you do." She could play this game too. Henfy is such an idiot, she thought, he thinks he's seducing me, whereas I already have him eating out of my hand.

"Yes," he repeated thickly, "my very best work."

She re-crossed her legs and sank further back in the armchair. "You know, James, maybe we should try to ... I'm not sure ... create a mood ... an ambience..."

"Absolutely," he eagerly concurred. "I'm inclined to ... come on a little strong ... But a mood ... definitely ... We're on the same page."

"If I may be frank…?"

"Of course."

"This wine…" She made the tiniest gesture of pushing the glass away from her.

He hopped up on his feet. "I get it. It's not hitting the spot. I have a bottle of Pinot Grigio somewhere."

She made a gentle see-sawing motion with her hand. "I think a sparkling wine might be called for, perhaps Champagne?"

His face fell, then brightened. "I can run out and get the best bottle of bubbly in the state."

"That would be great." She brought her hands together in a small clap.

He already had his anorak on. "Be back in ten minutes. Don't go anywhere."

"Take your time … Bollinger if they have it. I find that very mellowing."

"Hold that thought." He was gone.

When she heard the clunker start on the third attempt, a desperate crash of gears and a swish of gravel, she went about the real business in hand. In the bedroom the shelves revealed little; there were no 'How To' books by other authors, but rummaging through the drawers of his desk she found the 'original' long-hand manuscript of *Indoor Gardening*. There were so many deletions and insertions that it had the feel of legal originality. Flicking to the section on ferns she found a better flow, fewer amendments. Just the one lapse, maybe; it wasn't conclusive but it was something to go on. She folded up the manuscript and put it in her purse. She could have her assistant check it out further. With any luck she, and her firm, were in the clear.

For the first ten miles she drove above the speed limit, trying to put as much space as she could between herself and the barnyard rooster. The cheek of the little bastard, expecting her to wait for him in that ramshackle house, while he hunted for Champagne to put her in the mood, as if that was ever going to happen. She thought wryly of his book on *Techniques for Advanced Lovers*; maybe he had hoped to put some of these to the test.

Back in her apartment, which she appreciated more than ever, she had a hot bath, laughed a little hollowly, put silk sheets on her bed and slept soundly.

She didn't hear the news of Robert's abduction until Sunday morning.

At his country club Drew finished a languid tennis match with the pro who, because of the heat and in deference to Drew's position on the Courts Committee, merely patted the balls back to him, making them bounce about a yard in front of his left foot. After shaking hands at the net, as if it had been a Wimbledon final, Drew strolled into the changing rooms and emerged in his swimming trunks with a few towels draped across his shoulders.

As he walked towards the pool area, he seemed all torso, the inconsequential legs tapering down to surprisingly thin ankles and small feet, against the soles of which blue flip-flops smacked loudly. He sat at a pool-side table under an umbrella reading the latest Grisham thriller, until the life-guard in his umpire chair blew a whistle and announced an adult swim. After the kids reluctantly, and with plangent cries, clambered out of the pool, Drew eased himself in and struck out with a lazy breaststroke, keeping well away from the pinch-nosed belles engaged in synchronized swimming in the deep end. The water cooled him down as he ducked and bobbed, his tadpole legs doing little more than trailing behind like afterthoughts.

His enjoyment was marred by a young show-off, equipped with goggles and snorkel, who did a perfect front crawl without having to raise his head to breathe. After a minor collision which disrupted his barely established rhythm, Drew croaked, "Look where you're going, damn it." The swimmer, who didn't hear or possibly chose to ignore him, went forging ahead while Drew rocked in his wake, taking in a mouthful of water. Grimly, he continued until he'd completed his modest quota of seven lengths.

As he was hauling himself out of the pool he saw, through a haze of droplets and straggly hair, a familiar figure weaving through the tanning bodies and umbrellas.

"Well, for goodness sake, Sarah..." Using every ounce of strength he managed to lever himself out in one reasonably fluid movement.

"Why didn't you tell me?" she demanded, hot and dusty from the drive out to the club.

"I tried calling all day yesterday but there was no answer." Involuntarily he scratched his midriff where the elastic waistband of his trunks left squiggle marks on the folds of his cantilevered gut.

She let it pass; yesterday and Montauk Beach didn't bear thinking about. Her face began to crumple. "And to think I blamed him ... for standing me up..." The tears in her sad eyes sparkled like glycerin in the rays of sun that came slanting through a tree of furry yellow catkins.

"You weren't to know," Drew consoled her. He might have made a move to hold her except that he was wringing wet. He wrapped himself in his terry-cloth towels – with his coloring he couldn't take strong sunshine – and slipped on the flip-flops, hooking the thongs around his toes which were white with proud flesh from the water. He held his stomach in and smoothed forward the strands of red hair to cover the thin spots.

Sarah removed the jacket of her shot-silk suit; she wasn't dressed for the pool, felt clammy and out of place. The mingled smells of embrocation, tanning oil and sunscreen lotion made her queasy.

"Could we sit somewhere? I feel weak." She hadn't fully absorbed the news and found it difficult to believe that Robert was in real danger.

With his hand at her elbow Drew led her to the pool-side bar where they settled themselves under palm fronds and ordered a bottle of chilled Riesling. The plastic straps of the chair nipped the undersides of Drew's liver-spotted thighs as he leant forward to pour. For a while they watched the kids somersaulting into the pool or shooting down the slides shouting "can-opener," the sunbathers strewn on grass, some reading Kindles or tinkering with iPhones. Over to the left of the pool, golfers putted out on the eighteenth, shook hands and signed each other's score cards.

"I still can't credit it." Sarah's under-lip trembled as she sipped her wine.

"It takes some getting used to," Drew agreed grimly, giving the impression that he'd been through the worst of it. He donned a white cotton-planter's hat. It was a strange day, hot certainly, but the sun was blurred behind a layer of egg-white membrane, not cloud exactly, rather a sort of hazy mist which he knew from experience did not screen out the burning rays. The sandwich he ordered with the wine attracted wasps and he threw it in a nearby trash bin. With all the panoply of technology they still couldn't keep wasps off a sandwich.

"For me swimming is a kind of therapy," he said as if he had to explain his presence there. And it was partly true. The club which he'd joined after his divorce kept him busy during non-office hours, and he was on several club committees. It was making up for lost time too because he'd never been a member of a glee club or a frat house. "I'm glad you came," he said. "It's not good to be alone at a time like this." He patted her hand and found it surprisingly cool.

"And they won't negotiate … It's like a bad dream." She shuddered suddenly and sucked in her breath.

"It doesn't look good," he said wanly. "But Robert is a survivor," he added more positively. "If he keeps his head he should have a chance."

Sarah turned away abruptly and shielded her face with an upraised hand.

"What's the matter?" Drew asked.

"Nothing. Someone I vaguely know." Actually, it was a tabloid columnist, who had wandered towards her but since disappeared into the changing rooms. He was one of the most inventive and relentless muck-rakers in the business and she certainly didn't want to give him any ammunition. In fact she would have to be careful not to be seen with any man while Robert was incarcerated.

"An old flame?" Drew asked keenly.

"No. Just a copy editor who pesters me for work," she said fluently, waving away a wasp.

"I'm pestered too," he said, "by these spooks in my office." He went on to explain how the CIA had virtually moved into the KNYBS building. "Have they contacted you yet?"

"No." She breathed in deeply, a sigh that dilated her pert nostrils which were pink and translucent.

"They will. The guy in charge is called Limon, a sharp operator." He wondered if he should tell her about the peculiar angle Limon was working on but, for some reason, decided against it. He couldn't help noticing how well she looked, easily holding her own among the nymphs who lay strewn within the charmed acres of the club. Her skin gleamed, the make-up perfectly minimal, and her high cheekbones gave rise to smooth, intriguing shadows beneath. Not many women could take strong sunlight in their stride the way Sarah did; there were no blemishes to hide and the brown of her eyes retained its tawny integrity. Clothed, she was more alluring to Drew than any of the half-naked females who lay around the pool. But then he was old-fashioned and sighed for the days when a man's head could be turned by the arch of a woman's foot.

He wanted to let her know how he felt about her, but was foiled by the circumstances; Robert's welfare was what counted for now. He did, however, try to fathom the depth of her concern for Robert behind the veil of tears but was side-tracked into admiring her grave demeanor which was captivating in its own way.

How far did his feeling about the kidnapping extend beyond the proprieties? He couldn't deny the fascination of such an enormity, that feeling of standing at the summit of a mountain, watching a boulder begin to slide and gather speed as the potential for destruction grew and grew. Drew's detachment was complete; he owed nothing and was perfectly safe. Not like his father who gambled away everything and left them broke and busted down the social scale, forcing his mother to work in a sweatshop in Elizabeth. At the time, Drew was too young to be able to help in any way but he desperately wanted to restore the fortunes of the family, and raged against his helplessness.

He fought his way back inch by inch, putting himself through college and, in reaction to his old man's incandescent self-destructiveness, developed an instinct for success and a powerful urge to be in control. He didn't mind taking a back seat or indulging the famous with their childlike desire for visibility, as long as the means and techniques of production were vested in him. Lynskey, however, was an awkward cuss, not sufficiently malleable; for him exposure was not enough, not anymore; now he wanted to make a 'contribution'. To make matters worse he had it all, talent, clout, credibility and, of course, Sarah. And he didn't appreciate any of it. That was obscene, un-American. Maybe Limon had a point, or the kidnapping was a kind of retribution.

He touched Sarah's hand again. "When this is all over…"

"Please don't," she said gently. "Not now." Searching his face for some redeeming feature, she wondered if he wanted her more than wanting to acquire her. Maybe it came to the same thing in the end but it bore thinking about.

Drew changed tack but stayed on course. "I

don't know what we're going to do about the '*RL Hour*'. Maybe a guest host..." He hoped he wasn't forcing the pace. On the other hand she wasn't exactly a grieving widow.

Sarah recoiled but didn't say anything. She sensed that he was putting out a feeler or maybe trying to tell her something; either way silence was a useful bait.

"We have to carry on somehow," Drew murmured. Then he said, "I'm not sure Robert is interested in the show any more."

"Oh, damn the show." Sarah angrily crossed her legs, hooking an instep behind a slender calf. "Anyway, what do you mean by that?"

"You must have sensed it. A sort of ... disaffection or change of heart..." He shrugged, unable to explain it further, but his eyes didn't leave hers.

She took this on board silently.

Shortly afterwards Drew was dragged off to a club committee meeting. He thought he might raise the question of banning snorkels in the pool.

When Sarah got back to her apartment she was crushed by inactivity, by the long Sunday afternoon that still stretched ahead. She was just about to go out again when Limon called and introduced himself. She had little choice but to invite him in. He was polite and sympathetic as he went over some familiar ground.

"So you were to meet at seven in the restaurant...?"

"Yes. We made the arrangement earlier that morning." Even if Drew hadn't warned her she would have sensed that he was no ordinary flatfoot; his sharp, restless features gave the impression of several facts and possibilities being sifted and weighed at the same time.

"We know Mr. Lynskey left his broker at one. I understand he normally went to his place in the Heights afterwards."

"That was his routine, yes. But I called his secretary and he didn't show up there either." It suddenly struck her how awful these facts were, how callous in recitation. Robert was the victim of these brute facts. Poor Robert.

"I see." Limon had already spoken to Beth and this confirmed what she'd said. While he was there he had, to Beth's annoyance, insisted on reading Lynskey's work in progress. In the draft of '*Media, Myth and Metaphor*' he had come upon the passage: "...So the media still cultivates the notion that strength guarantees victory whereas there is now abundant evidence that small guerrilla forces can outsmart and defeat the most powerful standing armies. We have seen it in Vietnam, Afghanistan, Ulster, Beirut, Ground Zero, the aftermath of the war on Iraq. A campaign of Shock and Awe does not win the day ... Is it perception-lag or lack of objectivity that sustains this myth?" Limon had taken a copy of the manuscript for further analysis; he had also arranged for some of the bright young things at the Agency to go through all of Lynskey's published work with an eye to seditious sentiment of any sort.

"I suppose Beth is a protective sort?" Limon permitted himself a small smile.

"Aren't most secretaries?" Sarah remembered the rather strained phone conversation with Beth the morning after Robert's disappearance.

"Mr. Lynskey seems to inspire loyalty in people," Limon hazarded, leaning forward over his knees that rose up sharply from the low chair.

Sarah agreed wistfully, surprised that this line of questioning hurt more than she had anticipated.

Limon put the notebook into the pocket of his fawn lightweight suit as if to suggest that the formalities were over. "I've always admired his broadcasts," he confided. "Especially the way he stands up for the underdog."

"I know what you mean," Sarah said, then asked, "Is this relevant ... I mean...?"

"Sometimes it helps to have a psychological profile," Limon answered smoothly. "To know how a person might react in ... difficult circumstances..."

"What are his chances?" Sarah cut in, suddenly dismayed by circumlocutions and the apparent normality of the conversation.

"Try not to worry," Limon said slowly. "Between the Agency and the Police Department we have fifteen senior officers on the case. You can rest assured that no effort will be spared. I give you my personal guarantee." He could have mentioned several other agencies too, including the Security Council, but he felt it better to withhold that information. There was something about her, not untrustworthy exactly, but kind of flaky.

He hadn't answered her at all really and it occurred briefly to her that he might have been more forthcoming if she were Robert's wife. Indeed, he took his leave rather abruptly. Maybe it was just her imagination, which now had free rein to do its worst to her.

As Limon drove away he reviewed what he had come up with to date. It now seemed certain that Lynskey was snatched shortly after 1 p.m., in broad daylight and in one of the busiest parts of Manhattan. Were the kidnappers trying to prove something or was there an entirely different explanation? When he got back to his office – his weekend was shot anyway – he called Mahon and asked him to comb the Financial District for witnesses; shoe leather was Mahon's department. Limon didn't say so, but he felt there wouldn't be any witnesses. They'd got nothing yet from Jallud Fahd, who protested ignorance of any attempt to free him. Skilled interrogators had just been dispatched from Langley to Guantánamo Bay. Limon's main concern was that whatever information came from that source would be channeled through him. With so many agencies involved, anything could happen. He could find himself left out of the loop. Or it could end up in a total cluster-fuck with him left holding the can.

They decided to do another lap of the reservoir in Central Park. Chaim wore a sweatband to keep his tousled hair out of his eyes; he sometimes held Christopher's hand as they jogged side by side. This was their Sunday ritual and it made them feel special. They exchanged the odd breathless comment as they ran.

Christopher had come to New York a little over a year ago, making a complete break with his stifling hometown outside Billings, Montana. After some lonely weeks in the city he plucked up the courage to go to a gay discussion group which was chaired at the time by Chaim. The newcomer was welcomed in the normal way by Chaim and asked to sit closer to the front. As the meeting got under way it became clear that, despite a tough front and chiseled features, Christopher had a poor self-image. Empathizing with his embarrassment, Chaim tried to draw him out, made him the focus of the encounter session and showed him how much support and understanding there was for him in the group. When at one point Christopher's poise gave way and he started to sob, Chaim knew that he had taken that first and irrevocable step towards him. Within a week they'd moved in together. They struck a deal, common enough among gays, wary of the 'scene', to stay together for one year and remain faithful to each other for that period.

As he jogged the last lap Chaim realized that there was less than a month to go. It bothered him that Christopher had not said anything about renewing the arrangement and he didn't know how to interpret his silence. He tried not to project, not on this fine day as they ran stride for stride, the air cooled by the water of the reservoir and the overhanging foliage. Not unlike alcoholics, they lived a day at a time; there were no guarantees about the future. If Christopher wanted to renew the arrangement, then Chaim had decided he would propose marriage.

When they got back to the apartment, Chaim checked the pigeon hole for mail or messages, nodded to the surly doorman and rode up in the elevator with Christopher. They showered together, kissed and gave each other climaxes, watching the semen mingle in the soapy water and disappear into the vortex. Outside of the narrow cubicle they toweled each other down and dressed.

They prepared a late lunch on the balcony. Christopher lit the charcoal on the Hibachi grill, added some slivers of hickory, and painted barbecue sauce on the burgers. There were faint sounds from the balcony above; their unseen overhead neighbors obviously had the same idea. The sun was low, going behind the water tower on a building close to the East River.

"You're quiet," Christopher said, looking up from the grill. "Still worrying about Robert Lynskey?"

"I guess so." Chaim buttered the rolls and set the table.

"What if he isn't rescued?"

Chaim's head came up to meet the abrupt question. "It doesn't bear thinking about. These are … international terrorists."

"And what happens to you?" Christopher moved towards him across the tiny balcony, sauce brush in hand.

"Oh, I'll be OK." Chaim tried to sound confident; he didn't want Christopher to think he would lose out. Like it or not, credentials and jobs mattered to them all, maybe in part-compensation for not being fully accepted by society. They needed the profile, the roar of their own small crowd. He didn't blame him for it. But, Jesus, if he were to leave him … He watched the fair head turn towards the vista of buildings that prevented even a glimpse of the river, and felt the ache begin.

"Christopher, it's already May … We have to talk." Chaim rehearsed it over and over. But he couldn't say it. Not today. He passed him the corn-cobs; they ate in silence. Nothing was resolved.

Afterwards Christopher went to the basement to do some laundry. Chaim went down the corridor and emptied trash into the chute. He did the wash-up and then sat down to read the Sunday papers which were still full of Lynskey. He realized that he loved that man almost as much as he loved Christopher.

CHAPTER 13

IN HIS DREAM he walked up a hill shortly after dawn to serve early mass. There was no one else stirring; the sleeping town was his. Looking back before entering the churchyard, he saw the long line of his footprints in the snow, a single trail which grew fainter in the distance and finally disappeared around the corner at the foot of the hill. He carried his black draw-string bag containing surplice, soutane and canvas slippers.

The sacristan had gone up the spiral stairs of the steeple to ring the last bell which he now heard as he dressed, pealing over the town's crisp air, summoning the faithful from their beds. He brought the cruets of water and wine out to the altar, his slippers squeaking slightly on the marble floor. Some of the wine spilled on his fingers; it smelled rich and sweet. Behind the back of the huge sculptured altar of icing and marzipan, he climbed the ladder and, from a taper, lit the six tall candles. From that vantage point he could see the early congregants moving slowly up the nave of the church, women with hats, bare-headed men, genuflecting before taking their seats, coughing in the cold vaulted space. They seemed so ordinary, shuffling into the brown pews, whereas he was on the altar, separated from them by a golden rail, bathed in incense and candlelight. He went back to the sacristy and waited until the priest had finished dressing.

During the mass he knelt alone on the altar steps, ringing the bell, responding in Latin: *"Ad Deum qui laetificat juventutem meam ... Qui fecit coelum et terram ... Et cum spiritu tuo ...* To God who giveth joy to my youth..." Unlike the congregation he knew what the words meant; he felt special, inside the altar rail, a figurine on a wedding cake, and safe too, beyond the remotest reach of harm, surrounded by spotless linen, marble and gold, all lit by the sanctuary lamp right above his head. All was well, infinitely well, with a cleanliness of soul that would never be experienced again.

During the Eucharist he brought the bell to the top step, held the hem of the priest's chasuble as he genuflected, waited for those moving words, *"Accipite et manducate ex hoc omnes. Hoc ... Est ... Enim ... Corpus ... Meum."* Then he rang the bell, matching the beat of his heart.

Behind the priest at communion, he held the gold paten under the chins of the faithful as they knelt at the altar rail receiving the host. What strange, poor faces he saw, mouths open, eyes fluttering, grimaces of piety and strange passion. Mrs. Monihan, one of his teachers, clutched her stomach after receiving, and looked as if she might faint. She could not intimidate him again because he had seen into her soul.

He watched the priest replace the ciborium and chalice in the tabernacle embossed with gold letters, alpha and omega, and glimpsed the monstrance flaring like the sun...

And suddenly, despite the snow outside, it was Easter, the turn of the year, bells ringing in affirmation over the whole town, his world made safer by the risen Christ and promises fulfilled…

———————————

Robert wakes from the dream into a nightmare. The altar boy vanishes as he struggles off the filthy bed and looks around the cellar.

The desolation of that first night is still with him but now at least he has some knowledge of what happened, thanks to a small radio given to him by the man who brings food once a day. He also has a rudimentary metal lamp to light the impenetrable darkness of night. Is it really him, this smelling unshaved creature living in his own squalor?

By standing on a box and looking out the barred window he can see an overgrown meadow and a hill beyond; there is also the faint sound of running water, a stream perhaps. It could be anywhere. He has examined the cellar thoroughly; the earthen floor is underlain by rock, the walls are solid, built of stone. Though the scrutiny has not given any hope of escape, there is a strange comfort in being more familiar with the minutest details of his prison.

He knows they cannot negotiate. In logic there could have been no other decision but the logic still hurts. The Arab who came to visit him briefly, as if to check on his merchandise, didn't even try to conceal his identity. A bad omen on top of others. He is a dead man, already dying in his filth. *"Ad Deum qui laetificat juventutem meam."* He dreads the idea of ISIS-style beheading ... Desperation drives him to a plan of sorts...

Is he just going through the motions as he stands with hammering heart behind the door, a heavy log of half-rotten elm in his hand? It can't be real unless death is real. He hopes it will be more than a token act but can't count on his will. How long more for the man to come? A strong man; must hit him hard. Then run and keep on running even if his heart gives out. There is nothing to lose. He breathes deeply, hears the upstairs door opening, steps descending. He tightens his grip on the wooden club, hears the key turning in the lock. Courage deserts him. He drops the weapon. Tomorrow. Definitely tomorrow...

———

At Anna's bidding Bart removed the cardboard from the kitchen window at the back of the house. The sunlight which filtered in through the mottled, dusty panes served only to highlight the squalor of the room, the fly-blown tatters of wallpaper, rotting floorboards, the detritus of years of neglect. At least it was cool enough in the stone-built house, in which must mingled with the more recent smells of kerosene and sweat.

Bart went out to replenish the water tanks from a stream that ran down a hill, south of the barn that housed the car. Carrying a two-gallon can in each hand, he walked over the burnt grass, sweat trickling down his neck into the khaki shirt. Passing the tiny window he saw Lynskey's face staring out, the frightened eyes just barely above ground level. He turned away and got on with his job. Before he reached the stream he stopped once to look at an old rusted disc harrow half buried in a patch of nettles, and wondered what it was.

When he finished his work-out Richard came into the kitchen and sat down with Khaled at the grime-covered table still littered with the remains of yesterday's meal. Among the debris stood Lynskey's dish, scraped clean of beans and bread; the dish reminded him of a dog he once had when he lived in Atlanta.

"Do you have to do those exercises in this heat?" Anna turned from the sink. "You know we're short of water." This was aimed at Khaled too; his ritual washing.

"They keep me sweet," Richard said evenly. He was free-wheeling, relieved that the first phase of the job had gone well, and not too dismayed by the surroundings or by the waiting.

But Anna took a dimmer view. The slum conditions were beginning to get to her, especially the lack of hygiene, and it bothered her that she alone seemed so affected. It suggested a weakness, exposed her more privileged background and the fact that her radicalism had a different provenance. It raised a question which she tried to shrug off about her motivation and her part in this unholy alliance. Her grandfather would have been amazed to see her here with these people. But the world had changed since his time, and different allegiances were needed to fight the same cause. Yes, the cause was the same and it would never change; the pathetic attempt at statehood by Jews, cozying up to the Americans.

But her birthright did not include the patience that was acquired through pain by the dispossessed in long bleak alleys of time. She wanted results now.

"They're not going to deal," she said, fighting back tears of frustration. "The whole goddamn country has given the thumbs down." She should have known all along. But Richard used to speak about Khaled as if he was some kind of miracle man. As she turned away from them her hair brushed against her neck. It was greasy and dank and her skin was sickly like parchment. She might have borne this degradation with a better grace if there had been some signs of progress.

"A knee-jerk reaction," Richard said, munching a crust of dry bread. "What do you think, Khaled?"

"It takes time for pressure to be felt." He remembered when Israeli soldiers erected the first part of the dividing wall in Gaza. Palestinians and all true followers of Islam were stricken beyond belief. Young men cut their heads and staggered through the streets until their clothing was soaked with blood. They didn't exist any more except in their own pain; assassination became inevitable, suicide bombing. An imagined breeze began to lift the corners of the Hamas flag where it lay ... He had to shut his mind down before the horror was revealed.

"Maybe we should step up the pressure," Anna said.

"How?" Richard asked. "Send them his ears in a box?"

She gave him a withering look, annoyed by his new-found independence. He wasn't so tough without Khaled. "Have you got a better idea? We have to show them we mean business."

"Maybe we should demand a few million bucks," Richard suggested more seriously. "He's worth that at least."

"Instead of Jallud Fahd?" Tracing a pattern in spilt salt on the worn oil-cloth, Khaled didn't look up but his tone was icy. Fahd was the only man who could unite the Arab world. Even if this could only be accomplished by some departure from fundamentalist ideals, Khaled for one was prepared to accept that, as long as the basic tenets of Islam remained intact. But the disunity could not continue. The Palestinians had won a hearing at the International Court in The Hague and no representative from Egypt, Lebanon or Syria showed up. While Iran supported the Palestine Islamic Jihad in the past, the flow of aid in recent years had been reduced to a trickle. The growing divide between Shi'ites and Sunnis was causing even more disunity. Only Fahd could bring the countries together and give the Palestinian people the help they needed. There was no possibility of dealing with America or Israel in any serious way unless the Arab world was united.

Anna wiped sticky palms on her jeans. It seemed to her in retrospect that they'd rushed into it and perhaps placed too much reliance on Khaled's judgment. He seemed so quietly authoritative, whereas she had been expecting a fanatic who would have to be kept on a tight rein. It was hard to figure him out; she wasn't even sure if he had another agenda.

Khaled could have been meditating except that his lower lip jutted out, giving the impression of a cross child. He looked at a square on the wall where a picture once hung and wondered what it might have been. Except for those blessed years at Qom, he'd spent most of his life living in ruined homes and had developed the habit of trying to reconstruct what normal life might have been like.

She confronted them at the table. "It's stalemate then. We might as well kill him and get it over with. The longer we stay here the greater the risk." The ensuing silence indicated that her point had not fallen on deaf ears. By killing Lynskey they would be throwing away any leverage they might have, but since the authorities refused to negotiate, he wasn't worth anything to them alive. The act of killing him would have symbolic value at least and show that America would never be safe.

_____

When Drew first suggested replacing Robert with a new host for the show, Chaim was hurt and upset, and indeed, did not think there were too many candidates with the required gravitas. If a change had to be made, he thought someone like Diane Sawyer or Christiane Amanpour, both of whom he greatly admired, might fit the bill. Drew, however, had other ideas but didn't manage to put them into effect.

Conan O'Brien and Letterman had the good sense to turn down the job offer on the grounds that they didn't want to dance on another man's grave. Drew finally settled for Si Rembert, who'd started as an alternative comedian at '*Catch A Rising Star*' just three years earlier. He was lively and irreverent, and saw this as his big break. Though Rembert was compliant enough and suitably modest, his agent was not. Knowing the predicament that faced KNYBS, the agent insisted on finest terms, a new-face launch with all the trimmings and a completely different set which he described vaguely as "Miami art deco sort of stuff with a couple of plaster flamingoes thrown in."

When Drew pointed out that the contract might not in fact be renewed – if Lynskey returned – Rembert's agent was unimpressed and refused to reduce his demands. This was his big break too and he subscribed to the negotiator's dictum, 'Go for broke when you have their peckers in your pocket'.

"We deal," he said, "as if Rembert's for keeps. Or we don't deal."

"He has no say regarding content," Drew insisted. "None."

"I can live with that."

"And if Lynskey comes back, we go back to the drawing board."

"OK. But if you ask me he's not coming back."

Drew was reasonably satisfied. Rembert was a risk of course, but his amusing, laid-back brand of nihilism was very *in,* a sort of throw-back to radical chic but with a lighter touch. And it had elements of post-mod irony that appealed to the younger demographic. He liked the idea of molding a new talent.

Although Chaim had no say in the negotiations, he had reservations about Si Rembert, but these paled before the contract of his personal life which was coming up for renewal. He buried himself in the mechanics of launching the new star, still afraid to broach the subject with Christopher.

He was working at his drawing board with the designers and floor manager when Peggy entered and diplomatically beckoned him aside. "Drew wants to see you."

"Later, Peg. I'm tied up now."

"He says it's urgent. He's in the cutting room on the twentieth floor."

"Why there?"

"I think it's because of those ... people in his office. The ... agents."

Chaim didn't bother with the elevator but ran up the stairs; it gave him a fleeting reminder of his leisurely Sunday jog with Christopher.

"What's up?" he asked entering the darkened room.

Agitated, Drew pointed to the floor; his eyes, lit by flickering screens, were wide with the knowledge of some enormity. The red hair that stood in a coronet seemed charged with static. He pointed downwards again. "*They* don't know about it yet. Another note arrived. Through the mail, addressed to me. And get this..." His voice tailed off to a low register, "There's a cassette as well."

"A cassette?"

"An old-fashioned video tape. I've just played it through. It's hot. They want us to air it. It's one of their demands. Christ! Close the door and sit down." He kicked a stenographer's stool towards Chaim and rewound the tape. His movements were jerky and sporadic as if the news had shifted him into overdrive. The boulder was beginning to slide and he was at the summit, watching with a strange fascination. Closing the Venetian blinds, he punched the remote control and the screen flickered to life.

There were no preliminaries, credits or logos,

just a close-up of a map of Palestine and a heavily accented voice-over which described the carve-up by the Superpowers in the post-partition plan and the Israeli plantation. The film then showed the Palestinian villages of Yalu and Beit Ruba before and after they'd been razed by Israeli tanks. "It was not just an occupation," the unseen commentator said, "but a systematic destruction of the State of Palestine with the agreement and encouragement of the Western Powers." There followed shots of refugee camps showing the appalling conditions of the disenfranchised Palestinians, described as "A new diaspora deliberately created to accommodate the Jews." There were stills of Israeli detention centers in which, it was alleged, thousands of Palestinians were being systematically tortured.

The footage switched to up-to-date shots of Israeli raids on refugee camps. The segment, which had not been seen before in the West, was interspersed with shots of Jallud Fahd ministering to the wounded and praying with the elders of the camps.

The commentary continued, "But the West-supported Israeli aggressors could not foretell the inevitable revival of Islam which started in Iran and spread rapidly to Lebanon ... A handful of Shia militia, including the Hezbollah, gradually grew in strength. The march of the spirit and justice of Islam is relentless and must lead ultimately to victory ... Iraq became the Vietnam of America..."

In the final segment a different theme was introduced. Black Jews were interviewed about racism in the white Israeli suburb of Bet Hakerem. "Black Americans should know," the voice went on, "that racial discrimination is an integral part of the so-called Jewish State…" The tape ended with a close-up of Jallud Fahd praying in a crowded mosque and preaching about the inevitable restoration of justice to Palestine.

Drew hit the rewind button and opened the blinds. Slatted light flooded into the room with an intensity that made Chaim cover his eyes.

"What do you think?" Drew asked.

"Not much. The cutting is awful…"

"God, not the damn technique. That's rubbish. I mean the content." He took the pipe from his breast pocket but put it back again.

"Well, it's just propaganda. And very historical stuff…"

"Pretty powerful though?" Drew prompted. It occurred to him that Jallud Fahd, or maybe even one of the kidnappers, could have done the commentary. "How do *you* feel about it?" He could have been an analyst asking Chaim to bare his soul but there was a prurient catch in his voice and a lingering delicacy. He felt sure there would be more tapes to come.

"As a Jew, you mean?" Chaim made the question explicit. He shrugged. "I'm not exactly orthodox, you know." He left it at that because Drew's suddenly cancelled grin pointed up the double meaning. Besides, Chaim had no desire to serve as a sounding board. It was crazy, all of it. He had read about Jewish fundamentalism too. Zealots in Israel thought it blasphemous to proclaim a State before the Messiah came. In one corner the Torah, in the other, the Koran, red grievances and blue sorrows. Who, in reason, would fight over the defunct scribblings of desert-crazed 'prophets'? As a lowercase liberal with a yen for simple survival and the resolution of his own personal life, it was beyond him. Yet he couldn't deny the faintest tug of affinity with the Jewish cause which he tried to muffle with a silent plea for detachment.

"Religion has a lot to answer for." Drew, too, felt the unreality of history.

"Anyway, we couldn't possibly give it air time," Chaim said.

"Why not? You're the one who wants balance..."

"But it's so ... amateurish."

As he removed the cassette, Drew wondered if Chaim wasn't deliberately missing the point. "I was accused last time of putting Robert's life in danger. If we air this video we'll be doing him a favor." It should, he thought, also be a major coup for KNYBS. And a powerful probe into that inner space, dense as a black hole, of public reaction. His guess was that, the anti-Arab mood of the country would give rise to a hostile response and much controversy. But then, there was no such thing as bad publicity.

"You'd better check with Limon," Chaim

advised.

"But first, have Peggy' make a copy for us." He handed Chaim the cassette and winked.

About one hour later Limon viewed the tape in the same room, after which he stroked forward his widow's peak and said, "Don't even think about it."

"What option do we have?" Drew asked with an innocently helpless spreading of his hands.

Limon brought his hand down flat on the table, three large veins standing out. "We can't afford to agree to *any* of their demands. Don't you understand anything, the political fall-out..."

"You stood firm on the hostage release," Drew pointed out. "So, you're already in front. This is a reasonable compromise. *And* it gives Lynskey a fighting chance." He brought the pipe from his pocket and began the preliminary fidgeting, as if he were going to fill it with tobacco.

"You just want good copy," Limon shot back, strengthened in his view that Drew was a shit-disturber, though a more subtle, and hence more dangerous, one than he'd figured previously.

"The two objectives happily coincide," Drew answered smoothly, a faint tic appearing at the corner of his mouth. "We happen to believe that Lynskey is worth saving..."

"Assuming he's still alive," Limon shot out, wanting but failing to punish Drew for his hypocrisy. He merely delivered a mild shock instead.

"What?" Strangely, that possibility hadn't occurred to Drew. "Have you any reason to believe…"

"Forget it." Limon thought for a while. He didn't want to go to his superiors for a decision without adding something of his own. "You mentioned compromise. Here's one. Show the damn tape as if it were a documentary made by KNYBS…"

"That's ridiculous," Chaim cut in. "It's worse than the average home movie."

Drew agreed. "No one would buy it. And it would offend our even-copy policy…"

"The hell with that," Limon grated. "This is a matter of national importance."

"It wouldn't satisfy the kidnappers." Drew changed tack.

Limon didn't disagree. He paced the room cluttered with monitors and editing equipment, the screens of which seemed filmy with dust in the strong natural light. He covered his mouth and chin with a large hand, the long fingers splaying upwards along the jaw. "Then edit it. Take out all that bullshit about Jallud Fahd. That's my bottom line." It was a tough call and he wasn't sure the Director would go for it.

"Hmmm. Maybe…" Drew sat quietly, looking down at the pipe which lay in his brown-spotted hands, a touchstone as well as a prop.

"It's not negotiable," Limon said, wishing to pre-empt further debate in which, he sensed, Drew had the edge. Neither man admitted he would have to refer to higher authority.

Limon took the cassette. "I'm sure you've made a copy."

As Chaim walked him to the door he asked how the investigation was going.

"We're working on some angles," was all Limon said to this stooge with the big hair.

CHAPTER 14

HAVING DECIDED TO KICK the office dust from their heels, they went to their favorite watering hole across the street to watch the broadcast. They sat at the brass-railed bar and ordered their usual, a vodka martini for Drew, a lite Molson for Chaim. The TV sat unobtrusively on a corner shelf close to the ceiling where the light from the low-slung Tiffany lamps didn't quite reach.

Near the main window the floor was raised like a stage, corralled by a rail of turned wood balusters in the manner of an old-fashioned law court, designed to make the largely legal clientele feel at home. Here the sober-suited customers sat in clusters bathed in light filtered through stained glass. They sipped their cocktails and nibbled at Macadamia nuts, cheese sticks and pretzels, unwinding in that mellow interregnum between the close of business and the journey home.

No one paid much attention to the TV even after Drew asked the barman to turn the volume up. The broadcast was introduced by the President of KNYBS: "The documentary you are about to see was given to this network by the kidnappers of Robert Lynskey who demanded that it be shown. While it is against company policy, the circumstances are such that..."

Drew turned in surprise. "I didn't think the President was going to front the damn thing."

"I wonder what Limon will make of that," Chaim wondered aloud.

"Who cares?" Drew noticed a crowd beginning to form around the bar to get a better view. The background buzz of talk began to fade and someone asked, "What the hell is this?" The TV was no longer just a modest part of the ambience. Within five minutes the bar was unusually silent except for the strangely accented voice issuing from the elevated set. The images that came in jerky cross cuts and trembling long shots proved that this was no ordinary program. But what exactly was it?

"Turn up the sound." A couple of youths came in from the pool room, carrying their cues.

"Sit down and shut up."

Drew took stock of the audience who could have been watching the Super Bowl except for the absence of cheers and groans of disappointment. Indeed, the silence was dense, clotted with private reflection and amazement. Few drinks were served. It reminded him a little of the Twin Towers, when the nation became a single mute spectator of the unimaginable.

After the program concluded the puzzled silence ran on for a split second, then disintegrated into a babble of speculative and outraged sounds, an odd snatch barely distinguishable above the general level.

"Jesus, those crazies ... murdering bastards..."

"Tough on poor Lynskey..."

"Maybe they have a point."

"No way. It's filthy propaganda ... Who're they trying to kid...?"

"A lot of it is ancient history..."

With his head on one side, Drew listened carefully to this spontaneous vox pop.

———————

The morning papers were more verbose if equally confused: "...Unprecedented ... bizarre ... wholly unacceptable, a sad day for the media ... a reasonable price to pay for Lynskey..." KNYBS was alternately vilified and praised. Even the Times lurched into ambivalence: "The use of the air waves for this purpose is offensive yet what alternative was open to KNYBS? The hostage exchange has, as we advocated, been rejected, so perhaps this 'broadcast' could be seen as a pragmatic response ... But by the same token, compromise of this nature comes close to capitulation ... It is not clear what the downstream effects will be ... Freedom to choose must not be undermined..."

Over his boiled egg Drew scanned the headlines and chuckled to himself, "My god, they're at sixes and sevens." That was a bonus in a way; what really mattered was the publicity.

This view was echoed within the Administration, though without the cynical amusement. The ambivalence itself was seen as a deep and threatening wound. Eventually, the White House raised the ante. No more tapes of any kind would be broadcast. The National Security and Homeland Security Councils joined forces with the Intelligence Board; this was to be expected as the situation escalated.

Although Limon had covered himself with his Director before the program went out, he didn't avoid all the flak that cascaded down from the summit. He was still in charge of the investigation but he began to wonder with increasing frequency whether he might not end up as the scapegoat.

In Bridgeport, Gary wept for his brother. Sue did her best to console him.

From her bedroom, Sarah called Gary, gave and took what little comfort was available. She called everyone, repeating much the same words.

In Metuchen Robert picked up the makeshift club from the log box. And waited behind the bolted door for what seemed like hours. He heard those heavy familiar footsteps on the stairs. As they came nearer his courage failed him and the cudgel fell from his hand. He had to try something. This was his only chance. To save his life. He had to try. When he heard the key scrape in the lock he bent down, retrieved the weapon. He tightened his grip and raised the club over his head, waiting for the door to open.

———————————

The forensic report on the first demand note contained little usable information. There was nothing distinctive about the paper or ink, as indeed even Mahon had noted, and there were no fingerprints. A state-of-the-art technique had produced a DNA print from a minute trace of tissue. Unfortunately, having run this through the computer in Langley, there was no match-up with any known criminal or terrorist.

Limon glumly dropped the report on his desk. "This and five cents wouldn't buy you a crock of shit," he said to Mahon who sat opposite. To make matters worse the Agents planted in the KNYBS building hadn't come up with anything. "What've you got?"

"Nothing much. A woman thought she saw a man being pushed or helped into a car on Exchange Street shortly after 1 p.m. She thought it could have been Lynskey. But he didn't seem to be resisting..."

"He could've been doped," Limon said by rote, but he was still nursing his other theory about the possible involvement of Lynskey himself. "What about the kidnappers?"

"That's the funny part," Mahon said. "She only saw a woman with long dark hair." He tried to settle himself into the old disemboweled chair; it was like sitting on a commode. He was relieved that Limon had the lead role in this ball-breaker of a case. In a way he was sorry for the ambitious SOB who for some strange reason just had to be out front, right at the cutting edge. Frustrated bureaucrats could be a very spiteful and unforgiving breed; Limon could easily get himself caught in vicious crossfire. They'd have his balls for book-ends. Mahon preferred to keep his own well protected.

Limon tilted back his chair. "A wig probably." It didn't make sense, or did it? He looked out the window at the wall opposite, the mica and feldspar glinting. Concrete was the only view he rated; nothing sylvan or maritime. There were too many senior people muscling in on the case, too many bosses falling over themselves. It could all go pear-shaped.

"How about the tape?" Mahon inquired, mopping his face with a huge handkerchief. Limon, who lacked his bulk, clearly didn't need much air-conditioning.

Limon picked up another report and paraphrased, "Tape and cartridge of Saudi manufacture – as if we couldn't have guessed – spindles of Far East manufacture, probably Hong Kong … No match on the voice print … probably a professional commentator or actor…" Limon looked up bleary-eyed. "And finally, the package was mailed in Queens. Big deal." He let the unhelpful document flutter on to the desk and made a fist. "They must have help from inside the country…"

"Like who? Organized crime, mob maybe?" Mahon removed his jacket and laid it on his lap, using the cover to loosen the crotch of his pants. His cell phone sang out and he killed it with a fat finger.

"No. Some political group. I've been wondering about the Nation of Islam or the Black Muslims."

Mahon fingered the folds of his chin. "They're not strong nowadays. At least," he added in deference to whatever superior intelligence might be available to the Company, "at street level. Maybe they disbanded completely after 9/11 when the heat was turned up..."

"On the other hand," Limon said, "we have some reports that they're trying to regroup, cashing in on the whole Jihad bit. Jesus, who knows?" In his frustration Limon decided to level with Mahon. "Maybe Lynskey is in on it himself. He's been acting strange lately..."

Mahon sat bolt upright. "Aw now, I don't know about that..." The theory was too rich for his blood.

"These guys can go right out over the edge. A sudden brainstorm and they sell out completely. I've seen it before. Suppose the woman seen on the steps was a contact or a *femme fatale...*" He realized he was thinking aloud rather than trading information. Besides, there didn't seem much point in developing this theory with Mahon, and he had a meeting with the FBI in half an hour.

Just then his secretary buzzed through.

"There's a Mr. Lynskey here to see you."

"Who did you say?" Limon looked in amazement at Mahon, whose eyebrows shot up.

"Mr. Lynskey."

"Robert Lynskey?" Several possibilities flashed through Limon's head, all of them crazy.

"No, I think he said Gary Lynskey."

"Show him in." Limon shrugged; they'd have to talk to him some time. He didn't reckon on Sarah being with him.

After a brief refresher course of introductions Gary came straight to the point, "We want to help in any way we can." Since Robert had been kidnapped he found it next to impossible to concentrate on his work at the store and had brought forward his retirement. But that might have been a mistake; since it provided him with more time than he could usefully fill, it added to his sense of frustration.

"I can understand that," Limon said, concealing his exasperation. It never ceased to amaze him how well-wishers straight off the street presumed that good intentions were the only qualifications needed to crack a case. "But as I told you when we got your statement, it's best to leave it to us…"

"But what progress have you made?" Sarah asked. "Too much time is passing." She dabbed her eyes with a silk handkerchief which left a lemony scent in the compact room.

"We're working on several angles," Mahon put in unhelpfully.

Gary ignored the hand-off. "Look, why can't you release that mad mullah? Who cares about Jallud Fahd or whatever his name is? My brother is a good citizen. He deserves better. You don't know him like I do..." To his consternation his voice caught in a culvert of his throat, forcing him to stop.

With an inward groan and wondering why his secretary hadn't spared him this, Limon began the firm-but-fair routine. "I really do sympathize, Mr. Lynskey. But it's out of our hands. A decision has been made at the highest level..."

"It's so unfair," Sarah sobbed. "After all he's done for this country."

"Of course, that's why the kidnappers picked him," Mahon said, once again displaying how irrelevant logic could be.

Limon silenced him with a look. "Maybe if the media had kept it under wraps we might have had some room for negotiation. But not now. The Administration has to stand firm. Believe me, I understand what you're going through." The very thought of negotiating with terrorists sent a shiver down his spine. Why couldn't these people see that it was out of the question. They were too closely involved to see the big picture. This was a clear case of the national interest coming way ahead of individual merit.

Recovering his composure Gary said, "I served with CIA guys in the Gulf. I know about covert operations. This thing doesn't have to be handled in the full glare of publicity. You could pretend to go for the hostage exchange, use a goddamn actor for Jallud Fahd. Then at the last minute…"

"Mr. Lynskey, all such options have been considered," Limon answered. "We're in constant touch with Special Operations. Even if something were being planned, you know I couldn't tell you about it."

"Then there is something…?" Gary pressed.

"We do our job." Limon looked away from the earnest eyes, not entirely happy about his handy retreat into subterfuge. No such charade was being contemplated, nor would he recommend anything of the sort.

As if sensing this, Sarah asked aggressively, "How long is all this going to take? What happens if the kidnappers feel he's no longer of use to them?"

"We'll get to him in time," Limon said with as much conviction as he could muster. "Now if you might excuse me, I have another appointment…"

As Sarah dropped Gary off at his hotel she gave vent to her intuitions. "I don't believe Limon. There's no deal being done under the counter. They've hung Robert out to dry."

"They must be trying *something*." Gary was surprised at her cynicism; maybe it was because the CIA had such a poor public image. They had certainly taken a lot of heat for not knowing what bin Laden had been planning.

"Come on, Gary. Why would the Administration take any risk? There's too much at stake. It's completely politicized now." Walking with him up the steps to the hotel entrance, she sensed from his bowed head that he was beginning to question his faith in the system.

At the door he stopped and said, "Then I'm going to see my congressman tomorrow."

"I'll come too." She wasn't sure it would achieve anything but she needed, as he did, to keep occupied.

"You don't have to." He appreciated the offer; she was like family. He remembered the time Sue had brought them all on a tour of Manhattan after which the kids had met their famous Uncle Robert who stood them ice cream in Swenson's parlor and then whisked them off on a helicopter ride over the city.

"I want to," Sarah said.

"And if that fails I'm going to Washington. I have some savings. I can hire a lobbyist if necessary." His face was grim in the sodium street lights. Sarah embraced him briefly as she said good night.

He tightened his grip on the club as he saw the door begin to open. The old dried bark cut his fingers. No more tomorrows; it had to be now. The door creaked on rusty hinges. He waited for the sound of keys dropping in a pocket. The tin dish appeared first followed by large forearms. Bart looked around the cellar blinking. Just before the gaze found him, Robert sprang, brought the club down on his head. Bart staggered but didn't go down. Using two hands Robert hit him again.

With vomit in his throat, he climbed over the prone body and ran up the stairs. His legs were so weak he bounced from one side to the other. Only the walls of the narrow passage kept him upright. The door at the top of the stairs was slightly open. He pushed it further and his heart froze.

There was another man and a woman. He waited till their backs were turned. But, hearing groans from below, couldn't wait for long. He crept across the kitchen floor towards the back door, praying it wouldn't be locked. It wasn't, but he had to raise the latch, a stiff metal one.

The sound of the latch was echoed by a cry. Throwing open the door, Robert started to run. Through rubble at first, then long tangled grass and weeds growing on pocked clay. The sudden light blinded him. He heard his pursuers but didn't dare turn around. His foot caught in a pothole. He fell and scrambled up and ran again, his heart fit to burst, waiting for a bullet in the back. His mouth was wide open gasping for air, screaming for survival. The sky whirling over the hill was massive and overpowering.

He was pole-axed by a savage two-fisted blow

to his back that sent him sprawling forward on his face into a patch of stony scrub. He hardly felt the kicks that went into his side. The earth smelled fresh.

Richard dragged him back over the burnt meadow and, with Anna, manhandled him into the kitchen and down the stairs. He fell the last few steps. Richard picked him up bodily and bundled him into the cellar.

"Don't try that again, motherfucker!" He kicked him again for good measure, dragged him up to a sitting position on the floor and hit him with the back of his hand across the face.

When he left, Robert slumped to the floor, conscious though mercifully without feeling. Vaguely he heard the door being locked, words of abuse receding into the distance. He cursed his stupidity, the pathetic attempt that had been only a gesture after all. He'd seen the enemy, that strange woman. He was done for. He sobbed for a while, waiting to feel the pain flood into all the numb parts of his body. Then, he looked up crookedly at his little patch of sky, and was glad he'd tried to escape. That part of it was out of the way; he could die more easily now.

CHAPTER 15

LYING UNDER A TREE – he wasn't allowed go beyond the copse of maples at the front of the house – Bart looked up through the branches at the milky dawn. He had really screwed up. Richard and Anna had come down hard on him and he deserved it; he wasn't the smartest of men. The leaves were forgiving though, and he noticed how bright they were against the sky; he'd never seen that shade of green before. His head didn't hurt much anymore.

Hearing twigs snap, he turned over on his side to see Khaled approach; he seemed tall and ghostly, the sun at his back thrusting him forward within an aura of yellow. Khaled sat beside him but didn't say anything.

"I'm sorry, man," Bart said. "Really sorry." He seemed to cower against the roots of the tree, the palms of his hands resting in the grass still wet with dew.

"It wasn't your fault," Khaled said. In a way he was intrigued by Lynskey's dash for freedom; he didn't think he had it in him. "How is your head?"

"OK." Bart grinned, relieved that Khaled didn't hold a grudge. "I bin hit worse before." In the worn saddle of a face the whites of his eyes were glazed with mother of pearl, an old fighter without many pay days left. He wondered what 'walking wounded' meant, nothing good the way

Anna spat it out. Raising a heavy arm towards the house, he asked, "Is this all gonna work out OK?" He'd sensed a growing tension but couldn't figure out what it meant. He was sorry Daniel X hadn't come with them; he got on well with him.

"With Allah's help."

Bart nodded several times as if confirming something deeper to himself. "I got religion too."

"I know, Bart. You live by the law."

"I try to." Bart nodded again, took one last look at the sky. "Better go 'n put the coffee on."

"Did you know that Jesus Christ was a Palestinian?" Khaled put the question with a smile.

"No way, man."

"Yes. Bethlehem is in Palestine." He watched how Bart absorbed this information as if it were a precious gift. "Be careful when you bring Lynskey his food."

"He won't catch me again." Bart grinned and rubbed his head.

———

As she dressed in silence, Anna longed for a shower and a change of clothes but she couldn't risk going into Metuchen. She had watched the broadcast the night before and wasn't very impressed, but at least it was a concession which proved that the powers-that-be recognized their existence. She'd also watched Khaled, who was even less forthcoming than usual; he seemed to be slipping deeper inside himself. She still argued that they should kill Lynskey and cut their losses.

She combed her hair roughly, tearing through the tangles, and went out to the kitchen where the others were having coffee and bread. It could have been an ordinary breakfast scene in a log cabin. The point somehow was being lost in this retreat of quiet, slow-moving men used to waiting for the weather to change. She felt that she was losing control by a strange process of attrition. Though she and Richard still slept in the same bed they didn't make love any more and the heat, sordid conditions and proximity of Khaled only provided a partial explanation for the estrangement.

Pouring herself a cup of greasy coffee, she sat down with them and immediately gave vent to her concerns. "I'd like to know where we're going with all this. OK, the tape was something, but it's not what we planned. We seem to be drifting." To disguise its poor condition she had tied her hair in a ponytail which gave her a prompt, preppy look.

"We can't make progress," Khaled said, "unless we persuade Americans to face the truth."

"You can't convert a country with a few tapes. In any case, you could've used social media, instead of all this rigmarole." She looked to Richard for support but he was busy cutting a wedge of cheese. It seemed unreal to her, as if she had wandered with strange bedfellows into a quietly waiting dream.

Khaled wasn't offended. "Social media was

tried several times but we were blocked. 'Objectionable content,' they said." But those sites could also be dangerous, he knew only too well. Postings in the past had revealed enough information to enable the US to mount lethal drone strikes. "Awareness is a good weapon," he added, "however it is achieved." He thought of all the other strategies they had tried, including recourse to the UN. Nothing had worked. And The Hague didn't look promising. The Western establishment was an impenetrable block, incapable of admitting to any injustice. Bush and Blair were war criminals but who would prosecute them? What had Obama done to restore justice? He had effectively started a war against Pakistan using drone aircraft. Trump invited despair. There was no end in sight.

"Awareness," Anna sniffed. It was a million lightyears away. Maybe the peasants in Iran were impressed by Khomeini's tapes but hard-bitten Americans were a totally different proposition. "That's why you chose Lynskey, the media angle. You planned it all along."

"That was one reason, yes."

"What's the Black Muslim movement going to get out of this?" She asked on behalf of Richard, who hardly deigned to look up from the table. "The few that are left could be wiped out over this." She remembered the hostile reaction of Americans to bin Laden's tapes.

"The spread of Islam will help all minorities who seek justice." He looked closely at Anna across the fraught space, gauging his next remark. "It will weaken the Jewish lobby in this country."

Shortly after his own training he'd met a twelve-year-old boy who slept in a hut near the dividing fence on the West Bank; the boy got up at six every morning, loaded his rifle and went out to kill or be killed with the same detachment as a kid going to school. Jamal was his name and he'd known no other life. His parents were dead; all he had in the world were a couple of friends and his rifle, stolen from a dead Christian militiaman. Khaled had gazed at him in much the same way Jallud Fahd must once have observed him twenty-five years earlier. He wondered how he might help the boy but he left it too late. After a dawn raid by the Israeli army Jamal was killed. Khaled saw his body in a crater, lying across an oil drum, the strap of the rifle still twisted round his arm. The open eyes were as expressionless as they were in life. His younger sister, Fatimeh, came to claim the body of her brother. She didn't weep. Nor did she see the bulldozers...

"I doubt it," Anna said. "It will take more than that to break the stranglehold of Zionism." She gave off a bitter sense of an anarchist who begins to see that rhetoric is not enough, and yet remains driven.

She had been using, Richard knew, as he concentrated on the back of his hands. He hoped her supply of smack was running low.

Khaled still saw the eyes of Jamal and the dry eyes of his sister, Fatimeh. They haunted him more than the carnage left behind by suicide bombers.

"I don't think the American public gives a shit about anything," Anna went on. She now saw Khaled as quietly insane, out there somewhere in a desert of sacred certainty, closed to reality though surrounded by it. Again, she had that sense of being out of place, linked by some extraordinary change in fortune, to strange and powerless allies.

Unruffled, Khaled answered, "They will watch and they will listen. The rest is in the hands of Allah."

At the sink Bart nodded.

"What about Jallud Fahd?" Richard asked.

"The tapes will help," Khaled said, leaving the major part of the question hanging.

"Maybe we should demand money as well," Richard said. "As an insurance policy."

"Perhaps later…"

"Later. How much later?" Anna's voice was high and pinched. Provocation was her stock in trade but she could get no change out of this ponderous man. "Every day we spend in this hole increases the risk. They're out there right now beating the bushes. You don't know the kind of manpower and resources they'd put into something like this…"

"I can imagine," Khaled said, thinking of the mighty highways that crossed this land, the kind the Saudis tried so desperately to emulate.

"And it won't take them long to make the

connection with the Black Muslims. This has to be a quick score. That was the deal…"

"She's got a point," Richard said, his fears returning.

"I have to do it this way," Khaled said slowly. "I know it's difficult for you. If you want to leave I understand and thank you for your help so far…"

"No." Bart turned from the wash-up. "We should finish the job."

In his eyes Khaled saw something of the intensity that came with the celebration of the last moment of the last day of Ramadan. Bart's faith was as strong as his own.

With the FBI muscling in to share the spoils – though as usual with little to offer – Limon was in a sour mood. He was desperately looking for the proverbial break in the case but couldn't find it. He was being turned on a slow spit. His Director was breathing down his neck, demanding a written situation report every day and sometimes a breakfast conference as well. The Director had already received a veiled threat from the International Division of the Budget Bureau; no progress, no development funds. The White House was putting pressure on the National Security Council.

For Limon this was the unacceptable face of

the bureaucratic machine. At times of pressure the Company started to panic; memos and sitreps flew as senior people ran for cover in written words and thickets of files. To protect itself from outside attack the organization started to consume its own flesh, starting at the edges, where Limon's flanks were flapping in the breeze.

"Limon here," he barked into the phone.

"I thought you'd like to know," Drew's dry tone gave the impression that the call was a courtesy rather than a duty, "that another tape's arrived. Plus a photo of Lynskey holding today's Times..."

"Don't say anything else," Limon snapped. "I'll be right there." He hung up and shouted through the partition to his aide to get him a car. He left a message for the Director and, as an afterthought, told the aide to let Mahon know.

In the cutting room he studied the photo of Lynskey. "His face is bruised. They must have beaten him." Though it could, he thought, have been staged.

"It looks that way," Drew agreed.

"You're not going to broadcast this tape." From beneath tightened brows his glance of warning was like the pass of a blade.

"Lynskey's life depends on it." Drew pointed to the accompanying note. "They make that very clear."

Limon bridled. "Don't snow me. It's your ratings you're worried about." He snatched the evidence from Drew's hands, in no mood to fence.

Drew ignored the insult, reminding himself that he held the high ground and had already made a copy of the tape. "You're overreacting. This tape is just a rant about Islam, sayings of the Prophet, quotes from the Koran. That kind of thing…"

"Run it," Limon said. "Now."

They sat through it in silence. The theme and commentary were much the same as before though the technique was slightly better. There were the usual shots of Jallud Fahd at prayer, refugee camps and Israeli raids. Much of the footage was new but not all that spectacular, given the carnage from all corners of the world that appeared nightly on TV screens.

"I don't think this is going to undermine the nation's value system," Drew remarked drily.

"You still don't get it, do you?" Limon snorted. "It's fucking Chinese water torture. We can't be seen giving in to these people. The Zionists are flooding down the Mall in Washington. The President himself is taking a pasting in the polls. They're making monkeys of us. Don't you understand? It doesn't matter what's on the tapes. It's the fact of showing them. If you show this one you're stabbing the country through the heart." He stood up, breathing heavily through a tight, crimped mouth.

"Nonsense. We're trying to save the life of an eminent citizen…"

"Bullshit! Lynskey is your meal ticket." The

gloves were off; the inevitable confrontation could no longer be deferred or hedged by innuendo.

"I don't have to take that from you." Drew's eyes bulged in their reddish sockets. "If you must know, I have a replacement in rehearsal for Lynskey right now. What *you* don't understand is that we have free speech in this country…"

"Not in security matters." Limon cut him off. "I've spoken with the Director about this. If needs be," he paused with a dramatist's instinct, "we'll take legal action under the Patriot Act. We can close you down." He stood to his full height, glaring down at the shorter man.

Drew was unrepentant. "Nice try. But we've taken legal advice too. Remember Woodward's book? You couldn't stop that could you? The Justice Department was left twisting in the wind. Official Secrets doesn't wash in a case like this. You know it, so don't try that with me."

"You'd refuse a directive from the Justice Department?" Limon asked.

"Absolutely. They don't have a monopoly on truth."

Limon slowly took a recording device from his pocket. "I thought you might say something like that."

"Hey," Drew set his hands trembling. "I'm really scared now. Jesus, you've got me for treason. Wow." He was excited rather than scared; the tipping point was at hand, the boulder beginning to gather momentum. No one could predict how much damage it would do before it came to rest, if it ever did.

"You should be scared..."

"Here, let me put my head in the noose." Drew lent forward and said into the tiny recorder, "Limon, the reason you can't crack this case is because you're a fucking grade A asshole."

He carried that defiance with him into the KNYBS boardroom with the chief executives and company lawyers, and four hours later, his face still mottled with liver spots, emerged triumphant.

The tape went out at prime time. The response from the public was more voluminous and strident than before. There were death threats to the producer, Zionists screamed blue murder. The President of the World Jewish Congress wrote to the Justice Department more in sorrow than in anger. The Wiesenthal Center called the State Department. One viewer from Daytona said Lynskey was 'a rich smartass who talked down to people for years and deserved everything he got'. The agents resident in KNYBS relayed some of the messages to Limon who wondered, not for the first time, who was to be protected from whom. He might even have had some sympathy for Lynskey were it not for his abiding suspicion that the great man might not be such a victim as appeared at first glance.

The papers had a field day, editorializing from the safety of their city desks about the new reign of 'terrorvision', the return of the living-room revolution, mad mullahs and media moguls.

Time magazine, the cover of which Lynskey had made twice, carried a picture of him taken when he addressed the New York Film Society, with the caption: 'Victim of Sacred Rage'. *Newsweek*'s back-page was an encomium on Lynskey, a former colleague and mentor of the columnist who nevertheless took KNYBS to task for prostituting the air waves. In general Limon was proved right: it wasn't so much about what was in the tapes, rather the fact that they were shown. That action shamed America, which still hadn't recovered fully from the trauma of the Twin Towers.

In order to meet demands of a different sort, the White House held a special press conference. The President again ruled out any question of a hostage exchange and, for security reasons, refused to be drawn on the progress of the investigation, except to say that everything possible was being done, all the resources of law enforcement and security agencies were being deployed.

"What about the tapes?" several reporters asked.

"The matter is being reviewed…"

"Mr. President, what exactly does that mean?"

"Well, Jim, we're looking at the situation."

"Are you influenced by the fact that Lynskey

is part of the establishment?"

"Now, Bob, you know that's not true. We're being objective. Yes, Celia, have you got a question?"

"Mr. President, how does all this stack up with your policy of conciliation with the Middle East?"

"We deal with moderates, but not terrorists. I repeat, however, how important it is for America to protect its borders and keep out these crazy foreigners. Does that answer your question?"

"Mr. President, are you not reaping the whirlwind for the mess in Iraq and Syria, more importantly, for not condemning the Israeli policy of assassinating Palestinian leaders?"

"The answer is 'no', the President said coldly. "Now, ladies and gentlemen, if you'll excuse me? The Chief of Staff will deal with any other questions…" Before the President left the podium he had completed his 'review': there would be no more tapes. He knew some of the guys over at KNYBS.

CHAPTER 16

THERE ARE SASSAFRAS as well as maples at the foot of the hill. The field in the foreground has not been cultivated for years and is overrun with wild alfalfa, toadflax, goldenrod and what he thinks are black-eyed susans. Standing on the box he wishes he knew more about nature. In the jumble of birdsong he can detect woodchucks and grackles. Once he saw a cardinal break cover like a spurt of blood and fly across his narrow field of vision. At night he sometimes hears the cry of whippoorwills and sees fireflies dancing among the stars.

His cuts and bruises have just about healed though his ribs are still sore. He's glad he got that pathetic escape attempt over with; it proved something that he doesn't have to prove again. Though he's run out of beta-blockers, his heartbeat is regular. Indeed, he's so calm he wonders if they might be putting something in his food. Anyway, he's grateful for small mercies.

He regretted that he couldn't identify the stars; but it hardly mattered, they were beautiful anyway without names. He thought of his nephew, John, whose planetary innocence made his heart soar.

When he gave up serving mass he couldn't cope with Sundays any more. In that small, barnacled town he felt deserted, unconstituted. And in those bleached and lonely hours, mortality came too close and the sun sought him out for mockery. Where was everyone? He peered through windows for signs of life, fossils of remembered things. It was that shattering loneliness that drove him finally to seek the reassuring roar of the crowd.

He never conquered that lost feeling even in his thirties when his interest in the theater brought him into the company of actors and other colorful egomaniacs, hectic with the flush of footlights. But even then he would walk by *Sardis* with that same empty Sunday feeling, and envy the glow inside.

Here in this cellar he was at last on the inside, the innermost Chinese box. The kernel, outside of which everything was as light and trivial as thistledown. Whether they searched for him or not was no longer of major significance.

His life now was narrowly defined and it amazed him how little he resented being deprived of freedom; he valued his few props, the radio, lamp, watch and ballpoint, the latter kept in reserve. Though for what he was not entirely sure. More organized now, more in tune with the particulars of his cellar, he cultivated constipation and dug a hole for urine. He cleaned his teeth and nails with splinters of wood from the log box; a wooden flour scoop served as a flesh-scraper. These were his Beckett things. And he would go on … for as long as he was let.

He met his captors fleetingly. They didn't seem so menacing even though they would kill him in time, probably as a 'statement'. Unlike the coward he would die only once.

As the light began to fail and the window took on a pewter sheen, he dragged the log box over to the bed and put the lamp on it. Then he took a cardboard box that once probably contained eggs, and began to tear it carefully along its natural folds, from one corner to another. For two days now he shifted the carton around the floor of the cellar, keeping it in the narrow beam of sunlight coming from the window. It was now almost dry. He worked carefully and steadily until he tore it into eight planes of cardboard – the lid he discarded because it was too badly torn and soiled. He folded each of the eight sheets along two evenly spaced lines. Then he placed the entire stack under the log box to press and sharpen the folds.

Despite sore ribs he did some stretching exercises, hanging from one of the lower beams. Yesterday this particular exercise threw a scare into his jailor who burst in, as if to cut him down. He didn't read anything into that gesture to save him; it was a reflex action, nothing more. Today he attempted a few semi chin-ups. He would be the fittest corpse in the cemetery.

He urinated and cleaned his teeth with the devotion of a cat licking its face. Cleanliness never seemed so important before; it had become a rite of startling directness. He lay on the bed, hands under his head and looked up at the old brown rafters, trailing streamers and spores of dust. There was some kind of acceptance growing in him, more profound than he could ever have imagined. These days were precious, without distractions, or the incessant drive to be productive, or the seductive crush of the press and daily fix of recognition. Even more precious because he was sure they would kill him after his abortive escape. Every day now is a bonus. It has taken all of this to pin him to the moment and stop him running from himself. Was it conceivable that freedom was overrated? At any rate his mind had found some degree of acceptance.

The cardboard might be ready tomorrow. He slept easily.

———————————

Because of the agents crawling all over his office, Drew was in a bad mood. When the next tape arrived, as he knew it would, he was summoned to the boardroom again. It was clear that the top brass who confronted him across the polished table were uneasy, and the lawyers dithered more than before. After much agonizing they finally compromised: Keep the tape under wraps for a while and see what might happen, hasten slowly. With his bile rising, Drew reminded these men, whom he envied but didn't respect, that the kidnappers demanded it be shown that evening. But the decision stood: Wait and see.

As Drew left the penthouse suite he knew that pressure had been applied or a marker called in.

Or both. Maybe the White House had made a call.

"Maybe it's a reasonable compromise," Chaim said later, swaying his head judiciously. But he was torn. He wanted Lynskey back in one piece yet something in him rebelled against the forced propaganda, the reinvention, as he saw it, of history.

Drew jerked his thumb upwards. "The fix is in if you ask me. Well, I wouldn't like to be in Lynskey's shoes right now." He was still burning from the session in the boardroom.

"No." Chaim nodded sadly. He had seen the photo and the bruised face. More than that, the haunted look that replaced Robert's normal alertness, dredged up in him a sense of barely remembered fear. For relief he looked out the window at the building across the street. At this height the skyscrapers were on nodding terms, sharing a lofty informality. He remembered hill-walking last summer with Christopher in Virginia. The higher they went the more people saluted them and the friendlier they seemed; it was something Chaim couldn't explain. He and Christopher had laughed about it and tried to analyze it in psychological terms. In the building opposite he could see people sitting in a room. It had taken him two years to figure out that it was a theatrical agency. He regretted he couldn't see into the inner sanctum where, no doubt, the hopefuls were displaying their vaudevillian wares. At that moment a man in the waiting room waved to him. Chaim smiled back though he knew that small acknowledgment wouldn't carry across the street.

From under his rust-colored brows Drew watched him, noting how curved he was in every respect, movements, words from a bow mouth, curly hair, round glasses – as curved and gentle as a womb, and probably spineless. A cherubic blob of dough. The passive partner without any doubt.

"By the way, what do you make of Rembert?" Drew challenged him.

"I saw him in rehearsal. He's OK, I guess." Chaim shrugged to indicate that he had been given no say in the matter.

"As good as Lynskey, would you say?"

"Well, he's different." Chaim hesitated, then declared flatly, "No, he's not as good. There's no comparison." He noticed that the hopeful actor across the street had disappeared from the waiting room; he was probably doing his audition as if his life depended on it.

"I see." Drew was surprised by the clear statement. Lines were being drawn on all sides and he preferred it that way. It was good to know where everyone stood as the boulder began to roll down the mountain. He thought of Sarah. It was hard to make his move while Lynskey was in danger; it would make him seem heartless. The situation would have to be resolved one way or another. Drew could not wait indefinitely.

Nothing!" Anna got quickly to her feet and switched off the monochrome TV. "No broadcast ... Where does that leave us now?"

"It doesn't figure," Richard said, sweating through his T-shirt. It was a warm clammy night, the sky heavy with low, threatening clouds. "Maybe the pressure is too much. The President has gone down in the polls. Maybe we've achieved something after all..." He looked to Khaled for confirmation.

"You're missing the point," Anna said curtly. "There's no mileage in these tapes anyway." This was aimed in Khaled's direction. "Time is passing. I saw a helicopter today. They could be closing in for all we know. We should kill him and get the hell out of here."

"Or go for the money," Richard put in hopefully. "Look, they're not going to release Jallud Fahd. It's all politics, man. But they could pay a ransom in secret."

"Jesus Christ, it's not a game show," Anna retorted. "I say we abort now while we have the chance. Go for some other target. Or finish the whole damn thing." There was merit in cutting bait. Al Qaeda actions had thrown the whole country behind the Jews who, in her view, had far too much American support to start with. Maybe her decision to throw in with the Arabs was counterproductive.

Khaled didn't just refuse to be drawn; he excused himself and left the room, allowing Anna free rein.

"He's flipped with these fucking tapes," she said. "I just don't get it." She paced angrily, stepping back from the window as lightening flashed.

"Maybe he knows what he's doing," Richard muttered with less conviction than usual. He had registered her remark about the helicopter.

"You bet." Bart smiled.

Anna gave them both a killing look. "You really believe in that … fakir? He's on another planet." She chafed her hands and wrists, a sure sign of withdrawal.

"He's seen more real action than we have," Richard pointed out in extenuation. The rain came suddenly, a cloudburst that quickly found the weak spots in the old house.

"So?"

"He believes in what he's doing."

"Meaning I don't?" Her mouth was pursed and dry as she rounded on him.

Richard kept his own counsel for a while, struck by her reaction. "I didn't say that," He backed away from the confrontation she so keenly sought.

"He's got guts," Bart chipped in, out of synch, as he placed a bucket in a corner to catch a heavy drip from the ceiling.

"What's he achieved?" Anna demanded. "Nothing. It's all stupid symbolic stuff with him. Snatching Lynskey in the financial district, for Christ's sake. Who gives a shit about capitalism? I can't stand wasted effort. There should be something to show. Now."

"Maybe he's looking to the future," Bart said with unexpected clarity. She glanced at him as if he were mad as well as simple.

That morning she'd heard on the radio that a colleague of her grandfather's, who had been expelled from Bolivia, had just been brought to trial in France. He was ninety-four. Would Bush and Blair ever be made pay for their war crimes? On that at least she could agree with Khaled.

———————

Drew covered the mouthpiece with his hand and gestured furiously to Limon who picked up the extension.

"Why did you not broadcast the tape?" Khaled's voice was low and muffled.

"Who ... is this...?" Drew fought for time as he had been coached.

"Answer. You have two minutes."

"We had difficult ... scheduling problems..." The disembodied voice had scared him in a way he never expected and it undermined his attempt to stall. By some strange transference he had suddenly become the abused victim.

"Tonight. And no editing. Or you will have the blood of an innocent man on your hands."

"There are ... technical problems," Drew blustered. "We can't just ... Give us more time..."

"Tonight, or Lynskey dies." The phone went dead.

"Shit" Limon crossed the room in two strides. "Why didn't you keep him talking?"

"He knows what he's doing." Drew sat down weakly, gripped by a presence that until now had only been imagined. For the first time he had a full realization of the danger that surrounded Lynskey. He was in the hands of terrorists, possibly even al Qaeda.

Limon conferred with his assistants. They hadn't been able to trace the call but they had a good recording which he wanted analyzed immediately. The voice was definitely that of an Arab but it held an intriguing American undertone which might help narrow the field. But he wasn't that hopeful. He had, however, been pushing out on three other fronts. One involved Jallud Fahd, who was still being interrogated, another the Black Muslims. The third was the one which dogged him, the MICE theory of treason: Money, Ideology, Compromise, Ego. He was inclined to dismiss M and C. Lynskey had more money than he could shake a stick at. Having his pick of women, it was unlikely he would fall for the honey-pot ploy. That left ideology and ego, both, to his mind, distinct possibilities.

"You heard the man," Drew said. "We have to go with it tonight." He felt fairly confident that the top executives would now back him. They would have no choice.

Limon dragged his thoughts back to the matter in hand. "No broadcast. It's out of the question. We'll take legal action if we have to…"

"Not the Patriot Act again," Drew said. "Go ahead. It'll take five years. Then we'll appeal. Another five years. Then you'll probably lose. But even if you win you lose because we'll all be dead at that stage anyway. And," he added in a moment of clarity, "no one will have been promoted in the meantime." He stood quivering in his own force-field, inviting, almost pleading for opposition.

Limon pointed an accusing finger, began to say something but stopped. They'd been over the ground before and the time for threats was past. Anyway, he felt for the first time that a break might not be far away.

Another top-level conference followed in which Drew excelled himself in conveying the menace of the phone call. They were now dealing with an immediate life-or-death issue. An hour later, reeking of cigar smoke, he emerged from the board room with the decision he wanted.

Later, he had an exultant drink with Chaim in the bar across the street. Even in the semi darkness his face glowed as if he'd just breasted the tape ahead of a choice field.

"When it gets right down to the wire, they're not so tough," he gloated.

"How did you persuade them?" Chaim asked, perched on a barstool with his legs crossed.

"The old ploy." Drew grinned. "Made them responsible. Described that godawful voice on the phone. I told them that Lynskey's life was in their hands. I asked them to consider what they would say when asked by the media why they'd jeopardized his life. They clutched like a bunch of old women." His own moment of fear had passed and he was back to his old vicarious ways, pulling the strings in the safety of the booth. But something was let loose in him and he was already starting his second martini. He drank only when he was already high.

"What I don't understand," Chaim said, "is what the terrorists hope to get out of this. It's like a confession made under duress. Everyone knows it's just propaganda. They must be lunatics."

"Is it just propaganda?"

"Sure. What else?"

"I wonder." Drew popped an olive into his mouth and idly stirred his fresh drink. He seemed more interested in the event, the logistics, rather than the reasons. It didn't matter what started the avalanche as long as it was cataclysmic. But who would jump clear and who would be caught?

Chaim left early, having promised to take Christopher to dinner to broach the subject of a new contract. He had his own compromise worked out, a six-month extension of their partnership at least. He hoped against hope that Christopher would go along with that. If he did Chaim would propose marriage.

Drew had a few more drinks and then an idea. Armed with a bottle of champagne he turned up on Sarah's doorstep.

———————————

Sarah had been expecting Gary. She was dressed in a sand-colored jumpsuit with brown accessories that suited her eyes and tan.

He followed her into the lounge, his eyes moving up and down her slender back with the action of a razor being stropped.

"May I say you're looking especially radiant," he slurred slightly.

"Gary's gone to Washington." She resisted the blandishment, waved him vaguely into the brightly decorated room and switched off the stereo as if reluctant to share with him her personal taste in music.

"Wasted effort, I'm afraid. What can one individual do?" He stood swaying on the carpet, the tissue-wrapped magnum nestling against his stomach.

She shrugged. He might at least have phoned ahead rather than assume she had nothing better to do with her evenings.

He lowered himself gingerly into a modern chair and stretched out his legs with a sigh. He was glad of the few drinks. They made him more of a match for her; at least she didn't seem so intimidating.

She sat opposite him, leaning back in that superior, appraising way some women have. "Why do I get the impression you're getting a buzz out of Robert's misfortune?"

"Oh, come now, Sarah ... We all have to cope the best we can." A slack grin sidled over his face. He could see that she wasn't exactly ready to throw herself on the funeral pyre. He eased the cork out of the champagne bottle, grimacing in anticipation of the pop which never came.

They watched the broadcast together. Again it was introduced by the President of KNYBS who said with intense sincerity, "I want to make it clear that showing this program goes against the policy of the United States Government, a policy which has again been clearly enunciated by the President as recently as yesterday. We regret this action but believe this network has a specific responsibility to Robert Lynskey..."

Drew struggled upright. "Oh, the clever bastard. He's trying to save the President's ass. And his own." He had, however, a sneaking admiration for the stratagem. They'd probably spent hours on the statement.

During the broadcast Drew kept up a running commentary of his own, not particularly interested in the, by now, familiar heavy-handed proselytizing. Sarah shushed him periodically and he took advantage of those intermissions to re-charge the glasses. He drank steadily, sneaking an odd glance at her neat profile as she craned forward towards the screen.

"It's much the same as the other two," she said afterwards. "Do they really think this somehow going to get Jallud Fahd out of jail?

They're probably water-boarding him as we speak."

"They're not playing with a full deck. But I suppose as long as we humor them…"

"Poor Robert. In the hands of those maniacs … It doesn't bear thinking about." She closed her eyes and looked forlorn.

"Well, he's made it thus far," Drew said lightly. He went on to describe the photo that had arrived but omitted to mention the bruises. "Don't worry." He sat beside her on the pretext of offering comfort but within seconds was kissing her ardently, pushing her back on the sofa.

"Come on, honey … We're an item … You know what you mean to me." He clutched her stiffening body, trying to make it compliant.

She resisted, delicately at first, and then with surprising strength.

"Not now! How can you be so insensitive?" The memory of James H. Henfy's feverish overtures were also fresh in her mind.

"At a time like this." He sadly mocked the cliché but didn't yet succumb to it. His tongue tried to probe her mouth but met with a portcullis of enamel. "I need you."

On that plaintive note she wriggled free and stood up, smoothing her virtuous clothing. Men were indeed brutes but in a way she was glad of their weaknesses.

"I'm keeping him alive," he said valiantly, prodding his chest. "Me." He pointed at the screen. "I persuaded them to show the damn tape.

I'm giving him a blood transfusion ... a lifeline..." His voice tailed away and he slumped deeper into the cushions, a warrior exhausted if not quite bleeding.

He passed out a little later and she let him sleep on the sofa. Before switching off the light she looked at her crumpled visitor and smiled despite herself.

CHAPTER 17

HE WOKE EARLY and for a while lay on the straw mattress, delicately probing his mood as one might touch a newly formed scab; to his amazement he still felt all right. Getting to his feet, he lifted the log box and removed the stack of cardboard from beneath it. It wasn't quite ready yet, so he reversed the folds and replaced it under the box. That simple action, carried out with minute precision and care, gave him a sense of satisfaction.

Still in his underpants, he did some stretching exercises and running on the spot, careful to end the routine before the perspiration came. As he pulled on his pants he noticed how loose they felt; he could insert a closed fist inside the waistband. He'd probably lost up to twenty pounds in the nine days ... or was it ten? His beard felt full; it probably eclipsed his birthmark and, judging by the moustache he could just make out by pursing his lips, it was almost white.

Strange, that among the gamut of feelings he'd run since being taken hostage, anger had not yet appeared. Had he always been waiting for this leveling, for the second shoe to fall? Maybe there was something sadly apt about being stuck in this stinking place which exposed the sham of his stylish life. What had he really contributed anyway, apart from the occasional smart aphorism, a tepid plea for radicals to use common sense and – to preserve his image – a rather sardonic way of looking at the world? Not exactly a major breakthrough. He took the easy way out; instead of discovering a star, he became one.

But in the process he lost the ability that came so easily to Gary, to hang out with friends on a wooden porch to watch the sun go down. Had it been a conscious choice or did it just happen that way? There was so much he didn't know – and would never know because his time on the planet was rapidly running out.

The first friendship he could recall – before he went on that long solo trek towards a hopeless goal – was Spider Hastings, a weird and wandering soul, always in trouble at home and at school, laughed at because his father was a bin man and part-time drunk. But Robert and Spider got on well in that unquestioning way of twelve-year-olds. They wandered together across fields and drumlins under the pagan shadow of Ben Bulben. And Spider would beat the hedges with his stick, drink from streams, and sometimes yank a turnip from a field, impale it on his stick and eat it raw. He would shout and sing in gibberish as he strode the land with what seemed to be great purpose though there was never any.

Robert's mother worried about the friendship and tried to discourage it.

"He's a wild thing," she would say, "without a seat to his trousers. And who can understand that mad talk? Is it tongues or what?"

Once, venturing into a wood owned by mad

Colonel Fingleton, they knew they were trespassing but it lent excitement to the escapade. Daring each other, they emerged from the cover of the wood and approached the Palladian mansion in which, according to Spider, there were nude statues well worth seeing. As they circled a lawn at the back of the great house a shot rang out followed by a blitz of frightened crows, and saw to their horror the mad Colonel with a shotgun running towards them. Spider took off at speed with Robert hard on his heels. Another shot rang out. They had no way of knowing the Colonel was firing into the air. With the edge of the wood in sight they unfortunately ran into the arms of two estate workers.

"What're you two up to?" Fingleton bellowed at them. "Trying to get into the orchard, eh?" He grabbed Spider by the lapels of his threadbare coat and lifted him clean off his feet.

"No, sir. Just playing."

"Trespassing you mean." Fingleton took Spider's stick and broke it under his heel. The estate workers laughed and nudged each other.

"Gariantagh vamut amashin pershatonishaaa sucucrataighaieee…" Spider broke into his startled song, spittle forming at the corners of his mouth.

"What the facq…" Fingleton took one step back and looked to his steward for an explanation that didn't come. He smacked Spider across the face.

"You mad fucker!" Spider suddenly switched

to the vernacular, his forehead white as chalk, kicking the legs of the steward who held him from behind. "Don't lay yer filthy paw on me."

Fingleton struck him again, this time with the back of his hand, and split his lip. Robert waited in trepidation for his turn, determined not to cry out or struggle in any way. But Spider broke free and bolted for the wood. The diversion gave Robert his chance and he followed at full tilt. They kept running long after their pursuers gave up, and didn't stop until they'd leapt a stream and vaulted a stone wall to the main road.

"I'll get that fuckin' planter," Spider sniffled, a thread of blood on his chin, mucus coursing down his throat. There was more involved than shame; a deadly seed had been sown for the future.

Robert, on the other hand, just counted his blessings. Fingleton was mad of course but in general he had nothing against the gentry. In a way he admired their style as they came tweedily into town on Saturdays in their mud-spattered jeeps to buy provisions from the merchants who fell over backwards to give them credit.

Some years after that adventure their paths diverged. Robert got a scholarship – and the permission of the Bishop – to attend that 'Godless' college in Dublin. Spider joined the army and went to the Curragh for basic training. He obviously joined the IRA after that because Robert read about his death by hunger strike decades later.

In his first years in New York Robert lived in a room on Columbus Avenue. It was his study really because he spent most of his time with a young divorcee called Dorothy who had a good-sized apartment across the hall. He baby-sat her three-year-old kid while she was out working during the day. Dorothy and he were close and comfortable together and it was his first real affair. Because of his background he was a little shocked at how soon she went to bed with him – on the second date – to be precise, but he soon realized how innocent and direct a woman's desires could be. She was honest and up-front about everything. After their first encounter in the bedroom he made to leave her bed and pad back to his own room, shoes in hand, to mull over the dramatic thing that had just happened.

"Where are you going?" She sat up startled. And that was his second lesson; intimacy went beyond the act; more was required than just doing it. But it took him weeks to learn how to fall asleep holding her as she wanted to be held.

"It's all a myth," she once said, looking at herself in a mirror.

"What is?"

"That the female form is beautiful." Sadly she cupped her breasts and gazed at them forlornly. "Tits are stupid and bovine."

"You're mad."

She went on to tell him why many women suffered from low self-esteem. When they were young they noticed that their brothers had that extra little bit which was quite handy. Later on there was a compensation of sorts when the breasts began to form. But then the hips expanded, awful, shocking hair appeared and then, to cap it all, the bloody curse came along. She made it sound like some sort of existential dilemma which entrapped half of humankind. Although he couldn't agree with her, he liked the frank way she spoke.

Fortunately, she wasn't so modest or ashamed when it came to the point. She liked sixty-niners in the big old claw-legged tub with the shower running; she would take him in her mouth while she settled herself over him, her fine pink derriere with small puckered eye looming over him in such abandon that all his fantasies were gloriously realized. He'd never before experienced such a dimension of nakedness or honesty of the body.

It had to be the New World, a world that offered so much sweetness without any aftertaste. His old European genes grooved to this freedom but still hankered for a modicum of expiation, that exquisite narrow shaft that quaked through the Lutheran bowels. Dorothy was a good cook too and there was in addition a virtual city-wide room service that provided an amazing range of ethnic take-aways delivered in minutes at any time of the day or night. There was no appetite uncatered for. Towards the end of his first year in Columbus Avenue, Robert developed the first signs of a paunch which was all wrong for a struggling young writer.

In a way Dorothy and he were marking time, waiting for their respective ships to come in. They were both young enough to believe in unique super passion. If in the meantime they used each other it was at least mutual and enjoyable; they were like a couple of sophomores who studied together, compared notes, played to each other's strengths.

Her ship was the first to arrive, in the form of a wide-shouldered sax player with neon lights in his eyes and a promise of marriage. Robert was not exactly broken-hearted but it was a wrench to be evicted from his comfortable berth and yield his place in Dorothy's bed to another man.

"I'm sorry Robert," Dorothy said at the moment of parting. "He really likes me."

"So do I."

"In your own way I guess." She kissed him lightly. "But he wants me. We have a future together."

Even his usurper was kind, "No hard feelings, Bob," he said as Robert collected his few belongings in a shoe-box and retreated across the hall to spray his musk on his own four walls and wait like everyone else to become somebody in that proving ground called The Big Apple...

It seemed to him now as he moved around the cellar that he hadn't been fair to Dorothy or to any of the other women in his life, that he may have given little because for some reason he expected less. He had always pulled the Christmas cracker so that the trinket fell out his end. He was calculating and cold back then, maybe still. He regretted it. In these, his final hours, there was no possibility of redemption. Again, the contrast with his brother, Gary, came to mind.

What was the point of these senile reflections? Where was the unity which he desperately wanted to glimpse before it all went black? Maybe he wasn't entitled to such grace.

The door went through its ratchets of sound and opened slowly to reveal, not Bart, but Khaled who entered almost diffidently as if he were gate-crashing. Without knowing why, Robert saw immediately that he was the leader of the group.

"Are you being treated all right?" he asked, standing between Robert and the door as if waiting for an invitation to sit.

Robert couldn't help laughing. He was princely and the situation priceless. Gallows humor was the best kind.

"Does it matter? You're going to have to kill me."

Khaled ignored that. "You know why you were chosen?"

"Chosen? Chosen...?" Robert gasped for air. He thought of Moses wandering around Egypt with the chosen people before they settled in the land of Canaan. Maybe if he'd let them carry on worshipping the golden calf there would have been less conflict in history. "A hostage exchange and something about tapes. I've been listening to the radio." His eyes scanned the dark face for clues. The intensity he saw there was not reassuring. This could be the moment of his death. He wasn't as ready as he thought he was.

"Do you think the tapes will have an impact?"

"You're asking me?" Robert felt light-headed. Having come to accept captivity this was pushing perverseness to the limit, and it threatened his hard-won equipoise.

"You're a communicator. You must have an opinion." Khaled sat on the box adding welcome pressure to the cardboard underneath.

Was this real? Should he offer his visitor a drink and some canapés? Should he apologize for the ambient stench of urine? "I normally charge a consulting fee."

"There's so much disinformation. It's important to put the case correctly..."

"It's not that easy to bat the breeze with someone who's going to kill you." There, he'd said it, and in a fairly steady voice. He might even have enjoyed the irony were it not for the scary sense that Khaled seemed close to the edge. Robert's partial sense of resignation now bothered him because it meant he had no fight left; he had given in. Christ, he should really fight to the end, the bitter end.

"You'd kill me if the situation were reversed," Khaled said evenly. He looked away, apparently not too fond of eye contact.

"No, I would not. I wouldn't have kidnapped you in the first place."

There was something too calm about him, Robert thought with a tremor of alarm which suggested that he just might have some residual instinct for survival left in him. Eddies of fear nudged him towards a proposal. "I'd prefer to offer you money," he said, the words tailing away into a pimp's undertone.

Khaled smiled bitterly. "Money speaks in a language all nations understand."

"How much?" Was it possible that it was this easy, that this was the solution all along? The bottom line. He thought of Simkin's theory of money, buying claims on people, buying freedom from claims.

"You misunderstand. You're more use to us this way."

"Just to get your tapes broadcast?" Robert couldn't conceal his disappointment, though the offer of money had never been more than a long shot. "And when I'm dead the ratings go up, is that it?" It was like asking a doctor how far the cancer had spread; he would hang on every syllable and inflection of the reply. Would it be a bullet to the head or heart, he wondered. The head would be better if it were true that his heart had been moribund for years. Would he like it to be with or without warning? With, he answered himself immediately though he didn't know why. He hoped it wouldn't be a knife; stabbing would be bad enough but he couldn't stand the thought of his throat being cut.

"Abraham was willing to sacrifice Isaac." Khaled traced a pattern in the dirt with the toe of his foot. "I know we're regarded as fanatics in the West. That is part of the propaganda."

Robert knew the theory of building a relationship with one's captor to find the chinks, but this man's conviction was complete, unswayable; it put him beyond guilt, maybe even feeling. Of course he was a fanatic; he just couldn't see it. Having nothing to lose Robert took a flier, "The Koran is open to interpretation."

"No!" Khaled took this badly. "The Word is the Word." He remembered his two years in the States, the selfish rootlessness of Americans who had no code or point of reference. Individual conscience was no substitute for rules. "The fact that *you* hold these views shows how powerful the propaganda really is."

Robert couldn't let this pass, especially the suggestion that he couldn't think for himself. "You're using power over me, extreme power."

"No. You are being given an opportunity. Those who die on the Jihad will gain a place in Paradise."

Oh god, Robert thought, he means it, in his frightening warped sincerity. He restrained himself with an effort and said, "It's not my fight."

"Injustice is everyone's fight. The bell tolls..."

Sitting on the edge of the foul-smelling bed,

Robert suddenly felt the anger that had been strangely missing. This righteous pap sickened him to the core.

"And you decide who to enslave, who to kill? Where the hell do you get that right?" He held the edge of the bed to stop himself trembling.

"Divine revelation," Khaled said without a moment's hesitation, without even noticing Robert's anger that somehow seemed wasted and inconsequential. "I'm ready to die for my beliefs. Are you?"

"Yes!" Robert yelled though he hadn't had time to think about it. He was no Socrates or Spider Hastings; martyrdom was overrated. "For *my* beliefs, not yours. Mine!" He stabbed his chest with a finger, revulsion rising up in him.

"There is only one truth."

"Revealed to you alone, I suppose. That's bullshit and you know it ... Wiser men than you have tried ... What about Hitler, his revealed truth, his 'struggle'..." He was becoming incoherent, swamped by nausea as once, when a cub reporter, he'd seen a woman's body dragged from the East river, the nail polish still intact on the putrefying fingers. He covered his mouth with a shaking hand. There was more he wanted to say but Khaled had another shock in store.

"I took some of your classes in Columbia in the late eighties."

"Wha...at?" Robert's mouth hung open. Suddenly, despite all the odds, an image heaved itself up from the past, a lonely, bearded figure

who sat sullenly, never participating. "My god …
you sat at the back of the Physics Theater … near
the door…?"

Khaled smiled. A renewal of friendship with a
teacher he would kill. "In those days you spoke of
Sartre, 'Violence creates the self', 'I rebel,
therefore *we* exist.'"

"Not with approbation … you're being
selective…" Robert was more confused than ever.
Was this part of the reason he had been 'chosen'?
Was it possible that in dishing out the fast food
for thought all those years ago he had actually
helped create this monster? Everyone was a
radical back then. He, the king of irony, couldn't
take any more. The thought of other weirdos using
his lectures to bring grist to their haunted mills
unnerved him. Anger abated just enough to ease
the pain in his chest. He glanced at the door that
Khaled had left unlocked; this was the only real
debate; to try again or not. A failed teacher fleeing
in disarray, to be kicked again and ridiculed. No.

"Existentialism is a very poor philosophy,"
Khaled said, "because it assumes that God is
dead. People cannot live without God."

Robert wondered whether he should argue the
point, when Anna entered and said that she
wanted to speak with Khaled.

"Don't mind me," Robert said as lightly as he
could, trying to restore his countenance. "Pull up
a box and join the party."

"Shut your mouth." She didn't even look at
him.

"We were discussing the humanities," he went on, hating her on sight, using his almost lost drollery like a poisoned quill to deaden her effect. "Perhaps you'd like to take part. Maybe you're a former student too. We could have a seminar." He might as well rile her. He was dead meat anyway. She was pure gangrene. He knew it was she, in disguise, who had injected him on the steps of Simkin and Heller.

"There's nothing an asshole like you can tell me."

He mused on her viperish mouth and was compelled to push her further as if his death depended on it. "How did a nice girl like you get mixed up with Mullahs and Black Muslims?"

Her sudden glance towards Khaled told him he was right on the money. She tried to ignore him but with difficulty. After Khaled's sinister quietness he wanted a reaction. He now felt sure that she would be the one to pull the trigger or wield the knife and he wanted to make his stand, wanted to make her realize that it would take more than a mechanical act to end his life.

"Maybe," he continued, "you're a rich kid who likes to play with the rough set. It's a cliché of course..." And then he had a sudden spark that came from nowhere. "War criminals deserved the death penalty..." He didn't duck in time. Her scratching blow caught him full on the face. Only his beard prevented her nails from breaking the skin.

"Shut the fuck up." As she reached the door

she turned back. "You leave here in a box. Think about it." Khaled followed her out and bolted the door behind him.

Though he'd seen the enemy and stood up to them reasonably well, Robert was sodden with dismay because all he could really do was make pointless gestures. Saving small shreds of pride was hardly worth the candle. When the offbeat rhythms of his chest subsided he began to rearrange his quarters, fumbling for a while like an old man with fading sight. He checked the cardboard. Tomorrow, first thing tomorrow, if there was to be one. There was an early moon of woven air outside the window; it cast the palest light he'd ever seen, a purifying breath that washed over the pen he took from his pocket and held like a weapon.

CHAPTER 18

THEY STAYED IN ADJOINING rooms in the Washington Hilton and met for breakfast to plan the day's activities. Gary had already been to the State Department and the Department of Justice and was reading as much hope as he dared into the kindness shown, the expressions of sympathy and encouragement. But Sarah, as she topped her egg in the lavish dining room, was more cynical. As far as she was concerned Gary was being palmed off by minor functionaries well versed in diplomacy.

She had accompanied him when he went to see Congressman Wilkinson, Chairman of the Committee on the Control of Terrorism. He was a charming man who promised the earth and probably even meant it at the time. She was struck by Gary's credulity – it was hard to see him as Robert's brother – but was reluctant to deprive him of his hope. So she did the rounds with him as one might lead a blind man around an art gallery, trying to describe paintings that had no appeal.

Her cynicism went deeper on reading the previous day's *Post*, which reported on the activities of the National Security Council to the effect that Robert Lynskey would not himself wish to compromise the policy of the nation towards terrorism. It was disingenuous and patronizing. Even Gary, who normally believed in his country right or wrong, felt let down.

"I think the President is involved in dishing this stuff out to the press," she said. "It sounds like him, the phony rhetoric." Robert would be a small price to pay for protecting the presidential image. It took her a while to get used to the thought of Robert, with all his clout, as a scapegoat, but that was the only way it scanned.

It hadn't taken the Washington news hounds long to discover them. Gary was reluctant to give any interviews so Sarah stood in for him. On the second day of their visit, the *Washingtonian* did a small feature: "Mr. Gary Lynskey, brother of kidnap victim, Robert Lynskey, is currently in the nation's capital, pounding the pavements on his brother's behalf. He is accompanied by Sarah Horton, publisher and close friend of Robert Lynskey. They are being shown much sympathy but little action along the Mall, which has pulled down its shutters. Ms. Horton has made a moving plea for the release of Robert Lynskey. It is most unlikely, however, that the White House will be swayed by that, given its explicit policy of not negotiating with terrorists..."

That same evening as Sarah returned to the hotel the concierge handed her a note. It was from Drew and it said: "Nice one, Sarah."

"Nothing serious I hope." Gary inquired.

"No. Just business." Sarah crumpled the message in her small fist and put it in her alligator skin purse ... The press are so intrusive. Why can't they leave us alone?"

"Don't give up, Sarah."

"You're right ... Robert must come first."

After her boiled egg, she neatly dabbed the corners of her mouth, leaving specks of lipstick on the napkin and, pushing her chair back, brushed some imaginary crumbs off her linen skirt.

Gary finished his coffee in a gulp. "Well, up and at 'em."

While he went to get a cab she went upstairs to her room to repair her face, change her suit, and put those minute finishing touches to her hair. She was appraising the full effect in the mirror when the phone rang. It was her secretary.

"I'm sorry to disturb you, but Mr. Henfy called to demand the return of his manuscript. He seemed very agitated ... accused you of stealing something that belonged to posterity..."

"Oh Christ, the idiot." She doubted if it was posterity that discombobulated Henfy as much as the shock of returning with Champagne to find her gone. "Look, make a copy of the damn thing and return the original to him." She felt sure that a copy would serve to prove that the plagiarism was slight; with any luck that would be enough to settle modestly out of court. "Oh, and tell him he's no longer on our list." She hung up, regretting the loss of future percentages, but there was no other way. A rather unworthy thought occurred to her. If Robert made it, he might be persuaded to do a book about his experience; alternatively she might ghost one with Gary, memories of his brother, that sort of thing.

Their first port of call was to be the Senate. From there they would go to discuss terms with a professional lobbyist who had been highly recommended by Congressman Wilkinson. Within twenty minutes or so the cab turned down Pennsylvania Avenue into the Mall, that huge green axis of power which stretched right from the Lincoln Memorial to the Capitol Building. It was flooded with tourists doing the museums and art galleries, queuing for conducted tours of the White House. A kite-flying competition was in progress near the Washington Monument.

As he sat in the back of the cab, Gary hoped Robert wasn't giving himself a hard time in captivity. Gary still remembered him as an anxious brother who often had terrible nightmares. He would wake up wild-eyed and covered in sweat, crying out in the kind of gibberish Spider Hastings used. But he never spoke about those dreams.

The webbed harness creaked slightly as Mahon leant out as far as he could to gaze down at the Potomac that ran its sparkling course through the dense green woods of Virginia. Gradually the woodland gave way to the pastures of Maryland and finally the low bridges and white buildings of D.C. Limon watched him with faint amusement. Although Mahon hadn't contributed much to the investigation he meant well and he wasn't pushy.

Somehow, he had a relaxing effect on Limon, who needed that now more than ever.

Over Roosevelt Island the Huey chopper slowed and began its descent, landing impeccably on the circular pad at Langley. The pilot stayed behind to supervise the re-fueling and the two men, ducking out of the rotor wash – Mahon with a large hand clamped on his porkpie hat – walked briskly towards the building. Picking up their clearance badges in the reception area, they rode up in the elevator to the situation room where the Director motioned them to sit in designated places at the large oval table. The FBI delegation was led by the Deputy Director. Several aides sat near the raised podium by the map wall, each with his own laptop computer networked to the central mainframe in the climate-controlled room on the top floor of the building.

After some brief introductions, the CIA Director who sat at the head of the table, his reflection in the polished wood, opened the meeting by giving an overview of progress to date. This was old hat to Limon, who nevertheless listened attentively and nodded every so often. His mood wasn't good. He realized they were still using him as an operative, way below the policy level to which he aspired. Even worse, the FBI had scooped him on the Jallud Fahd angle and had even used the CIA's experimental truth drug. From his contacts in domestic security he'd heard two days ago that the drug had worked. So it came as no surprise when he heard the Deputy Director say rather smugly, "…on the fourth attempt and by doubling the recommended dose, Fahd revealed the name of Khaled Hassan on whom you have a dossier, I believe." Having announced this coup he graciously yielded the floor.

"Over to you, Captain Limon," the Director cued him with a nod.

"We do have a make on him," Limon said, "though it's shadowy. He's been with various terrorist groups, the PLO, PLF, Hamas and now, we think, the Palestine Islamic Jihad. He was involved in certain actions…"

"Al Qaeda?" someone asked. The question hung in the air.

"It looks likely … but we can't confirm that yet…" Limon regretted sounding so half-assed but he had to be damn careful what he said in this exalted company. Any false steers would return to haunt him.

"We don't need a complete profile at this stage," the Director cut in, keen to exercise his chairman's role, especially with the Bureau present. "What of his movements in this country?"

"We don't know how or when he got in. He may have used an Italian passport. But we were able to tie him in with the Black Muslims and the Nation of Islam…" Limon hesitated. There was additional information which he wanted to keep close for the time being. The cryptographic report on Lynskey's collected works had been revealing although not definitive. What was absolutely damning, however, was the recently uncovered fact that Khaled Hassan had been a student of Lynskey's in Columbia. Limon knew the risk he was running by not revealing this connection right now, but having been given the mushroom treatment by his own Director and beaten to the draw by the Bureau, he was determined to keep his own powder dry until the time was right. *He* would be the one to lower the boom on Lynskey, no one else.

"...Surely the Black Muslims are a spent force," the Deputy Director was saying.

"Not really, Sir," Limon responded politely. "Our information is that they went underground but never really disbanded, not completely." The Deputy Director tried to conceal his surprise by looking unconvinced instead.

Limon's view was buttressed by his own Director who argued, with a broader political perspective, that the Black Muslims had regrouped somewhat as a result of the rise of Islam in different parts of the world. They had of course lain low since 9/11 but they hadn't gone away.

"Well then is it not merely a question of rounding up the usual suspects?" A senior FBI agent asked. Several heads nodded sagely.

"Since we made the connection that is precisely what Lieutenant Mahon has been doing." The Director asked Mahon to elucidate.

"We've been beating the bushes in Harlem," Mahon rowed in, unaware of how his street cop's vernacular clashed with the language of the intelligence community. "Right now we have a hood called Daniel X in the tank. We're leaning on him but so far he hasn't spilled. I think he knows something…"

"Then maybe you should lean a little harder," the Director said. "I would suggest that Captain Limon might lend his particular skills to that objective."

"Fine by me." Mahon shrugged. He had no axe to grind and when it came to matters of national security he wasn't in the least territorial. They could all have a shot at Daniel X as far as he was concerned, using so-called enhanced interrogation techniques if needs be. He wondered if they were going to have lunch here at Langley; to him it would be like dining at the White House. They didn't; the meeting broke up at twelve-thirty and he and Limon boarded the helicopter immediately.

Mahon wasn't too disappointed about lunch. It wasn't every day a flatfoot was ferried by Government chopper between Washington and New York. Besides, there was a hamper of club sandwiches and a huge flask of coffee, courtesy of the pilot.

"I want to see Daniel X this afternoon," Limon said shortly after they'd taken off.

"Sure, no problem," Mahon mumbled through a mouthful of BLT. "He knows something, I'm sure of it."

"Then we're close." Limon smoothed forward

his narrow promontory of hair and moved his hand further down his forehead until it rested like a calipers gripping his temples. But close to what, he wondered. If Lynskey was in league with the kidnappers it was going to be hard to prove. Judging by the photograph and the very real looking bruises, everything had been orchestrated to the last detail. He decided there and then to follow normal procedures as if it were a genuine kidnapping, and then in his own time pursue the deeper truth, if it took forever. So far he hadn't exactly covered himself in glory, but nailing Lynskey in the full glare of publicity would change all that.

Having been picked up on a trumped-up charge, Daniel X was surly and uncooperative, sitting restlessly at a table in an otherwise bare interrogation room. He'd been roughed up more than usual and knew that something big was going down. His eyes were watchful behind their hostile glaze.

Mahon dismissed the officer on duty. "Now, Daniel," he said, "you know what we want. I don't have to lay it out for you again."

"I know nothing, man, and I want out of here. You can't hold me." He wondered who the other mean-looking dude was.

"This is bigger than you realize, Daniel,"

Mahon went on looming over him almost parentally. "Trust me. You don't want to get your tail caught in the wringer. We know you're into this Muslim thing. Hey, that's fine, no problem. Religion is a man's own business. I'm Catholic myself. But this Arab thing, Daniel, now that's where we part company. They've been fucking up this country for years. Do you want another ground zero, Daniel? Is that what you want?"

Daniel squirmed, gripped the edge of the table. He didn't want to jeopardize Khaled's mission. Who was the other guy in the room? His albumen eyes swiveled sideways towards that quiet specter.

Mahon's voice had taken on a lilt, almost a kindly refrain. "You've seen the President on TV. He's in a jam over this thing. The towelheads are giving him a hard time. Now you don't want to make it tough on him, do you?" He walked heavily to the other side of the table and sat down opposite Daniel, man to man. "Just tell us which brothers have teamed up with Khaled Hassan and where they're at. We can cut some kind of deal."

"I don't know what you're talkin' about, man. What brothers? Who's this Hassan dude? You got your wires crossed. I'm walkin'." He made to get up and as he did Mahon's hand descended on his shoulder like a big paw, the weight of which made him resume his seat.

"You're not listening, Daniel. We're talking national security here. Know who this is?" He gestured towards Limon.

"Father Christmas." Waves of disaffection rose from Daniel to the harsh light of the ceiling but there was a give-away slackness about the mouth.

"The Company is who," Mahon said in hushed tones. "The Company ... We've just flown up from Washington together," he couldn't resist adding. "The man has come to see you."

Limon moved closer to the table and stood over Daniel, who refused to look at him as if doing so would betray a weakness.

"Loyalty is a fine quality," Limon said quietly, "but in this case it is misplaced. We know the Black Muslims have been trying to make a comeback and we've been turning a blind eye to that. But if you don't cooperate now I'm afraid we'll have no alternative but to wipe you out. Now I'm going to propose a deal which not even Lieutenant Mahon could offer you. It goes like this. If you help us now we'll give your people a chance to get out. You know who we mean and you know where they're hiding out..."

"I don't know what..."

"Let me spell it out, Daniel," Limon started to circle him with measured pace, his footsteps hardly audible. His sinister calmness wasn't entirely studied however; after two weeks of frenetic activity which yielded nothing, he now felt as if he had all the time in the world. It was odd how time didn't seem to matter when there was something tangible in store. He knew Daniel was lying and he basked in this knowledge; such endearing certainty had to be savored and so he paced in slow ellipses. There was almost a feeling of anticlimax; in retrospect all cases seemed as if they could have been broken much sooner. Of course there were layers to this one, and there would be consequences, but first things first.

"The reason we've come this far is because we used truth drugs on Jallud Fahd. He gave up Khaled Hassan's name. We can do the same to you. It's no problem. We don't have to use any rough stuff, just an injection, that's all, and you'll cough up your liver. Everything. It's all high-tech nowadays, Daniel. All I have to do is sign a form. But here's the deal. If you make me go that route you lose the chance to save your friends. So they'll go down and they won't forgive you for that. We'll let them know that you snitched. You'll be a marked man." He consulted his watch and made a mental calculation. "I reckon about five days … no, more like four … you'll be dead within four days. But if you tell us now, you save their skins and your own. Hassan is all we want and you owe him nothing. But if you don't talk now, we'll fill you so full of sodium pentathol and other cocktails you'll sing for a year. Then they all go down – twenty years, no parole. And you'll be dead."

Daniel was silent, wedged into his thoughts. This was the crucial moment, Limon knew, the crossover from denial to the contemplation of its opposite; it was also a very delicate moment.

Mahon knew it too, and let the silence develop

for a while. "Listen to the man," he urged in little more than a whisper. "No one but him can give you a let out like this. I can't do it. You're lucky he's here, damn lucky."

"Your people will thank you," Limon enjoined, "for saving their hides. I know about your movement. The surname 'X' meaning loss of identity. I sympathize with that. I do. But if you all go down you'll lose more than identity. The future is on the line here. What do you think your old man and Malcolm X would do? Live to fight another day or self-destruct now? Do you want to be remembered as the guy who disgraced the name of Malcolm X?"

Daniel shook his head not in denial but to indicate he'd enough to think about. Limon and Mahon exchanged glances above his bowed head. They sensed the scree was loosening and that something was about to give.

CHAPTER 19

FOR HIS FIRST SHOW and partly in response to his own preferences, Si Rembert had as his guests Britney Spears, Lady Gaga, and that zany Italian artist who wanted to wrap the Chrysler building in purple cloth. Pop, soap and tat, Chaim thought with sinking heart, setting up the camera angles. For even lighter relief there was a comedian out of the same semi-alternative stable as Rembert who interspersed his gags with trumpet solos played on a watering can. The set was an art deco caricature down to the contractually-specified plaster flamingoes, set against a postcard-blue sky with pink-tinted clouds.

To Chaim's annoyance Rembert missed his mark several times and spoke to the wrong camera twice as he strutted about the pastel set, bird-dogging his guests. Chaim might have been able to compensate by skillful cutting and insurance shots but he didn't bother. It was never necessary with Lynskey, who had a natural rapport with the camera. Besides, it was outrageous to launch this burlesque show while Lynskey's fate still hung in the balance. Even though the promos and advertising hype had been at pains to avoid the impression that the show was a replacement for the *RL Hour*, Chaim regarded the whole idea as callous and crass. In fact, if he read Drew's mind right, it was all based on the assumption that Robert Lynskey had absolutely no hope of survival.

He really would have credited Drew with better judgment and even a semblance of style, if not artistic integrity. But without Robert's guiding hand Drew had gone off like a cheap firecracker at a Frat party.

Rembert was cavalier if not downright rude with his guests, asking Britney if she'd look as good as Madonna at her age, badgering Lady Gaga to reveal the latest episode of her romantic life. He was determined to make his own mark by debunking established stars. If the guests reacted badly on camera that was money in the bank for him; he was stealing their astral light. As far as Chaim was concerned, Rembert abused his privilege as host, something Lynskey would never have done. The whole thing was shoddy, a nightmare of debauched style. If this was Postmodernism, Chaim wanted nothing to do with it.

Drew didn't see it that way. He wanted Rembert, his protegé, to establish himself quickly by whatever means. New York was loud; he wanted decibels, polka dots and plaid. He wanted impact. Controversy was good. Insulting stars was good. Rembert would claw his way up into the firmament.

With the show in the can, and the humidity less intense than usual, Drew suggested a few holes of golf to loosen up the joints. Though not a golfer, Chaim had nothing better to do so he went along. To walk, not play and certainly not caddy.

He sensed it might be the last time he would go along with Drew on any of his ventures.

Teeing up on the first, Drew said, "It was a lively show. I think we're on to a winner."

"I doubt it." Chaim was no longer afraid to take issue with his boss, whose decisiveness could no longer command respect because it had gone that short but critical distance beyond reason. He seemed out of control. "It's cheap."

Drew raised his head to look curiously at him from under his eye-shade. "Now don't go snobby on me, Chaim. It's hard to overrate the public." After a few practice swings he took an almighty swipe at the ball, which started well but faded left and skittered into the rough. He picked up his tee, rammed the driver into his bag and set off down the fairway. "You move in a … rarefied group, but I believe I know the man in the street. He's not interested in all that Zen stuff about excellence. He wants a laugh and a bit of color without having to concentrate too hard."

Maybe he had a point, Chaim reflected. They had all at one time or another depended on audience reaction as a measure of worth. Except for Lynskey. Goddammit, he might have been off beam at times but he had the guts to get out front and lead. Chaim never realized before exactly how much he admired him for that, and now he was beginning to understand. Only it was too late.

"Rembert is an asshole," he said quietly as the freshly cut grass of the fairway snagged softly at his shoes. He should have persuaded Drew to hire a buggy.

"No argument." Drew grinned. "But he's going to be a successful asshole. And he's going to be my asshole." He walked jauntily, secure in the knowledge that he had his finger on the pulse. The smile that floated over his face was as much for Sarah, as he envisioned her swanning around Washington, like a grieving widow. They would make a stunning team, a canny partnership of equal foibles. It was a glorious day, the heat tempered by a breeze that ruffled the pines and turned into spindrift the jets of water rising from the sprinklers. Atoms of flint glinted in the sand bunkers, bleached almost white by the sun; a stand of cedars threw slate-gray shadows on the grass.

Drew hacked his way out of the rough taking a huge divot. The ball faded upwards as if melting into the sky then re-appeared in the distance, landing dead just short of the green.

"You'll have to commit more to Rembert," he said without looking in Chaim's direction. He took out the wedge in anticipation of his next shot and swung it idly as he walked. "It would be wrong to cold-shoulder him just because he's new. You could have fixed some of those blips."

"Are you criticizing my work?" Chaim was conscious of sounding pompous but the situation called for it. And he had always prided himself on his professionalism.

"Yes. Don't be a dickhead. There's no point in going down with the ship. Where's the percentage in that?"

"Forget about Lynskey, you mean."

Drew duffed his chip and three-putted but he didn't seem to mind. "I didn't say that. Sympathy is one thing but martyrdom is another. If you want to self-destruct, that's fine. But do it cleanly. Don't agonize over it."

In a way Chaim was relieved the breach had finally come. And he knew that Drew was really putting down his marker: if Rembert bombed it would be partly Chaim's fault. Lack of commitment, his old bugbear. Controlling his anger, Chaim began to review his options, dreading the decisions that might have to be made, instead of just getting on with his life. Maybe a clean break was called for, West Coast, even Hollywood? Christopher would jump at the chance but, god, that could be a double-edged sword. The thought of losing Christopher made him tremble. He wondered if he would ever be free or have the guts to go his own way, wherever it might lead. Was that the question that had obsessed Lynskey before the kidnapping, and had he somehow therefore ambushed himself? The shadows lengthened over the golf course and hope seemed to fade with the light.

Back in the clubhouse, Drew was the center of attention. Any word of Lynskey? What's the latest? He grew expansive, filling in his cronies and fellow committee members. He hardly noticed that Chaim had left. Remember the name, Rembert, he told them; he's a pistol.

The first show went down well, even allowing for the novelty effect. There was some debate in the print media about the propriety of substituting Rembert for Lynskey in the given circumstances, but nothing that hurt the network. The next show would be the clincher. As they said in the business, one for touch, two for go. Drew felt confident about the show and about Sarah.

Partly because he'd studied so hard and with such grim determination, he didn't have a girl to leave behind when he emigrated, but he remembered his last view of Trinity, framed by the arched main gate, the campanile flanked by maples, the cobbled squares and irreproachable granite buildings from which wonderful music often issued late at night, making his heart soar and forcing on him the resolve, the hope of someday reproducing that feeling in others through his own medium. That was the nature of the power he craved as he left the cloister for good. This campus he'd dreamt about in the northern fastnesses now spewed him forth upon the world. The days of Dublin ended quickly. The wrench of beauty separated from a dream kept him brooding like a jilted lover until Shannon. Then, somewhere over the Atlantic there was a subtle change as the New World beckoned.

About two years later Lynskey was driving

over Brooklyn Bridge and for no apparent reason started to weep violently. He lost his breath completely. He got out of the car and waved frantically for help. No one stopped. He thought he'd die right there and then. An unknown blue corpse on the asphalt, with no obvious wounds. Until finally a young African-American woman risked slapping him on the back. His throat freed up; he gasped his thanks. Moments of unresolved grief were to recur later in his life but never again in such overwhelming torrents. In fact, after that experience on the bridge he never really looked back, or went back, apart from that trip years later when his soul was more inured...

He held the bars of the cellar window and looked at the fresh day, wistful as a sigh, beyond his reach. His desire to go into the world had come to this. No self-pity, he told himself, you've had a good innings. Don't end it like a wimp. You wanted to establish a reputation, be a national figure, and now you're paying the price. He knew that if he hadn't become a man of substance – a personage – he would never have been kidnapped. So, he had to accept it. He had authored his fate.

His mind returned to a theme that had haunted him in the last couple of years. Where had the balance lain between his desire to make a contribution and his wish to be credited with it? The answer came clean and fast and it did nothing to soothe his conscience. First and foremost, transcending everything including that much vaunted shudder of enchantment, he had wanted recognition, wanted it badly. Was he then so blind he could live only in others' eyes or in mirrors, in the Swiftian glass "wherein beholders discover everybody's face but their own"? Jesus, some pathetic epitaph.

And Gary, by contrast, was peerless; he didn't need to cry out for significance or conceive himself from air. He came ready-made, safe and secure inside his own skin. And it was all so effortless.

How Robert had fought and clawed for his share, suffering the stabs of form-letter rejections, snarling at the established glitterati, and all the time grooming himself, rehearsing everything even his 'spontaneous' ripostes, mirroring his audience, when he had one, until he became almost like that Woody Allen character, *Zelig,* who ballooned up in the company of fat people. Then he got smarter. In his first TV appearance he used the subterfuge of forward referencing so he couldn't be edited or clipped; he learnt how to interrupt with a ready-made epigram and force it to be relevant even though it might have been out of context. He discovered and used the shock value of reverse psychology. Leaving Hollywood in a huff, actually walking off the lot because the director departed from Robert's script, was another major coup. His stock soared. Who was this guy? they asked. How could anyone do that unless ... unless ... he's got something really special? Finally he developed what could be called the total-image concept of packaging. Sam

Beckett's plays were austere, he looked and acted and was austere; nothing about him was *other* than austere. Take it or leave it. The complete package. Robert Lynskey programmed himself. His work was droll; so was he. Enter his unified world or back off. The man and his work could not be differentiated. In a cybernetic age it had to work; it did. The total image.

And then the final let-down, the discovery that being a celebrity confirmed other peoples' existence, not one's own, the realization, ghastly when it came, that the gulf between wanting and having could not be bridged – indeed after he 'arrived' he suffered acute anxiety attacks for all of a year. And most sinister and damaging of all, because of his role-playing, he lost the ability to trust, except for children whose innocence he worshipped, though only from a distance.

It was a disheartening inventory and he came badly out of all comparisons. However misguided Spider Hastings might have been, he at least spoke his own tongues and when he had no language left he closed the book with extraordinary courage, a hunger strike. Dorothy came to terms at last with her body. And Gary … was … Gary.

He realized how quickly the morning had flown when Bart brought his food.

"What is it today?" Robert asked as if he were a resident in a first class hotel, asking about the *potage du jour*.

"Beans, bread." He laid the tin dish down on

the box. There was no animosity but he seemed reluctant to talk, had probably been warned by the others to keep his distance.

Robert sniffed the dish. "Smells good." He looked up with a grin, "How's the head?" He knew that this kind man would not be his assassin.

"OK." Bart didn't say any more but moved away carefully. Was it possible that he was afraid of *him*? Did he see him as a dead man walking?

Robert spent some time over his meal, making it a formal repast. It was necessary to break up the day so that time would not swamp him, and to have some little ritual. He spooned up the beans careful not to lose any juice and chewed slowly and thoroughly to fool his stomach. Nothing had ever tasted as good. He kept a piece of bread in reserve to mop up the juice, no longer concerned that he might also be mopping up foreign bodies from the bottom of the dish. His stomach had adapted, as he had, to such surprises.

When he was finished he left the dish and spoon on the earthen floor just inside the door. Then he clapped his hands as a prelude to action, moved the box and brought out the cardboard. He started to tear carefully along the folds, a half inch at a time. When he'd finished he had twenty-four foolscap-sized sheets which he assembled in a neat pile and laid on top of the box. He placed his ballpoint pen beside the stack and sat on the edge of the bed smiling to himself.

Notes from underground. This would be some memoir. No word processors, recorders, or research team this time, kiddo. Just rotten cardboard, half a refill and perhaps a few days if he was lucky. Of course it wouldn't be a memoir at all, just a few scribbles that would probably never be found. Good, that old *bête noire*, recognition, wouldn't sidetrack him then. From what? His apologia? No, a search for that one little nugget that must reside somewhere in the shaft he'd mined almost to death.

He'd often fantasized about this kind of set-up, an old monk in his stony cell on an outcrop of rock in the Atlantic, trapped in his own faith, with nothing to distract him from the gentle hovering cloud – as he imagined it – of inspiration. He should be so lucky.

It was one thing to be faced with a blank sheet of paper, but twenty-four pieces of cardboard were even more intimidating because he was denied the luxury of a running start to be followed by as much revision as he pleased. He would have to settle for staccato notes and key words, each one as definitive as he could manage. No outside descriptions or padding of any sort, no style either. Just the mathematics of the soul, hopefully leading to a solution, if there was one. QED.

On the plus side he was free of that stylistic encumbrance that ruled out sincerity because it lacked sophistication. He tried to remind himself of the advantages as he sat with pen poised, and was still reminding himself one hour later without having written anything. He had thought of: 'Conception, a process not an event', but it lacked something, wasn't quite whole enough to waste ink on. Then he'd considered, 'The tyranny of the inner eye', by which he meant the extraordinary gyrations and destructively jealous forces let loose by the fact of human consciousness. But that, too, wasn't encompassing enough to justify the expenditure of scarce ink and cardboard. This was rationing as he had never known it. His own office used up several ink cartridges a week.

The afternoon passed slowly and he couldn't get flowing. He was quite unable to get beyond one thought that seemed so pervasive and yet superficial. Fame, the thing, the concept preyed on him. He had devoted most of his adult life to it, worshipped at its shrine and yet couldn't explain its fatal attraction. Why had no one attempted to explain it? If you asked all well-known artists and scientists what motivated them, the answers would be predictably precious and vague: some inner light, because it was there, desire to make a contribution, love of beauty or structure or truth. If you threatened them with torture or a polygraph you might get: wealth, power, to show those other bastards. But they would never admit to fame, in fact would decry it as a *cost* of success, being hounded by one's fans, forced to sign autographs, having one's privacy invaded. And this from the cream of the truth-seekers. Then, what reason for hope was there?

Yet the cry for significance was real; it probably underlay wars and revolutions. Look at me, I exist. Look at us. Do not go gentle into obscurity; rage, rage for recognition. That must come first before being assigned a place upon the earth; it was the high-octane fuel whose only substitute was blood. It was what put Robert in this prison. He might have written something about that but doodled instead. He was too sick at heart to want to prove anything.

CHAPTER 20

EXITING FROM THE LINCOLN TUNNEL into the harsh morning light, Limon reflected again on how easy it had been in the final analysis. All told, it had taken less than three hours to break Daniel X, who cannily insisted on having the deal in writing. Given what was at stake Limon had no compunction about letting the Black Muslims off the hook, for now. They were almost a spent force anyway. Besides, it would be a relatively easy matter to nail them on something else later, especially that National Front woman, Anna Heckschler, who was wanted in several different countries. He was certain that she was the woman in the black wig who had helped kidnap Lynskey, or at least stage a kidnapping.

Limon could have delegated this reconnaissance but he wanted to see for himself the lie of the land; it would help him plan the rescue mission which, all going well, could be mounted that night.

With the aid of a computer-generated map, and following Daniel's instructions, they left the New Jersey Turnpike just south of Elizabeth and drove through Metuchen until they came to a turn-off north of Baldwin Hill.

"Pull over here," Limon said to the driver.

Through the high overgrown hedge which sprouted stray wisps of woodbine and the wild antennae of boxwood, they could just about see the ramshackle house a half mile up the rutted drive. It was more or less as Daniel X had described it.

They got out of the car and stayed close to the hedge; Mahon examined the earth just inside the rotten redwood gate.

"No fresh tire tracks," he said. "If they're in there they've stayed put."

"Naturally," Limon said. "They wouldn't want to draw attention to themselves." He examined the iron hinges and found some particles of rust beneath. "That gate's been opened recently." He wanted to look at the latch on the other side but couldn't risk leaving his cover. Instead he found a small gap in the hedge which he widened with his hands and peered through. Standing behind him, Mahon grinned nervously to see a Chief of Intelligence with his head stuck in a bush as if he were bird-nesting.

"See that old barn up there to the back of the house," Limon commentated. "It's big enough for a car."

Mahon took his turn in the ancient hedge, musty with cobwebs, dead insects and pupae. He removed his porkpie hat and waved away a cloud of disturbed gnats.

"I dunno. It looks deserted to me." The collapsing shingle roof, broken windows and lichen-covered walls didn't inspire confidence. "Look at the length of the grass and weeds at the front. No one's been through that door in years."

"Daniel wouldn't have lied."

"No," Mahon admitted. "It doesn't add up. Maybe they didn't tell him everything."

"There must be a back door," Limon said, "But there's no way we can go round the back, and a chopper would be spotted immediately." He fetched a pair of high-powered binoculars from the car and spent some time focusing them.

Just then a tractor came chuntering down the road in a cloud of dust, smoke billowing from the vertical exhaust.

"Just what we need," Mahon groaned.

The driver stopped the tractor. "You folks need any help?"

Limon withdrew from the foliage, the binoculars hanging from his neck. "No thanks. Just … bird-watching."

"You won't see much in these parts," the local man said leaning over the steering-wheel. "Except maybe a few woodchucks." He wagged his head at the ways of city folk.

"Well, we'll be moving on soon…" Limon had an idea. "That's an interesting old house up there. Deserted for years I suppose?"

"Yessir. Ever since old Manderson died. Must be all of seven years ago…"

"I guess kids or vagrants make use of it from time to time," Mahon said, picking up on the drift.

"Naw. I pass this way every second day and I never seen a soul near the place. It's too outta the way." He tipped back the peak of his *Burpee Seeds* baseball cap, revealing a white proud-flesh forehead, and scratched the crown of his head.

"Pity to see a place go to rack and ruin but that's how it is sometimes."

"Still, it could probably be renovated," Limon suggested as if he were a prospective buyer. "At least if the wiring and plumbing were in reasonable shape." He walked closer to the tractor to reassure himself that it couldn't be seen from the house.

"Hell, Mister that old place's been gutted, cleaned right out. Doubt if there ever was much plumbing to speak of."

"Probably a well." Limon nodded sagely.

"No. Manderson never sunk a well. But there's a stream over by the right of the barn. Comes down from Baldwin Hill. I'll show you if you're interested." He made to get down from the tractor.

"No. Thanks all the same. I was just curious. We have to be going now."

"Well OK. But if you're interested there's a realtor in Metuchen by the name of Collins. He could show you over the place." He put the tractor in gear and gave it full throttle. The sound of the engine was deafening but Limon doubted if it would carry as far as the house. The smoke that rose up straight in a black jet concerned him more.

When the tractor had gone, he focused the binoculars again, this time more purposefully. "I see the stream," he reported back to Mahon. "And get this," he added excitedly, "There's a patch of flattened grass. Someone's been drawing water there. It can't mean anything else."

Mahon stepped forward and had a look. But he wasn't convinced. "I dunno. It's a bit flimsy." The grass was tamped down all right at one point beside the stream but it didn't exactly form a trail leading to the house. "It could be embarrassing if we go in like dam-busters and ... Jesus Christ" His bulky frame went rigid.

"What is it?"

"There's someone at the window..."

"Let me see." Limon reached for the glasses. "No..."

"There was. I'm telling you."

"You're sure?"

"Absolutely. A dark face. Could have been Hassan. He probably heard the goddamn tractor."

"'Then we go in tonight." Limon's mind shifted to a new gear. He made mental notes of the terrain. It should be possible, he reckoned, to bring in at least one chopper and land it between the barn and the hill, just out of sight of the house. Judging by the height of the windows and the way the foundations sloped, there was probably a cellar to the rear of the house. Using a zoom lens, he took photographs to complement his memory. His ordnance training helped him to estimate distances and lines of sight.

Mahon kept his eye on the window. The figure didn't reappear.

"OK, we have enough for now," Limon said. "Let's move out slowly."

The driver slipped the car into gear. Rather

than reverse past the gate, they went straight on, following the road until they found a safely distant turn-off. Sitting quietly in the back, Limon had already begun to plan the mission. In deciding on the logistics he had to work on the assumption that it had been a genuine kidnapping. Mahon wanted to talk but he had no audience.

It just wasn't fair to be blocked at a time like this. He'd spent three days getting the cardboard ready, virtually reinventing papyrus, living in anticipation of putting pen to paper and then, after half a sheet, he dried completely. The dulling impotency cut him to the quick, especially as he had been on to something important, converging on a rich vein. He could feel it but couldn't develop it. He sensed a frightening kind of self-sabotage right on the verge of what could have been the only real breakthrough of his life, something far more important than a memoir of his pathetic existence. What really irked him was that he knew the reason. This was the toughest deadline he'd ever faced and it made him panic and seize up. Diagnosis, unfortunately, was not the same as cure.

He pushed the box aside, stood up, tried to get the circulation going – blood at least – and didn't hear Khaled until he was right behind him.

"There will be one more tape," he said matter-of-factly as if he were confirming a prior agreement. There was no way Robert could have anticipated what came next. "It would have a bigger impact if you participated in it."

Instinctively, Robert took a step backwards. "You ... can't be serious."

"I can help you with the facts. We could agree a script." Khaled's face seemed fuzzy, out of focus, the dark eyes smudged in the depths beneath the heavy forehead.

"A script," Robert repeated weakly, reaching blindly behind him to touch the wall for some kind of support.

"Yes. Most of the tape is already made," Khaled explained. "But we could add ... what do you call it ... a voice-over ... I have some rough notes here." He handed him a sheet of paper which had been torn from a spiral-bound notebook.

The hand which accepted the page didn't seem to belong to him, nor the eyes which scanned it. "...I have come to understand the nature of dispossession ... the fundamental truth of Islam ... would urge the American people to see through new eyes ... Democracies also engage in terror ... American Presidents are not elected by the people but by big business..." For a moment he felt as if Drew had just handed him his cue notes for the *RL Hour*, although that seemed a lifetime ago. Looking up, he saw in Khaled's passive face, the reflection of his fear that life-times came and went and were of no more consequence than the void that preceded them. Fighting for more reality than that intimation, Robert blurted, "I don't support your cause." Was he mad? After the national trauma of 9/11, the international condemnation of the Madrid and London bombings, how on earth could he hope to win acceptance for his message?

"You must."

Robert tried to interpret this. A threat or a plea? It didn't make much difference either way. Would he die for his beliefs? What the hell did he believe in anyway? His imagination was up and running, giving him previews of televised retractions that astounded the nation: Lynskey recants, regrets his former support of Western values, finally sees the light. Finally.

"You're going to kill me anyway. So why should I lie for you?" His voice shook, unsure of whether this conversation was actually taking place. He hoped the method of execution would be a bullet. The thought of decapitation scared him.

"You would be telling the truth..."

"Oh Jesus, don't start that again." He moved towards the light that slanted from the window. It was fading though still held a comforting sepia quality; that shaft of light had been his salvation during the past two weeks and it was natural that he should now be drawn towards it. *Quid est veritas?*

"If you cooperate you may save your life." The proposition was insinuated so softly into the silence it took Robert several seconds to grasp it.

"You mean…" He turned back from the light, a spurt of adrenalin shooting through his veins, to see Khaled nodding. But was it a false uplifting? He began a wary reckoning. A lie for a life. He would of course be a laughing stock afterwards, assuming … It wasn't that he cherished his own views so much; they were just scaffolding in a way, erected around a tower that hadn't yet been topped out. But his image, the monolith would collapse, leaving a vacant lot in the Manhattan skyline where once he stood immutable. Just like the Twin Towers. He played for time.

"It would be obvious to everyone I did it under duress. No one would believe me." Could he laugh it off afterwards, say he'd been drugged? There were always ways to mend fences after the event.

"We can take that risk," Khaled said just like a producer planning a change in format.

Robert was floundering badly. Here was his chance to survive. There was a deal on the table, a devil's contract of probabilities. Suddenly a gambler's instinct rose up in him and he saw the core of certainty. They were going to kill him anyway since they couldn't afford to leave a witness. This insurance policy had a high deductible; he would demean himself for nothing. "You *may* save your life", that's what Khaled had said, because he couldn't lie outright. *May*. The clever bastard. Oddly, though it shouldn't have concerned him, Khaled went down in his estimation. There was only one thing worse than a fanatic and that was a fanatic who compromised. No deal, a voice shouted inside him. Where had he heard that before? He was sickened by this commerce of the soul; even Simkin was more honest.

"No. Absolutely not."

"That's too bad," Khaled said, tightening his lips at the corners. He withdrew a cassette from the sagging pocket of his jacket. "It's the most important tape yet. Maybe it will stand on its own." He conveyed the impression that Robert's foolish recalcitrance had just deprived him of a leading role in a mega production.

Robert peered at him from under his brows, this stupid, deadly-earnest *schmuck*, re-inventing the wheel of PR, grossly overrating its power, believing, like some simple-minded crusader, that if the world hears it will also see. He couldn't decide whether he hated him or pitied him and the ambivalence set off a bilious feeling in his chest. The madness had come full circle; he couldn't even despise the man who would do him the ultimate harm.

After he'd left, Robert tried desperately for perspective. He was sure he'd made the right decision, almost sure. He was being pragmatic not heroic. But he cursed Khaled for raising his hopes if only for a second, and giving him that agonizing moment of choice. Then a strange thought came to him. Was it possible that this remote underground place would yet prove to be a hub of history on which the geo-forces of holy or nuclear war would converge, he a clone of the Archduke Ferdinand and his captor the personification of Götterdammerung? Shit, he would die a megalomaniac, still striving for a stupendous exit from the world stage, his image more important than his life. There was more to repent, much more. As he leant against the wall tears came to his eyes. But he recovered quickly. He could almost feel the stupid, vain ego begin to seep like a bad spirit from his body. Maybe when it all went he could follow peacefully without a murmur. He felt old and almost ready.

CHAPTER 21

BY MID-AFTERNOON an Inter-agency SWAT team was brought together and briefed by Limon, with the odd corroborative interjection from Mahon. Using the hastily taken photographs and his own excellent, though short-term, memory, Limon had supervised the construction of a three-dimensional mock-up of the location which he now used for the deployment of this crack force.

Despite his own predilection for policy rather than operations, he insisted on being part of the mission so that he could see it through right to the end. But more importantly he wanted to be one of the first through the door, to witness the staged set-up first hand and catch Lynskey *in flagrante*. 'He'd better be in chains', he thought, 'for his own good'. The element of surprise had never assumed such importance.

During the briefing, which was direct and to the point and had the usual air of nervous expectancy, Limon had to fight off a recurring sense of artificiality as if he were just going through the motions. He had to remind himself that for the purpose of the exercise it had to be *assumed* that Lynskey was at risk. Limon was acutely aware that by keeping his suspicions to himself he was playing a very dangerous game. There were several scenarios, each one more fraught than the next; the one which concerned him most was the possibility of Lynskey being taken out by friendly fire. Limon would carry the can for that all the way and would never be able to exculpate himself by proving Lynskey's complicity in the kidnapping. Now that it was coming close to the moment of truth, Limon wasn't sure any longer why he had taken so much on himself. Certainly the weeks of false leads and FBI hegemony had gotten to him. Nor did the media-conscious Homeland Security machine help. But behind all that frustration he was driven by something that was all his own and which at this moment he could not explain.

The session ended with a few questions and points of clarification. Limon stressed again the absolute necessity of surprise and keeping in radio contact at all times. After he wished them well, the men went to draw their weapons, side arms and folding-stock Uzis. Bullet-proof vests, camouflage fatigues and balaclavas were mandatory. The marksmen spent a little longer studying their positions, selecting scopes and pre-adjusting the sights of their rifles.

On Limon's instruction the FBI had arranged the transport, including one Black Falcon helicopter which stood by fueled and ready. The operation was timed for twenty-one hundred hours. There would be no moon but enough light for the marksmen; there was a possibility of rain.

With less than an hour to go the Director called Limon and wished him well, conveying also the good wishes of the President, who wanted to be informed of the outcome later that night.

The Director reminded Limon of the paramount importance of protecting Lynskey; the President himself had adverted to that. Limon knew that behind the good wishes a marker was being put down; he also knew that his survival now depended on saving the life of a traitor. It was one hell of a charade.

He drew an automatic pistol and flak jacket. Mahon checked his old service revolver and replaced it in his special shoulder holster. He wasn't looking forward to this; his stomach was a mess.

———————————

Richard picked his nails as he paced the familiar floorboards, wrestling with his conscience. It was still light outside; and they hadn't yet put the cardboard on the window. A gray squirrel played in the grass and suddenly ran up a tree, darting along the arterial branches until he disappeared in the denser foliage at the top. The surefootedness of the animal and his ability to hide impressed Richard. He was sorry it had come to this, though the message from Daniel X hadn't really surprised him. Anna was right; Khaled had not put them in the picture from the start. He was following some lonely, distant ambition which he hadn't shared with them. Richard was hurt by that but he sensed that his grievance was nothing compared to what Khaled must have gone through in his own country, the accumulation of wounds that would have finished a different man. Bart in his own way had picked up on that right from the start, but it had taken Richard longer, and now it was too late; there was no time left to put their cards on the table. So his conscience, which had lain dormant since those Gospel days in Atlanta, continued to churn in the face of the enormity that was planned.

He looked at his watch. Eight-thirty already. He wished there was another way. It would have suited him to accept Anna's verdict that Khaled was mad but he knew that was too easy. He studied her as she sat at the kitchen table, her face set and determined; it was clear she had no doubts. Meeting his gaze she nodded slowly.

"Bart, you go out and wait in the car," Richard said.

As he laid the sweeping brush against the wall, Bart looked at him in surprise. "Where're we goin', man?" Sweat in the cleft of his throat trickled down his chest to form a dark wedge-shaped stain on the front of his T-shirt.

"Just into town…"

"How about Khaled?" Bart's expression was one of uncertainty mixed with resignation that he probably wouldn't understand anyway. He sensed that something was going to happen and relied on Richard to make it right.

"Later. We'll catch him later. Go on now." Richard's voice rose in pitch, bullying him into silence.

Shortly after Bart left, Khaled came out of the adjoining room, his hair wet from ritual washing. He seemed relaxed; prayer renewed him.

"Maybe you've ... reconsidered?" He put the question neutrally, not as a plea.

"No. I'm sorry, man," Richard answered. "It has to be this way."

"Then I'm sorry too. There was much we didn't agree on but we did well together." Khaled stood in the middle of the room, which seemed a little tidier. Bart, he noticed, had swept the floor and cleaned off the table-top; the few remaining tins of food were neatly stacked on a shelf by the old porcelain sink, and the water tank had been replenished. The irrevocable signs of departure were all around him. He had seen those signs many times before.

"Yeah ... well..." Richard hesitated, his eyes hooded with what could have been extreme fatigue. His left hand gripped the door jam, the fingers gouging powdery flakes from the rotten timber.

"Let's go." Anna heaved a duffle bag on to her shoulder.

"The mission is almost over," Khaled said. "Two more days at most. Maybe you...?"

"No," Anna interrupted. "We've invested too much in this already. With no pay-off. It's time to get out." She couldn't wait to leave. This had been a disaster from day one, and she wanted to sit on a beach somewhere, swim, get the stench of this place out of her nostrils.

"Maybe *you* should quit while you're ahead," Richard suggested although he knew the answer. His eyes carried a more urgent plea.

"No," Khaled replied. "There's one more tape. The most important one. I have to see it through."

Anna swore under her breath. He just didn't know when he was beaten but it wasn't her responsibility to reason with him now. He was on his own.

"I'm grateful for your help." Khaled embraced her and Richard in turn. "Goodbye. I wish you the peace of Allah. Say goodbye to Bart for me."

As he walked towards the car which Bart had brought out of the barn, Richard hesitated, almost stumbled. "We can't just … leave him." Concern clawed at the skin of his face. This was the unforgivable act; all his experience of the ghetto told him so. They might avoid the usual consequences of such an act because Khaled was a foreigner, but this did not ease his mind. They were setting him up to save their own skins. Daniel X had explained the deal in great detail.

"Yes we can," Anna said in a stern whisper. "It's over. It's his fault." She walked more quickly towards the car.

"Maybe we should … warn him." Richard dropped his bag on the grass and made to turn back.

She caught him by the shoulder and spun him around. "Don't even think about it. We've got our marching orders. If they don't take him there's no deal for us. Then we're finished, the cause is finished. Get in the fucking car."

He let her make the decision for him. As the car moved off Anna grimly chalked up another failure. It occurred to her that she was getting too old for this; the privations were grinding her down and the noose was tightening. Yet her purpose was still intact, growing stronger with the years and uglier with the accumulation of frustration. She hated Richard for his weakness. These people were so fucked up they didn't know how to fight. She would have to look for stronger allies, or strike out on her own. Either way she had reached a personal watershed; she decided to go back to Austria for a while to take stock.

At the bottom of the lane Richard looked back once to see the deserted house. There was no sign of life. He'd left something there which would never be his again.

In the cellar Robert heard a car drive away and wondered what it meant. His window didn't reveal much except the setting sun and two lapwings flitting across the sky. Purple streaks entered the cumulus which crowned the hill, patchy with the rusts and lichens of ancient stones. The wind had a sad lyric; he hoped it might be a stormy night. It would be better than the silence, even if the rain seeped up through the foundations or dripped from the ceiling. He remembered one winter years ago when he and Gary woke simultaneously to the sounds of a snowstorm and gradually became aware of a hammering noise coming from the other side of the village street. Through the window they saw Spider Hastings' Dad in his night-shirt frantically trying to break the ice in the water butt at the gable end of his cottage. They didn't know at the time that Mr. Hastings kept his emergency bottle of booze in the water butt, and in retrospect the incident didn't seem quite so funny. It may have explained why Spider spent so much time on his own stalking the countryside, bellowing away in a language known only to himself – and finally paying the ultimate price.

Robert looked in the dish but there was nothing left. Still, there was a lot to be said for enforced dieting. Maybe he wouldn't need beta-blockers again; of course death was a good cure for blood pressure, as some comic had said. He lay on the straw mattress that by now bore the imprint of his body. But he couldn't rest; something was different. Suddenly he was galvanized. The car! Suppose they'd lit out, leaving him. He sprang from the bed. But before he reached the door it opened and Khaled came in.

He didn't say anything for a while, just lay against the jam of the door and seemed to be absorbed in his shoes, which were cracked and worn.

Robert threw caution to the winds and asked him how a man of faith could justify atrocities like the Twin Towers or Bali or Madrid. Behind the question there lurked the fear that maybe, just maybe, his role-playing radicalism at Columbia might have been taken too seriously by his former student.

"I don't justify it," Khaled said. "You think all Palestinians jumped for joy when three thousand innocent civilians were blown up? You judge us harshly. We are all God's children. But we should be treated equally."

Robert was knocked off his stride and he tried to rally by suggesting that Khaled had to be linked to some terrorist group or even a sleeping cell of al Qaeda.

"I am a priest," Khaled answered him. "I do not believe in terrorism. Your former President is closer to the bin Laden family than I am. Neither of them represents the poor or the dispossessed." He looked out the small window at a patch of gray sky. A spider was busy spinning a web in the corner where two rotting mullions met. For an instant he could have been a cellmate.

"But Allah welcomes martyrs who've blown up innocent people."

Khaled shook his head slowly. "There is so much misunderstanding between us." He saw again the crumpled Hamas flag and this time, against his will, it fluttered away, revealing the broken body of Fatimeh, the young girl who had tried to save her brother, Jamal. One track of an

Israeli bulldozer had crushed most of her head, but one staring eye was recognizable. Khaled leant against a wooden pillar and fought for breath.

Robert looked at his abductor carefully and noticed the distress. For one crazy second he thought he detected something of Gary's earnestness in this man, the presence of a conscience. He quickly reminded himself that this was his kidnapper and probable executioner.

"So the attack on the US was not a jihad?"

"No. We have to … put the record … straight…"

"That's too much to ask." Did he not know that the average American didn't know the difference between a Palestinian and any other Arab – and didn't care if there was any difference? The Jewish lobby was far too strong anyway.

"In one of your lectures you said that although truth was the first casualty of war it was the necessary precondition for peace."

It sounded like something Robert might have said; he couldn't deny it. But nowadays he belonged more to the Pontius Pilate school of relativism. The pages of blank cardboard underlined his failure with absolutes.

"One man and a few tapes…?" Did he really think those mediocre tapes would change anything, given the preexisting level of hostility and hatred? "Did you really think Jallud Fahd would be released?"

"I thought there might have been a chance."

"So then, even if ... you kill me ... your mission will have failed?"

"Not necessarily..." Khaled looked him in the eye and then turned away.

A long silence followed; they had nothing left to say.

"I heard ... a car a few minutes ago." Robert broke the silence. He noticed for the first time the metallic butt of an automatic pistol that protruded from inside Khaled's open coat.

"The others have gone."

"Gone?" The prompt was more strident than he intended.

"It's nearly over," Khaled mumbled, still looking down. "Just that one tape left."

Robert's blood went cold; every moment counted now. He stalled. "You really think ... it'll make any difference?"

"A dent in awareness. Can we expect more?" Khaled seemed weary beyond words, almost beaten.

But it didn't reassure Robert, who was certain his time was coming soon. And it would be Khaled after all, this morose man his executioner. Yet killing, for such men, might be nothing more than a necessary chore. The gun suggested it wouldn't be a beheading. Recriminations overcame Robert. He should have ... what? Tried to write more? Love more? Prudence had been the bane of his life. There was no point in pleading or attacking. Khaled was younger, fitter and armed.

Maybe one chance in a hundred but he couldn't muster the energy for such odds. And he didn't want it to be unseemly. Dignity was all that was left. Strange, he'd always laughed at that idea of dignity, but it was important. Keep talking at least. Every second was precious.

"What will you do when … you leave here?"

"Oh." Khaled shrugged as if trying to free his shoulders of a heavy weight; the effort made him silent.

In the midst of his own thoughts, which should have been more important, since final, Robert heard a susurration in the trees outside. Maybe it would be a stormy night after all. But the wind seemed to die as quickly as it got up. Something about the strangely abrupt sound drew his attention to the window. In the failing light he saw a black shadow move across the field, ruffling the grass, and disappear. His heart froze. A helicopter! It had to be. It seemed miraculous that Khaled didn't notice.

With pounding heart he moved between Khaled and the window. He tried to say something to distract him but couldn't think of anything. The pain of hope restored the beating in his chest. Because he had a chance. So close to freedom he knew real fear. He could hardly breathe. Or think. He bunched his fists. Yes. Go down fighting on this chance. Yes. Jesus, there was just a second either way.

"I know they're out there," Khaled drew out the pistol.

Robert launched himself but was repulsed by an elbow in the chest. He fell to the ground. Then he heard a shot that in the confines of the cellar almost deafened him. He could smell the cordite. But he felt no pain. Khaled had fired through the window at random. Oddly, the glass had fallen inwards. Robert stayed on his hands and knees.

Then a voice through a loud hailer: "Khaled Hassan, you are surrounded! Do not harm Robert Lynskey. Come out with your hands in plain sight. Repeat, do not harm Lynskey!"

The sound of his name electrified Robert. He struggled to his feet, his mouth open for air. He was about to be rescued, or was he? The thought of being shot now, so close to freedom, was unbearable.

Methodically, and without any great urgency, Khaled removed the clip from the gun and threw it on the ground. His eyes met Robert's. "See how our fortunes change. You are free now…"

"You … never intended…?"

"No. You were a good teacher." Khaled reached into his pocket and handed him the tape. "Use it as you will." His gaze transcended the invisible screen between them as though he had a direct, though secret, route into Robert's mind. "Despite what you think, you are an honest man."

Robert couldn't answer, even when he felt the cassette being slipped into his pocket. Something more than a tape was being transferred.

"Maybe you would like to see how this ends." Khaled's hand brushed his arm.

In a daze Robert followed him upstairs. He was much weaker than the last time he'd made that climb but some reserve of energy drove him on.

Khaled walked slowly through the house and paused at the front door, drenched with light from the spotlights outside.

"Stay back," he said, opening the door. Even more powerful light flooded in. Robert was blinded but thought he saw Khaled's arm move. Immediately there was a shattering barrage of fire. Khaled was flung back into the middle of the room. Screaming ricochets whined after the first bursts. At a command the firing ceased. When he hit the floor Khaled's body clenched in one last spasm as if testing its ebbing strength, the legs buckled, arms pinned awkwardly. Then with a long sigh his limbs straightened and relaxed and all the last moment's tension seeped away. There was a second, more muffled, sound as his body crumpled into its final position. Having thrown himself down when the firing started, Robert now found himself staring into Khaled's still open eyes, dead orbs of glazed brown. Because of the eyes he didn't see the destruction of the skull or the rosettes of blood spreading over the threadbare suit.

"Are you OK, Mr. Lynskey?" Limon was first through the door. He helped Robert to his feet and signaled to a couple of men to lend a hand. He then went into the room to examine the body.

Robert's legs were so weak he had to be half

carried to the waiting car. The open space frightened him, the sudden immensity of the sky. In the car he almost passed out, clutched the seat in front for support. He remembered the last time he'd been helped into a car. Was it beginning again? No, just shock. He held his knees to stop them trembling. Mustn't cry. His nephew, John, once hit by a baseball, fought back tears. As he must do now. Christ, he'd survived against all the odds though couldn't quite believe it. But he was used up. He had spent all his meager strength to adapt to prison and had nothing left to cope with freedom. It had happened too fast. This rescue could be the death of him. Thank god for humor. And for the friendly cop with the brandy.

"Bet you could use another belt," Mahon said, passing him back the flask.

Robert put it to his lips, drank, gagged and drank again. Rich fire, raw life. No sensation ever felt so good. The fumes went straight to his head. Or maybe the night air sweeping from that enormous sky. The gratitude he felt was shaming. Must hold back tears. Look around for bearings. The outside of the house, much as he'd imagined it. Helmeted SWAT police swarmed over the building and outhouses. Riflemen boarded a bus further down the lane and moved out. Others boarded the chopper. Mission accomplished. He was stunned. A small army had come to save him. He hadn't been abandoned. He felt again the gratitude of a young immigrant saved by this generous and resourceful country.

"Are you all right, sir?" Mahon asked.

"Yes ... thanks..."

"We'll get you to hospital straight away." He nodded to the driver.

"I'm so ... grateful..." Robert couldn't finish it. As they drove away he saw the police carry out a body bag that sagged in the middle.

CHAPTER 22

AS HE DRIFTED in and out of sleep, he glimpsed blurred fragments of white and silver, sensed an order and cleanliness that were almost an affront. And far from being in danger there were starched figures fussing over him, their murmurs like prayers. For that whole day they ran tests on him, fed him with chicken broth and what he guessed were sedatives, and mercifully kept visitors at bay. He dreamt of a looming dark figure walking towards a stream to fetch water, but the stream was dry and, for some reason, the man collapsed.

He woke once to find a tall, angular man looking down at him; he thought he may have asked him something. When he came to later the man was gone.

The next morning he woke renewed. He went into his private bathroom and had a shower that made his toes open and shut; he actually moaned aloud under the cleansing jets. Drying his legs, he watched the old flaky skin peeling from his shins and drift like confetti to the tiled floor. He covered himself with all the unguents the well-stocked bathroom provided, talcum powder, cologne, hair gel. He trimmed round his beard making it look more full and defined; this was his new crest and he wore it with pride. He clipped his nails, filing them smooth, and brushed his teeth until the gums bled. Then he brushed them again and gargled with mouthwash to staunch the bleeding.

Another even more sinful pleasure was in store: breakfast. He started with pineapple juice, sitting at his little functional table, then attacked Eggs Benedict – there was a lot to be said for private medicine – and finished off with hot croissants and coffee, the taste of which he had all but forgotten.

Propped up in bed, spruce and shining, he received his visitors, Sarah and Gary the first admitted to the presence. She fell into his arms and they exchanged hungry kisses; he could taste the salt of her tears. "Oh Robert … it's so good to have you back … You've no idea how I … we all worried about you. Darling, it's just wonderful. But forgive me. You're probably still weak…" She withdrew and, still appraising him with shining eyes, plumped up his pillows, arranged flowers and cards, her hands fluttering with a will of their own.

"It's good to see you, Sarah." Robert grinned from his pillows, a wounded satyr recovering other sensations.

Gary who had been standing in the background came forward and warmly shook hands, then embraced him too.

"Great to see you, Bob. I knew you'd make it … And you're the guy who worried about guts." Gary moved his head from side to side, marveling at his redoubtable brother.

"Well, there were times…" Robert left it

hanging, smitten again by the thought that somehow or another he had beaten the rap, and was restored to his life of comfort. It was hard now to imagine how, before the kidnapping, he had questioned and bemoaned the perceived limits to his freedom; in retrospect they seemed so paltry. He hoped he'd learnt his lesson.

"It must have been awful," Sarah sighed, plucking off her gloves, finger by finger, as she sat on the edge of the bed, her delicate lemony perfume finding its way through Robert's astringent excesses. "Those dangerous fanatics. Was it just terrible? You must talk about it. Let it out. We spoke to so many people in Washington. But the press was so persistent." She shuddered so that a wisp of hair broke its moorings at the base of her slender neck. "We felt so … ineffectual."

"I'm sure you did all you could, and I'm grateful…" Robert faltered, regretting how, in the dark hours, he had misjudged people, assumed they had abandoned him. His expression crumpled, canceling the image conferred by the beard.

Gary came to his rescue. "Take it easy. You've all the time in the world. If you want us out of here just say the word. I mean me," he added, realizing he shouldn't speak for Sarah.

"No. It's just … images come back…" The effects of his shower and breakfast were wearing thin and he knew the adjustment would take longer. In the cellar he had begged for his life, he had tried to run away, tried to bribe his abductors and he had considered selling out whatever principles he had left. Nothing had worked and yet he survived.

"You'll have to write about it," Sarah said enthusiastically. "It would be therapeutic apart from anything else. And people really want to know." She leant forward and kissed him again. "It tickles." She stroked his beard.

On an impulse Robert struggled out of bed, went to the closet and checked the pockets of his suit. The tape was there. For some reason he locked the closet and transferred the key to the pocket of his robe. He got back into bed weaker than he realized. He wondered what had become of the cardboard.

"What was all that about?" Sarah fussed over his pillows again, her finely-wrought gold bracelets tinkling. He hadn't seen this maternal side before and was rather ashamed to find himself wallowing in it.

His reply was baulked by the arrival of Drew and Chaim armed with gifts of books, magazines and booze. After a fierce fusillade of greeting and back-slapping, Drew stood jovially with stomach distended. "You old survivor. It takes more than a bunch of kooks to punch your clock, eh?" The camaraderie was more than their normal relationship would have permitted but the circumstances seemed to warrant it.

"Welcome back." Chaim said. He joined his hands together and made a Mandarin bow.

Drew removed his green corduroy jacket as if

he were going to make a day of it. "KNYBS has been flooded with messages of goodwill. Wait till you see them. It'll do your heart good. Hey, that beard is cool. Makes you look like Papa Hemingway. But seriously though the folks are glad you made it."

"The fickle populace still wants you," Chaim said, the barb aimed in Drew's direction, a pointed reminder about Rembert.

Drew let it slide by. "I'm sure you have tales to tell and stories to write."

Robert smiled feebly. They meant well but it was all getting a little much for him. His stomach was reacting badly to the invasion of rich food. A nurse came in to say the press were milling outside, demanding a statement

"Oh Lord," Robert groaned. "Could you get me out of this?"

"I'll take care of it." Sarah volunteered, swiveling on her heels. Drew followed her with his eyes; she really was something else. He marveled at her. "Has Limon been in?" Drew turned his attention back to Robert.

"Is he the tall one?"

"Yeah. Looks like a hawk."

"I think he was in yesterday. But I was half zonked."

"Probably waiting to hear if you talked in your sleep." Drew occupied the edge of the bed recently vacated by Sarah. Gary had surrendered the only other chair to Chaim. There were never enough chairs in hospitals.

"Why would he do that?" Robert asked.

Drew hesitated, not sure if he should mention Limon's odd theory. "You know what these spooks are like."

"He's CIA?"

"Yep. Mind you, he did a good job in the end. Got you out without a scratch." Drew fiddled with his pipe, took a reamer to it which dislodged the odor; having stopped smoking didn't mean he had to stop sniffing. After twelve years the unlit bowl still smelled of Balkan Sobranie.

"They weren't going to kill me. Not Hassan anyway..."

"Oh come on Robert. You're dreaming. From what I hear those guys were heavy."

Chaim nodded. That had been his impression too. Terrorists held life cheap; Lynskey was definitely lucky to be alive. It seemed as if they all wanted to be part of the most dramatic story possible.

Robert felt his eyelids begin to droop. Drew was so vibrant and combative it underscored his own weakness. They were all beginning to fade, or perhaps he was receding to a quieter place. Was there something called survival fatigue? Like an animal coming out of hibernation after a long winter, he needed time to blink in the sun, feel the air on his pelt. Birth must be a little like this, if one could remember.

Announced by her heels in the sounding corridor, Sarah returned. "I got rid of those news hounds. But they're hungry for meat. They want you to hold a press conference soonest." She fastened her stare on Drew until he got up and gave her back the best seat in the house.

Robert tried to rouse himself. "I don't know if I'm quite … up for that…"

"You'll have to, Bob," Drew said. "It's important. In my opinion it's the biggest story since 9/11 and Uncle Sam could sure use the kudos right now." He flashed his all-weather smile.

"We'll see." Robert reckoned he probably couldn't escape. He looked at Gary standing in silence, nursing his own thoughts, and longed to talk with him.

"I think Robert is tired," Sarah said proprietorially, placing a cool and delicately perfumed hand on his forehead.

"Maybe we'd better skedaddle at that." Drew was lost in admiration for how she'd reentered Robert's life and taken charge, soothing his brow, curtailing the audience. He was her main project again. Drew should have felt jealous but he didn't. There was a tensile complicity between them which could be stretched to infinity without breaking. She might deny it but was nevertheless tethered by that strong invisible thread. He could wait; waiting was his game.

"Take care," Chaim said, holding up the palm of his hand.

Sarah saw them out and returned with more flowers and cards from well-wishers including Simkin, Nita, Robert's own staff and the staff of

KNYBS.

"There's an email from the President," she said excitedly. "Shall I read it?"

"Shoot." Robert's strength was ebbing but he rallied to hear this.

Sarah gave a little formal cough and began, "My Dear Robert, I salute your courage in what must have been a most trying situation. We are all delighted to have you back safe and sound. Be assured of our deepest affection."

"Nice," Robert murmured. Someone had ghosted the message; the President would never have written, 'My Dear Robert'. He wasn't sure if he was doing it deliberately, but his eyes began to close. The images that raged inside his head were becoming fragmented, senseless.

"I think maybe we should give him a break," Gary said.

Sarah reluctantly agreed, planting a farewell kiss on the pale forehead.

Not long after they'd left, Robert got a spiritual second wind – he couldn't sleep anyway with those disjointed pictures flickering in his mind – so he sat up and opened the bottle of Jameson Reserve sent by Michael Moore with a card that read, "Have a belt or two for derring-do." He poured the whiskey into a little plastic medicine cup about the size of a shot glass and knocked it back. He sipped the next one more slowly and switched on the TV, hunting and pecking at the remote control. He caught a news flash about the rescue on Channel Eight. "...is undergoing tests but is said to be in good health after his ordeal. According to FBI sources the operation, mounted late last night, was a complete success. Robert Lynskey was not harmed in the surprise raid though arch-terrorist and fanatic Khaled Hassan, who came out of the house firing an automatic weapon, was shot dead..." In the upper left-hand quadrant of the screen there appeared a still of Robert taken, he surmised, from the dust jacket of his latest book. This was immediately replaced by a shot of Khaled's body in a mortuary; the sudden superimposition made Robert's sedated heart leap. The newscaster continued, "This morning, speaking from the Rose Garden, the President complimented all of the Federal Agencies on the success of the mission, which proved that the forces of law and order could triumph over terrorism. He praised Robert Lynskey for the courage he had shown in what he described as 'a most trying situation' and expressed his personal delight that his former friend and colleague had been delivered safe and sound from the hands of his abductors." There followed a clip of a smiling, sunlit President, reading from a head-up device, waving to his personal friends among the press corps. His stock was up in a bullish market. "In Washington circles," the anchor man continued, "the success of the operation is seen as a major plus, possibly even a turning point in the President's efforts to defuse the situation in the Middle East." He paused to receive a message through his ear piece and continued, "We have just learnt that Robert Lynskey is to talk to the press about his experience at an early date. Stay tuned to this channel for further details…"

After switching off the set, Robert's initial exhilaration turned to dismay. The bulletin was so finely nuanced in favor of the authorities and so self-serving it seemed to support everything that Khaled had said. And he felt aggrieved – though he knew it was churlish – that the President's 'personal' message to him had been so obviously transcribed from the official statement. Then there was the barely concealed self-promotion of his erstwhile colleagues in the media. But what bothered him most, though he couldn't explain it, was the electronic fusion of Khaled's image with his own.

Later that day the results of his tests came back. His blood pressure was slightly elevated and he was put on beta-blockers again, but apart from that, the doctors smilingly informed him, he was in good shape. Robert didn't tell anyone he'd been discharged, and to avoid the press staking out the main entrance to the hospital, he made his escape through the Outpatients Department and went home in a cab. It was good to drive through the streets again; he imagined a mock-heroic refrain: 'Lynskey is back in town.' But he knew his freedom to walk those streets would be curtailed in the future.

He had the cab drop him off a couple of houses away from his own brownstone, and to avoid his staff – he had visions of a standing ovation or 'surprise' party – went straight up to his apartment which had a slight musty, unused smell about it. The tortoiseshell shades seemed to cower against the chintzes as if a stranger had invaded their precious privacy. Eschewing the high-backed regency furniture of the lounge, he went into his study, which bore some of his own mark, and sank into a well-worn armchair. Afraid to look at the papers on his desk, he poured whiskey into a glass that smelled stale and began to drink. That plus the beta-blockers added to his fuzziness. But he wasn't going to drive any heavy machinery. He was home, be it ever so humble and foreign. The luxury of being alone and free was almost unbearable.

He was drifting finally into peaceful sleep when the phone rang. With a not so muffled swear he answered it.

"Limon here. Glad you got a clean bill of health."

"Thanks…" The man clearly didn't go overboard with social graces.

"We'll have to have a debriefing session soon. When would be good for you?"

"There's really nothing I can tell you." Robert had a vague intuition that it wasn't over. His own whiskey breath was referred back to him from the mouthpiece; it smelled rank and sickly rich, worse, it seemed, than any of the stenches of the cellar.

Limon was not to be put off by that. "In cases like this it's necessary to hold a ... to rake over the details. It's an intelligence matter. I'm sure you understand..."

"All right," Robert conceded wearily. "Tomorrow afternoon." They had saved his bacon after all, at least as far as they were concerned. He owed them that much. They weren't to know that Khaled was not going to kill him.

"That would be fine." Limon rang off.

Robert tried to settle back to his nap but the moment had passed. He sat in the darkening room wondering if he were trying to re-create the atmosphere of the cellar in the same way that soldiers returning from the front, sometimes headed for the hills, to seek a redemption which civilization could no longer provide. He shrugged off that notion – he was still too fond of his creature comforts to crawl willingly into the final bolt-hole – got up and did a few chores.

He emptied the pockets of the suit he'd lived in for the last two weeks. It was beyond saving, virtually stood up on its own, so he left it with the trash for his daily, Mrs. Knowles, to dispose of. He stood on a chair to put the cassette on top of a tall bookcase behind the pediment. Partly by rote he went to the kitchen and looked in the icebox which Mrs. Knowles had kept reasonably well stocked. God bless her; she had obviously made an optimistic calculation about his chances. There was certainly enough for a sandwich, but on reflection and given the state of his stomach, he didn't bother. On the way back to the study he glanced out a window and saw a car parked in the quiet street outside his house. He filed it away as something to look into later.

When he was reasonably inebriated he decided to check his messages. The first one was from Sarah, fuming about being stood up. This was followed by Nita, reminding him about the alimony check. Voices came and went, Drew, Peggy, Simkin, Beth, different voices, different messages. Nothing urgent, just touching base, call me when you get in, call me, please get back to me ... Life was a series of minute transactions. Then the sudden break. Sarah again, "Darling, forgive me ... I had no idea..." This sentiment repeated by other voices in varying degrees of distress. Some crying, that fine girl, Peggy sounding genuinely upset.

Then another sea change *after* the rescue. Simkin: "Well done, Robert. Now you know about claims..." And of course Drew: "All I said was memoirs. I didn't say you had to go and make history."

There were many other messages too; it was as if he'd cast his net upon the wide sea of finely meshed lives. That was enough for the moment; he couldn't face emails or social media just then. Through the window he saw the same car, the driver pouring coffee from a flask into a plastic cup. Protection? Was he still at risk even though they'd blasted Khaled to pieces? Maybe it was just routine, though if so Limon might have mentioned it. On the other hand *he* hadn't mentioned the tape to Limon, and wondered why not.

Later that afternoon Sarah rang to see how he was. Reluctant to accept his assurances she said, "You sound a little odd. Are you sure you're all right?

"Drinking a bit, you know. Getting the feel of the old pad." He tried to sound jaunty; the affectation surprised him.

"Have you eaten?" she asked suspiciously.

"Yes, sandwiches. Don't worry, Sarah, I'm fine. Really. Going to turn in soon."

"By the way, don't forget the press conference. It's set for ten tomorrow at KNYBS.

"OK." There was something else. Oh yes, Limon's 'debriefing', but that was in the afternoon. His calendar was filling up already. How had anyone coped while he was out of action? Maybe life ceased when he turned his back.

"'Bye for now, darling. We'll have to get together soon." Her voice went low and lingered over the words.

"Absolutely." He drew out the syllables too in a sympathetic reflex.

For some reason he went downstairs to wander about the sleeping offices where all the high-tech equipment stood mute on desks. He wondered what the staff had been doing these past weeks. Had he left enough ideas in the pipeline? Beth of course would have found something to do. Indeed, judging by her desk, she had put together a comprehensive folio of newspaper clippings. He riffled through it without absorbing anything but the most graphic headlines. Then he noticed a satin banner draped across a chair, 'Welcome Home Robert'. They were planning something for tomorrow; he felt guilty previewing it.

As he looked over his little empire he thought how easy it would be to write up his experiences-stroke-memoirs. Could have a bestseller out in six months, use tomorrow's press conference to promote it. Thinking of which, he would need to work out some *bons mots* for the press, little silver fish for the seals to leap at and applaud. Yes, all the options were open. He was back.

By the time he'd re-acquainted himself with all the nooks and crannies of the house, he couldn't postpone any longer what remained for him to do. The mood in which he approached the tape had something of the embarrassed fear of reading one's own first galleys. He steeled himself as he went back upstairs to the study. But why should he care? Maybe he should just throw the damn thing out with the greasy suit, or pass it over to Limon. But he couldn't. For some reason he could not do that.

As he prepared for this most private screening, he slotted the tape into an old video recorder and sat in the dark, clasping a glass to his chest – he no longer had a paunch to balance it on. The radio commentaries he'd heard in captivity were right; the stuff was heavy-handed and gauche. And, as he watched the unobtrusive screen half-hidden among the bookshelves, he had to admit the awful relativist truth that, compared with recent coverage of African famines, shots of Palestinian refugee camps did not tear the heartstrings, at least not to the degree assumed by the overblown commentary. Another demeaning thought: it needed a slicker presentation, better production values, as Chaim would have put it.

But he sat and watched, reassured in a way that it lacked punch and therefore didn't commit him to anything. Much of the footage pertained to different periods, some far back in time. He began to sit up and take notice, however, when he saw hitherto unknown shots of US destroyers in the Gulf firing indiscriminately at civilian targets, and Fl-11s bombing the refugee camp of Bourj El Barajneh. He didn't realize that America had been so directly involved in these 'reprisals'. Indeed the White House, backed up by the Defense Department, had repeatedly denied any such direct action. The tape, if shown, would not help America's credibility.

The next clip, though jerky and smudged, was more damning. It showed what appeared to be US Marines shooting two Palestinian prisoners at close quarters. After an interval the camera moved in on one of the bodies, a boy who couldn't have been more than fourteen. Then there was the assassination of the stroke-crippled Ahmed Yassin. Further atrocities against the Palestinians were shown, including the results of the bulldozer attack which had killed a young boy and girl in a brutal way. An unseen hand draped a green Hamas flag over their dead bodies. Several times Robert had to cover his eyes; he was no longer a numbed observer.

At one point he had to stop and rewind the tape to check on something. There was footage of a Palestinian reprisal, a suicide bomber in a shopping center. It wasn't all one-sided; Khaled was trying to be even-handed. Shortly afterwards, his commentary suggested that there was fault on both sides. Palestinians and Jews were cousins who should live in peace. The West should not favor one side over the other or be influenced by votes, oil or commerce. Only Jallud Fahd could reconcile the factions in the Middle East, including Israel. He renounced terrorism, was wrongly imprisoned and was a man of God.

There were scenes of Jallud Fahd being tortured and degraded in prison, scenes much more horrific than those in Abu Ghraib. Robert felt bile rising into his throat. He could scarcely believe that the US military could behave like that. Khaled pleaded for an end to violence on both sides and argued that the voice of reason had to be heard. That was why he chose Robert Lynskey, a man whose humanity was obvious in his works and lectures. Coming from an Irish background, Lynskey knew the meaning of diaspora and dispossession. He and Jallud Fahd would have much in common.

Astonished, Robert listened to that familiar, though slightly distorted, voice outline his plan to persuade American networks to show the tapes. "There is no other way. Robert Lynskey will not be in danger. When this tape is shown I will be dead, but the effort to improve awareness must continue..."

Robert had to take a breather; he could not explain why it affected him so much. It wasn't just the reference to himself, though he had been moved by that. He felt the stirring of a radical instinct long repressed. As a cub reporter he had hounded Nixon and been critical of most of his successors. What right had a plutocracy to impose democracy on the rest of the world or lie to its own people? Even now there was too much imperial hubris about the role of America in the world. They had strayed very far from the vision of the Founding Fathers.

Khaled had planned it right from the start, Robert thought, getting unsteadily to his feet, every detail. *He* was the production, not the tape; the singer not the song. He had made Robert witness his death, the body crumpling inside the cheap suit. It was the craziest PR stunt of all time, one that had no chance of working. And he left the decision to Robert. Thanks a lot. Although he was moved by some of the images, he doubted if America as a whole would be influenced in any way, even by Khaled's death.

Then he went back to the tape; there wasn't much left. He expected some more rhetoric or a few more out-of-date images. But what he saw shook him to the core of his being.

CHAPTER 23

THE 'SURPRISE' PARTY with Beth and the team was pleasant and endearing though a little strained. After the initial salvo of applause and greeting, they stood around having cake and coffee and chocolate-chip cookies, Beth fussing and, as usual, taking responsibility for everything, including Robert's state of mind. At times they waited to see if he wanted to talk about his experiences but didn't press him, so the conversation was a little makeshift, cobbled together across the smiling silences. One of the junior researchers wore an expression of such obvious respect that it was touching and also a little frightening. The modest party cleared up his morning hangover. But it did nothing to reduce the shock effect of the last segment of Khaled's tape.

As he crossed town on his way to see Limon it dawned on him that he'd forgotten all about the press conference; it was the first gig he'd ever missed. The hell with it, he thought, but still he felt guilty. The old social scruples were back; the cellar was already becoming a memory.

Moving hydraulically in his long cylindrical suit, Limon folded himself into a swivel chair and thanked him for coming in.

"I hope, after your ordeal, you're not finding it too difficult to get back to normal." The pleasantry was stilted because chitchat didn't come easy to him.

"Thanks," Robert replied uncertainly. "I've commenced re-entry. By the way, I wonder if you might convey my thanks to Lieutenant Mahon. He was very kind." He observed the functional, almost Spartan office which had as little personality as its occupant. You could almost tell it was Agency because it was so anonymous and shell-like, except for the stars and stripes that hung limply in a corner, and a well-touched-up photograph of the poorly-touched-up President. Everything was locked away or encrypted on computer; even the in-tray was empty. There was nothing on the desk apart from a blotter pad and there weren't even doodles on that. Limon seemed husk-like too, not quite belonging, and his voice had a hollow metallic ring.

"May I ask," Robert continued, "how you discovered the ... location." He was going to say, 'hide-out', but that would have sounded childish.

"Well, the Black Muslim connection helped." Limon didn't elaborate. The information flow was to be one way.

Robert scratched his unfamiliar beard. Khaled probably reckoned the Black Muslims would sooner or later deliver him up. How easy it must have been to depend on others' weaknesses to achieve his goal of self-destruction. Had he enjoyed the process, watching his predictions pay off one by one like falling dominoes, sweeping towards the last act of the melodrama? Limon of course was entirely predictable, probably hadn't even considered taking Khaled alive. Limon believed in fire power, shock and awe; if you have it, use it.

As he poured two cups of coffee from a percolator, Limon started with the obvious questions: What had Robert heard about connections between Black Muslims and foreign terrorist groups, had Hassan mentioned anything about other missions being planned, were any names mentioned? Despite Limon's admonitions to take his time and not to regard anything as unimportant, there was little Robert could tell him. Except for the explosive tape, and he wasn't going to mention that until he, himself, had gotten it into some kind of perspective. Feeling defensive, he described how isolated he'd been in the cellar, how he'd only seen the woman once. He had the feeling Limon was unimpressed. He took no notes; maybe there was a hidden tape-recorder.

"Incidentally, I wasn't in danger, at least not from Hassan," Robert felt he should say this.

"Really?" Limon's face was a mask, resting on a bridge of long interlocked fingers.

"Yes. Hassan emptied his gun before you shot him. Well, I guess you know that by now."

"Why do you think he wasn't going to kill you?" Limon asked with a casualness that didn't quite conceal the underlying intent.

"I'm ... not sure." He faltered because it suddenly occurred to him that he didn't know the reason. Maybe Khaled wasn't a cold-blooded killer, or maybe he wanted Robert to run with the goddamn tape. Limon would laugh at the first explanation and the second would create a whole set of problems which Robert was not quite ready to face. "I don't really know," he ended lamely.

"I see." There was a break in the proceedings as Limon excused himself to take a phone call. After that, Robert, who had used the opportunity to gather his wits, threw him a curveball.

"Maybe you could stand down the agent who's been 'protecting' me."

Limon smiled. "That's just routine. But if he really gets in your way, call me." He stabbed the blotter pad with a letter knife. "So you don't know why you lucked out?"

"No. He didn't seem like a killer to me." Robert sipped his coffee which tasted excellent, but then his palate had lost its discrimination. He drained the polystyrene cup, crumpled it and threw it in the waste basket which, he couldn't help noticing, was empty. There was no evidence of any work having been done in that office and yet it wasn't exactly tidy.

"That wouldn't be consistent with our research," Limon replied. He didn't elaborate but paused for a reaction which wasn't forthcoming. Then he continued, "By the way, I was interested to discover that Hassan was a student of yours in Columbia." He sat back in his chair to see how the interviewee would field that unexpected bunt.

"An extraordinary coincidence," Robert agreed . "Of course I didn't really know him. He was a loner..."

"Still, it must have been a shock to be kidnapped by a former student. Maybe he didn't like your lectures." Limon permitted himself a tight smile.

Robert laughed a little uneasily. "Could be. I'm no Jordan Peterson."

"Or maybe," Limon leant forward, "he *did* like them."

"Meaning?" Robert felt a chill on his neck that spread slowly down his back. His question wasn't answered and he ruminated on the sinister non-response.

After he'd left, Limon opened a locked drawer and took out a piece of cardboard which contained some interesting notes. He also studied again a piece of paper torn from a spiral-bound notebook. It seemed to refer to another tape which was not found on Hassan's body or in the farm house.

Dressed in blue leotard and tights having just returned from a ballet class, Sarah met him at the door of his own house.

"Hope you don't mind. I just let myself in." Her features flickered with uncertainty as she read his face.

"Glad to see you, Sarah." They kissed in the hallway. He loved her with her hair up, that prima ballerina look that made her untouchable to others but not to him.

She ushered him into the dining room. "I brought some food. We can't have you wandering around Manhattan like a scarecrow." She sat him down at the head of the oval table and began to decant sweetly spiced seafood and saffron rice from an array of cartons.

Robert slipped his jacket over the back of the carved chair. "Limon gave me a hard time, put me on the defensive. I just don't get it." His voice sounded more petulant than he realized. He was supposed to be the hero after all.

"Oh, that Limon. He has some weird idea you were implicated. All those people are paranoid if you ask me. Mmmm, that's not bad." She tasted the shrimp and lobster tempura that came from one of her ethnic 'discoveries', and sniffed delicately at the subtle aroma. The only thing that marred the meal was the higgledy-piggledy cairn of tubs that littered the polished table. Still, it was a small price to pay for convenience.

"Implicated? Me?" He loosened his tie and shirt cuffs, wallowing in the cool, recycled air. That might explain Limon's attitude, he thought, but it still didn't make sense, and he couldn't deny it affected him. "How did you come across this ... this theory?"

"Drew mentioned it, I think." She helped him to some of the scallops in shrimp sauce and sprinkled sesame seeds on the rising mound of his plate.

"Drew?" How large and intricate a web had

been woven in the last three weeks? He didn't know. Maybe that time was utterly lost and could not be reclaimed by memory or narration. But he returned to the more immediate point. "So Limon thinks I was in on it. Good god, what next?" His savior now his accuser; it was lunacy. He couldn't cope with it at that moment. In the last couple of days he had developed a passion for milk and now drank it copiously, leaving the wine for her.

"Mysterious ways," she said indifferently. "But, Bob, how could you miss the press conference?"

"I forgot about it. I'm sorry." He teased with his fork what seemed to be a butterfly shrimp and thought better of it, reverting to his tumbler of milk.

"How could you forget about it?" Her face wore a frozen smile. "Everyone was there, all the frontline journalists. Even your friend Downey from Newsweek."

"Maybe my subconscious was trying to tell me I wasn't ready for a grilling." He felt sure the real reason had to do with the final segment of the tape which he still couldn't believe. Between the leaded glass china hutch and the French doors he noticed the slightly discolored patches of wall from which Nita had removed two paintings. One was a landscape by Turner, the other a dreadful portrait of Judge Thomas McKean, one of the signers of the Declaration of Independence with whom she claimed a tenuous relationship. In better times Robert used to rib her about her Great

Uncle who didn't exactly rush in with his John Hancock but waited to see which way the wind was blowing. Even with these omissions, however, the room was still overstuffed and was as foreign in its own way as Limon's office. And yet he was home.

"They wouldn't have pressured you," Sarah said. "Anyway they've probably forgiven you by now." She appraised the wine in its fluted glass and took a tentative sip. "By the way, Drew wants to talk to you about a new-look *RL Hour*."

"What did they do with the slot while I was … away?"

Smoothing an eyebrow with a ringed finger, Sarah thought for a while before answering, and then spoke in a rush. "Don't quote me, but they used a new guy called Si Rembert. He went down well the first time out, but then he bombed."

"And now they want me back? Nice." Robert couldn't say he was surprised. Drew was incredible, so obviously devious it could be funny at times. Anyway he didn't really pose a threat. But Robert was glad she'd told him; it cleared up the matter of alliances.

"Now don't stand on your pride, honey," she chided him. "You're still king of the mountain." She drew him towards her and planted a kiss on his forehead.

He found himself laughing. It sounded and felt strange as if a whole new set of facial muscles were suddenly pressed into service. Adding to the novelty was the sight, in his peripheral vision, of the white whiskers rising up on bunched cheeks. She joined in, tentatively at first, and then with unbridled merriment as the infection caught hold.

"Oh god," he gasped. "That felt good."

"And it's going to get better," she assured him, "We've so much going for us. Let's grab it with both hands." She could make him happy; it was a quaint old-fashioned thought but she believed in Robert as a man and as a partner. Maybe after his ordeal he was ready to make a commitment. Looking around the cluttered room, she itched to purge it of Nita's closely patterned fabrics spitting at each other. Why couldn't women of little taste settle for simplicity? Sarah, of course, had cultivated taste, largely under her mother's influence, had studied fine arts and color theory. She was currently into minimalism and the latest variant of *Feng Shui*. Having failed as a ballerina, she had been catapulted by her then husband – who indulged her every whim – into publishing as a consolation prize but it had never really appealed to her. She sometimes felt she was in orbit, scanning the horizon for somewhere to land among the tower blocks of the Manhattan skyline.

They brought their coffee up to the roof and sat among the trellised vines. She brushed the backs of her fingers against his beard, then stroked the back of his neck as if soothing away the chill Limon had given him. Her kisses were a light and fluttering prelude. There was a lot to be said for abstinence, he thought, fumbling with the satiny leotard, the secret exits of which she found for him. They made love on the roof, not fully hidden from the taller buildings or low-flying aircraft. Before his mind swam away on the ineffable tide he remembered the shadow of the helicopter that brought salvation from the skies. Through her loosened hair he could see the stars and still couldn't name them.

Much later, dressed and returned to more normal senses, he mentioned the tape though he wasn't sure why.

"Is it a rant like the others?" she asked, pouring him a brandy.

"It's different. Packs quite a punch." This was an understatement., but he couldn't reveal the full story that continued to prey on his mind. "I don't know what to do about it." Limon's suspicions of course made it more dangerous for him to hold onto it; of that he was in no doubt. Neither was she; the word 'treason' came to her mind; it had a frightening ring to it.

"Give it to Limon."

"I didn't mention its existence to him. He'd be even more suspicious if I gave it to him now. He'd wonder why I'd kept it a secret."

"Then get rid of it," she said without hesitating. Sometimes she couldn't understand why he made such a meal of quite simple things. As far as she was concerned there was no point in staying in a loss-making situation. "Junk the damn thing."

"But…"

She placed a finger on his lips. "No 'buts', darling. Just destroy it. And you will re-schedule the press conference?"

"I guess..."

"And consider the new-look show?" She smiled disarmingly at her own persistence.

"We'll see," he grumbled, reaching for her, to forget again, pleased that amnesia could become a habit, pleased also that his recent experiences had not affected his libido.

CHAPTER 24

IT WAS SEPTEMBER and the sun was less punishing, though it still held sway in an enamel sky. The city was beginning to unwind from the stifling heat of high summer, its pulse more measured and regular; the less congested air floated the hope of survival for another year. The three men sat in their shirt-sleeves.

"The old firm together again." Drew laughed and beckoned the waiter to the table where they sat under the awning of a street-side restaurant. The celebration lunch was on him. His forearms were knotted and bulging, the watch-strap lost in the folds of the wrist and the fuzz of orange hair. His breast pocket, stuffed with redundant pipe materials, protruded from his chest like a bung in a barrel.

"Don't get carried away." Robert entered a caveat. "If I do the show again it'll be on my terms." He was in a tetchy disoriented mood. But it was hard to be mad with the world on a day like this, the blond light streaming into the hexagonal patio in which they sat, or rather sprawled. Of course there was little real about it – even the passers-by seemed impressionistic, laid on as afterthoughts with a flick of a palette knife – but it would have been churlish to dwell on that. Reality was overrated.

"Sure. Of course." Drew's assurances came in gusts as he patted his arm. "And listen, Bob, that

Rembert kid was only a stand-in. A poor substitute, if I may say so." He waved his ceremonial pipe, a bent carved meerschaum with a Turkish bowl. Occasionally the pipe got him noticed when some fellow diner assumed he was smoking and ordered him to extinguish it immediately if not sooner. Drew seemed to delight in shoving the empty bowl under the nose of the complainant and extracting an apology.

Chaim might have cringed except he was glad to have Robert back. Maybe it would work out after all. He certainly hoped the water that had gone under the bridge wouldn't back up with the detritus of bad memories. To his relief, his partner, Christopher, had agreed to renew their arrangement for another six months, although he had taken a raincheck on Chaim's proposal of marriage. It was probably as much as he could hope for. He had often wondered why gays were so fearful of more solid, institutional arrangements, like marriage, why they preferred to coast along on a wing and a prayer. Naturally, Chaim didn't expect relationships to be pensionable or set in concrete, but the pervasive assumption that nothing good could last constantly amazed and unsettled him. Indeed younger gay men tended to laugh at loyal old queens as if the latter *had* to settle for marriage for want of something better. Anyway, he was glad Robert was back though he had a sneaking suspicion he'd left something behind him in Metuchen. He had certainly become more distant.

"But," Drew went on expansively, "do yourself a favor. Forget about that tape. Sarah is absolutely right. You owe those whirling dervishes nothing. *You* were the victim, remember. The public would never forgive you for showing the damn thing now when there's no need." In fact this was a matter of regret to Drew, who had put the proposal to the top brass in KNYBS only to receive a very dusty answer. Now that Lynskey was safe there was no justification for showing the tape. To do so would be a gratuitous act against the national interest, so the lawyers said, and one which would play right into the hands of the Justice Department, who were anxiously casting about for a test case of the Patriot Act. Reluctantly, Drew had to agree. Besides, now that Rembert had bombed, he desperately needed Robert back and didn't want him to disembowel himself in public. If necessary he would have to save him from himself. The rock-slide had petered out. For now.

"You aired the other ones," Robert pointed out, staring at a wine glass which he revolved slowly between thumb and forefinger. Here he was in another leafy bower like his own rooftop; all these pleasant spaces gave a bewilderment of choice. Yet the cellar was in his blood. One window was more than enough to look at the day. He had communed with every blade of burnt grass and stem of goldenrod as the seconds passed into minutes.

"That was to save your neck," Drew explained

again, wondering why Robert was being so obtuse. "And if we broadcast another one, they'd have our balls for book-ends. Don't forget, Limon suspects you of treason." He laughed, showing red wattles inside his mouth.

"What about good old free speech?" Robert asked mildly, debunking the question even as he put it. He had not told Drew how explosive this last tape was.

"Speech, not gibberish." Drew clapped him on the back, male-bonding. "*The RL Hour* is going to be bigger than ever. Have you seen the papers? You're hotter than a red pepper." The truth of this cut both ways, Drew realized. As Robert's star rose his own would fade in Sarah's eyes. He didn't as yet see any way out of this dilemma but his mind was working on it. Maybe Robert, with all his inhibiting scruples, wasn't as interested in her as he should be. Drew could wait and he wasn't proud. What a woman she was; she somehow thwarted all his selfish instincts and made him want to indulge her. He longed for that because it would be much the same as pampering himself. God damn it, he knew her so well it was unnerving. They were made for each other.

Robert didn't pursue it. Parked outside a drugstore across the street was his 'minder', not any longer bothering to conceal his presence. Driving with one hand on the wheel and his elbow resting on the sill of the open window, he followed them back to KNYBS where Robert tried to interest himself in material for the show.

As he left the building later that afternoon Chaim walked out with him.

"I wanted to tell you something," Chaim said. "While you were away there were these two agents planted in Drew's office. I overheard them talking once." He lowered his voice. "I think they may have bugged your apartment."

Robert stopped in his tracks. It was so obvious and yet it hadn't occurred to him.

"If you like," Chaim continued, "I'll go back with you and check it out. I know a little about electronics."

"Thanks Chaim, but I don't think there's any need." Robert had done some quick reckoning. He hadn't had any conversations in his apartment except for that 'social' evening with Sarah. It was conceivable that the bug had picked up the soundtrack of the tape the night he'd played it, but what did it really matter? He resolved, however, to find a better hiding place for the tape. What kind of fool was Limon? Anyway, he was going to have his work cut out … Robert would see to that.

They walked together for a while. Even with the light fading Robert drew stares and double-takes from passers-by but, mercifully, no approaches. Without looking behind him he knew that his faithful agent was cruising quietly close to the curb.

"I really am glad you're back," Chaim said. "And that you'll have control."

"Thanks. We'll see how it goes." He felt he

owed him a warning and added, "Maybe I've lost something ... I don't know." Or gained something? He wondered. Like relativity it depended on where you were standing at the time. "What did you think of the other tapes? Propaganda or something more?"

"I'm not sure," Chaim replied, sinking his hands in the pockets of his modish pants. "There was the usual amount of selective corroboration, I suppose. But there was something sad about them. Because the impossible is sad."

"I know." Robert nodded. A group of Hispanics jogged past. They all looked dark and regularly handsome.

"Jews and Arabs," Chaim said. "Even the words sound like insults. Maybe we should all get together and call it a day. The weak have no business fighting each other." He shook his shaggy head, the longish swathes of hair following the movement with a lag.

Robert carefully absorbed what he had said. Chaim was nothing if not fair. However, he had missed one point. Israel had the bomb and was allowed to have weapons of mass destruction. He noticed how slender and young Chaim's neck was. He didn't know this man, who always hid in someone else's shadow, but felt he would like him if he did. It wasn't easy for gay men who didn't play the scene. Looking up at buildings in the distance, he fell into an old habit of extrapolating lines and planes towards their vanishing points in the sky. He was intrigued by space, the absence of things, now more than ever.

———————————

Gary had come back again to New York to be on hand for his brother who, he felt, would need a lot of support after his ordeal. Because of the likelihood of a bug in his apartment, Robert chose to meet Gary in his hotel room, leaving his 'tail' perusing a drinks menu in the lobby, to all intents and purposes happy with the job he was doing. Robert knew he should be as mad as hell with the way they were invading his privacy but somehow he lacked the energy, or maybe he had to conserve his strength for whatever lay ahead. He had experienced the same kind of suspended animation in the cellar.

Sitting in the cramped room which Gary hadn't disturbed at all except for a shirt collar that drooped like a Dalí clock from a half-open drawer, Robert thanked him for all he had done on his behalf, adding, "But you really should be with Sue and the kids now."

"I'll probably leave soon," Gary said, but he wondered if Robert was fully recovered yet; though back in harness he seemed to be floating just above the surface of his normal life.

Robert told him about the tape which, for security reasons, he had brought with him. Gary asked him what it contained and Robert gave him a summary of the earlier segments. On impulse he decided to tell him about the ending; if not Gary then who? Gary listened without interrupting but his eyes widened with incredulity, then alarm.

"Are you telling me..?" he paused for breath, "that bin Laden may have died in his bed ... from natural causes? My god, Bob, you can't be serious."

"It certainly looks that way, Gary. There's footage of him collapsing in the street in a small town that looks like Bilal. Then he was helped into a taxi where he was driven to his compound in Abbottabad. His youngest wife helped put him to bed. When he died, there were shots of his wife and kids mourning him ... I recognized his son Hamza."

"It could all have been staged..."

"There is some possibility of that, but I don't think so." Robert began to pace the floor of the small bedroom. "I'll play the tape for you if you want..."

Gary stood up as if to follow him. "I don't want to see it ... You do know what it means ... if it's true?"

"I think so," Robert said.

"Let me spell it out ... It would mean the attack on bin Laden's compound was a lie ... No SEALs, no burial at sea ... the Administration lied about everything..."

"Not for the first time..."

"It would also mean that 9/11 ... Jesus Christ, it would mean that the 9/11 conspiracy theories are right ... that Mossad agents might have been involved, along with ... our own covert-ops spooks ... It would mean that there was no justification whatever for the wars in Iraq and Afghanistan..."

"All reasonable inferences." Robert turned towards his brother, waited for a while and said, "I think I'm going to broadcast the tape."

Gary grabbed him by the sleeve. "Are you fucking insane..? Even if the authorities disprove everything that's on the damn tape, you'll still go down for treason."

"That's beside the point..."

Gary tightened his grip and shook his brother. "No! No, it *is* the point. Look, I don't know what went on in Metuchen. Maybe you got a dose of Stockholm syndrome. But, listen to me, you're not thinking straight. From what you told me, Khaled wanted to die. That was his problem, not yours. You don't owe him anything. You've been through hell. Don't make it harder on yourself. That's always been your problem ... looking for obstacles. It's over, Bob, let it go. Destroy that fucking tape ... or hand it over to Limon."

"I know it sounds stupid, but Khaled died for his beliefs. I wouldn't do that." Robert hardly recognized his own voice above the purring of the air-conditioning. He found himself staring at a brochure in a transparent plastic wallet that advertised the facilities offered by the Holiday Inn. "I wouldn't die for my beliefs."

"So, you're rational. My god, Limon already thinks you were part of the scam. Do this and you're sunk. Listen to me, you hophead, have I ever steered you wrong?" Gary sensed he wasn't getting through and his lean face darkened under its tan.

"It's not that easy." Robert continued to wrestle with shadows and frayed memories. He felt the cassette in his pocket. This chance was given to him; it was more than a coincidence that he who had a voice and countenance should use them for the powerless. The people could decide on the veracity or otherwise of the tape.

"Aw Christ, Bob, I think they brainwashed you. There's no moral issue here. It's just the breaks. You got lucky, he didn't. Actually, he did get lucky because he died the way he wanted to. Maybe he was swayed by the thought of seventy-two virgins." Gary relaxed his grip on his brother's sleeve.

"I think he was basically a good man." Robert cringed slightly even as he said it.

"A fanatic, you mean," Gary threw back without looking in his direction.

"Maybe. But I'm not sure that's so wrong anymore." There were so many people who didn't go one step beyond themselves and Robert numbered himself among them. Whether Khaled's 'cause' was right or wrong hardly seemed to matter. What was important and rare was that his conviction was selfless. Maybe he was slightly mad but if Robert denied such a man identity he would be truly cursed.

"You're still … tired. Go and get some sleep.

You've got that press conference later and Sarah wants to see you at KNYBS beforehand…"

"He told me I was an honest man…"

"Who?"

"Khaled Hassan."

"And what…? You're flattered by that so you want to finish his job for him? Jesus Christ, Bob, get a grip. We all know you're an honest man." Gary was a little hurt as well as irritated; it seemed as if his brother attached more weight to the opinion of an Arab fanatic than to anyone else's.

"You think that…?"

"Yes. Absolutely. Damn straight."

"Thanks."

"For what?"

"Everything." It's only by denying the impulse to be recognized, Robert reflected, that one becomes whole. Like his brother. He knew he couldn't lie low much longer; pressure was building. Limon's agents were out there. Drew was planning a bumper show, the press were advancing on the citadel and publishers wrangling over the spoils. The crush wasn't winning any more. The crowd could also roar for blood.

"Just don't do anything rash. Promise me," Gary pleaded with him. "You could still be in shock."

Without warning they embraced. It seemed only yesterday when they stood shivering in their nightshirts at the window, watching Spider Hastings' misfortunate Dad hacking desperately at the unexpected ice in the water butt to rescue his last bottle of booze.

Robert went down to the floor above the lobby, a mezzanine from which he could see the agent watching the world go by, a diligent man doing his twilight work. Robert walked through a function room being prepared for some convention and left the hotel through a fire door. He took a cab to his bank in Exchange Street not far from Simkin's office, and put the tape in a safety deposit box. Feeling light-headed, he went back to the hotel and walked up to his gumshoe. He patted the startled man on the shoulder and said, "I'm ready to leave now, if you've finished your newspaper."

CHAPTER 25

DURING THE NEXT couple of days Robert called on other TV Networks. He was welcomed by old colleagues and pummeled affectionately, given sherry and coffee, but the *bonhomie* wore thin when he put his proposition about the tape. They offered guest appearances, consulting contracts, and a few even tried to wean him away from KNYBS with platinum handshakes, but they invariably lapsed into awkward silences when the subject of the tape came up. He formed the impression that they had been warned in advance; maybe Limon had put the word out. Maybe they were just chicken. The Patriot Act reached far and wide.

Though the rejections were apologetic and finely nuanced, they reminded him of the time thirty years ago when he had pounded the streets with manuscripts under his arm which nobody wanted to read. But then he had the compensation of youth and a slightly thicker skin.

During his perambulations around the city his alter ego stuck to him like glue, refusing to acknowledge Robert's frequent waves and gestures. Sarah refused to accompany him on what she called his fool's errand. Indeed many of his friends spoke about him in worried tones, hoping he would snap out of it. Drew advanced the theory that he'd been brainwashed and that people with an academic bent were vulnerable in that respect, lacking, as they did, their proper share of street smarts – "bullshit baffles brains." But, like a rogue elephant, Robert plunged on, undeterred, through the thickets of Manhattan.

He missed the next press conference too and was fast becoming an enigma. Rounding on him in print, the tabloids asked what he was trying to prove and accused him of arrogance. The country, they said, had watched and prayed for him when he was in captivity and now he responded with a deafening silence. But despite the petulant rant it was clear they were hooked by the mystery, drawn in by his reclusivity and the snippets of odd behavior that had reached them. They were at pains to unmask him and, by a strange perversion, endowed him instead with false plumes. But the volumes which his silence spoke could not yet be interpreted.

On Saturday, against his better judgment, but to make up to Sarah, he accompanied her to a publishers' bash in the Waldorf and found himself among portly possessive men in black suits squiring their glittering consorts dressed in the season's color, smoked palomino, among the buffet tables laden with canapés, hot plates and confections sculpted to look like the year's bestsellers.

Sarah draped herself on Robert's arm – it was not a night to prove a woman's independence – and met the bantering thrusts of all who welcomed him back. In a way, she chaperoned him and enjoyed the role reversal.

"Glad you beat the rap," an art book publisher called from the nearby raw bar where he had just quarried into a huge salmon whose dead eyes mocked its own pink flesh. Robert raised his hand in acknowledgment. He already had pains in his legs from standing around, and felt that faint unreality that comes after a few cocktails, when the highlights become misty and coalesce into the softer lozenges of a camera fade-out. The guests put him in mind of the lobsters in crushed ice, one giant claw washing the other. More generously he saw them all, himself included, like toys that came to life at night to work out their animated natures in the hazardous world of the nursery, to be found in the morning lifeless and still, tear-stained and slightly scratched. They were all fleeing the inertia of the grave, strutting their stuff in the fleeting moment.

The President of the Publishers' Guild grabbed him in a pincer movement, one hand on his arm, the other on his shoulder. "Wait till you hear my speech, Bob. I've built it around you." He bore down on him beaming. "You should have a ticker-tape parade, boy, if you ask me. What you have to do now is capitalize on your assets, get out there and hustle. Hell, you know that better than me."

Sarah rushed to fill the silence. "That's what I've been telling him, Dave." Writers, her rueful smile said, don't know which side their bread is buttered on; we have to show them where the bathroom is, but we love them all the same.

Robert caught her look just before she turned it off.

"You actually toughed it out with those terrorists." Dave continued the eulogy. "That's what makes it so special. You're not just an observer anymore; you've been there. That gives you real clout."

Total image, Robert thought. My god, he had it now, thrust upon him, at a time when he wanted to retreat into the wings or join Gary on the porch. He gulped his martini and gagged slightly.

"I presume we can expect a book...?" Dave extruded an impish look to soften the proposition.

"Back off," Sarah laughed. "I've got first refusal." Her free arm encircled Robert's waist in a proprietorial way.

"Well, whoever," Dave conceded. "It'll be a mega winner, that's for sure."

And this from a man, Robert thought, who rejected his second novel on the grounds that the 'genre' was not immediately obvious. Indeed, the book was post-mod and so defied simple-minded categorization.

"Let's auction it now," Robert said in a monotone.

Dave laughed and peeled off to mingle with another group.

"I'm leaving," Robert said suddenly. He longed for quietness and a scene that stood still. If he stayed he would start to drink heavily. These people weren't real; yet there was a time when he fought to cultivate them. Networking – or 'schmoozing' – had, he now regretted, once been his stock in trade.

"You can't be serious…"

"I don't want to be here. You stay if you want to…"

"He's going to mention you in his speech for god's sake." Her fingers gripped the cloth of his dinner jacket but, because of the long nails, couldn't maintain a firm hold without risking breakages.

"Accept the Oscar for me…" Without meaning to, he extricated himself rather abruptly from her grasp. He thought he might throw up.

"Robert, don't do this." On the verge of changing from alarm to dismay, her face had never seemed so heavy.

"I'm sorry, Sarah. I'll leave the car for you." He was finding it difficult to breathe. It was years since he'd had an asthma attack and didn't relish the thought of being laid low by one now. He had survived awful privations for three weeks in a filthy cellar and here he was in luxurious surroundings on the point of passing out.

She watched his departing back, and felt raw with unexpressed anger. But she decided to stay even though she resented having to explain his absence to others who gusted forward, asking "Where's Robert?" as if she didn't exist in her own right. So she stood in her paneled lace skirt with bowed mink hem and crêpe-de-chine cavalier shirt and damned him under her breath. He had never treated her so badly before and she had an inkling that behind the calm exterior something strange smoldered inside him. She wasn't disposed to spend too much energy trying to unravel it right now.

The party developed in squalls of greeting and recognition, sophisticated foreplay and the plying of the art which conceals business. Sarah stood, perforce, a little apart from it all and was glad when Drew sidled over in her direction. He gave her a countenance and a fresh drink. Although he had seen Robert walk out, he knew the time was not yet right to make his move. He broached a neutral subject: her plagiarizing author.

"You sorted out Henfy then?" he inquired. A blue cummerbund encased his tubby waist and a ridiculously ruffled shirt foamed out over it.

"Yes. Mr. James H. Henfy and I are no longer doing business."

"Too bad." With that opening gambit out of the way, he forged on. "Incidentally, if Robert does a book I'll be glad to help in any way I can, maybe a little TV exposure."

"We'll see." She wasn't sure what Drew would get out of it but there was bound to be something. She could recognize a fellow commission-seeker at twenty paces.

"You know," Drew continued, "Robert's behavior hasn't escaped attention. The gentlefolk of the press are pretty annoyed about being shut out. There's even talk that he's turning into a sort of Howard Hughes. I've seen this happen before. The greatest showmen on earth suddenly, for no apparent reason, start to spurn the media that helped put them up there. You know what this business is like; there's no time for shrinking violets. I wouldn't like to see Robert turn into yesterday's man."

"You wouldn't?" She gave him a canny, slightly disbelieving look.

"No."

"Oh, I don't think there's anything to worry about," she said lightly, wondering if it was a lie or whether she had chosen not to be concerned. In any case she had no desire to pursue it. He lifted two glasses of champagne from a hovering tray and handed her one. He looked around at the marble pillars, gilt ornaments and ice sculptures. "What's it all about? I sometimes wonder?"

"Gravy," Sarah said, debunking his philosophical speculation. "Gravy. What else?" She looked at the walking laundry basket beside her and felt better; he was homely if nothing else.

"What else indeed." He sighed at the foibles of the world.

Sarah laughed and used her paper napkin to mop the condensation running down the sides of her glass. "By the way, don't ask."

"What?" His eyes strayed over her face and upswept hair held in place by tortoiseshell combs.

"Where Robert went."

"Gone off, I suppose. To meditate," he added disparagingly. He picked his teeth with a cocktail stick, then used it to free an imaginary obstruction in his pipe. Despite all these manipulations he still managed to wave the pipe at people as they came and went. Because of his bachelor habit of getting out and about he had built up a large number of acquaintances, most of whom turned up at the same parties. It was a form of social capital that could be drawn down from time to time and pay surprising dividends.

"Right in one." The verification cancelled the carefully glossed curves of her mouth. The question formed and re-formed in her mind: if Robert could walk out on her like that what claim had she? "I don't know what's gotten into him. He won't do the press conference. He's going to let it all slip away."

"And he embarrasses you in public," Drew rowed in. This might just be the cue he was waiting for. It was monstrous that Robert, who had everything including damn good luck, should treat Sarah so cavalierly and get away with it. "He's self-destructive if you ask me, hawking that damn tape around the place." He took her hand in his and continued in a low voice for her ears only. "You should detach, I mean it. Or he'll bring you down with him. Listen to me, Sarah, I know you better than myself and I ... want you, have done for years. Hell, you know that. I've waited and watched from the wings while you wasted yourself on that prima donna who doesn't know the meaning of commitment. He never loved you. Not really. I said it before and I say it now. We're an item, you and me…"

She listened in silence to this earnest poem,

weighing up the unscannable verse, reading the lines of effort in his survival face. Was this it, she wondered, the end and the beginning? By comparison Robert was a zillion miles away. His light reached her but maybe he didn't exist anymore.

"Let's get out of here," Drew said in a hoarse voice. He hadn't planned to force the issue, but such an opportunity might not come again. Robert had treated her appallingly and deserved to pay for it.

She felt the pressure of his hand on the small of her back and the force of his suggestion.

"But the speech...?" It was a half-hearted, residual expression of doubt and regret.

"If he doesn't wait, why should you?" His logic was impeccable.

She laid down her glass, and tightened the wrap about her shoulders. Taking her hand, he led her through the thronged and watching room.

When he got home Robert discovered that his front door had been forced and his apartment turned over. The wall safe was torn out, drawers and closets gutted, beds ripped from stem to stern. He stood in the middle of the debris trembling with a helpless rage. His anger was not diminished by the perversely whimsical thought that it was one way of finally erasing the presence of Nita. Not one room had escaped what must have been a frustrated, vicious search. The offices downstairs had suffered the same treatment, filing cabinets forced open and shelving units swept clean. Thankfully, as far as he could tell, the computer hardware had not been damaged. Upstairs, he discovered that even the scanty furnishings of the roof garden had been ransacked. In his mind he railed against the invisible and untouchable image of the perpetrators, servants of the State, paid for by his tax dollars.

He had never been the victim of legalized violence before and even as he surveyed the evidence, could hardly believe it had happened. Indeed, until now he would probably have justified such a raid in situations of national emergency. But as he wandered through the wreckage, he realized just how callous and downright sleazy so-called covert operations could be. Judging by smashed porcelain figurines and other small antiques which couldn't possibly have concealed the tape, the operatives – civil servants by another name – had clearly enjoyed their work. He felt powerless; it was as if Khaled was giving him an object lesson in American polity. At least he didn't have to worry about the cassette which was safe in his bank.

He spent the night at Gary's hotel and regretted it because Gary stayed up for hours trying to convince him to hand over the tape.

"It's an albatross around your neck," he said

more than once in the cramped bedroom. "Give it to the CIA for god's sake and be done with it. If they toss your apartment like that where are they going to stop? Don't you see what you're up against, Bob? Not even your influence is going to get you out of this hole. Stop digging. Settle down for Christ's sake, marry Sarah. Since when were you a rebel? Never..." He stomped around the room in his striped pajamas, using his hands as if he wanted to throw them away from him.

Robert lay fully clothed on the spare bed, appreciating what Gary was trying to do, but not really listening to him. "You know Khaled asked me to participate in the tape and I almost agreed. Maybe I should have done it."

"I don't want to hear it." Gary shook his head and raised a hand to fend off such nonsense. "I think you're losing your marbles. Look, I'm for the underdog too but no one expects you to sacrifice yourself. Don't you get it? Limon is after your hide and you're playing right into his hands. The last part of the tape will do you in." He paused but not for long in case the silence was construed as capitulation. "Remember that trip you offered me? Let's all go on a long vacation together. We'll bring John, lie in the sun..." He kept up the barrage for most of the night, alternating between dire warnings, well-meaning abuse, and inducements to get away from it all.

———————

Robert's righteous anger was an impenetrable shield which he carried with him when he barged into Limon's office the next morning on the stroke of nine.

"How dare you ransack my house," he grated, standing before the bare desk. "I've put up with your bugs, that idiot who follows me around, and your paranoia. But this time you've gone too far, Limon. Your miserable agency is not above the law. You can't hide behind executive privilege any more. I'm going to sue you for what you've done..." He wiped away a slight dribble of saliva that appeared on his bottom lip.

Far from being fazed, Limon lay back in his chair and brought his long hands together in an attitude of prayer. "You're going to sue me? That's rich, coming from you. Do you happen to know what the penalty for treason is?"

"You must be crazier than I thought. Maybe it's an occupational hazard with you people, living in a sewer..." He quaked with rage, feared he would lose control. The shield protecting him from the reality of madness was beginning to disintegrate.

"The evidence is incontrovertible." Limon began to notch off the most telling points. "Hassan was a student of yours. No violence was used in the kidnap. You were bent over the body when we broke in. We found some ... interesting pieces of writing in the cellar. You were clearly collaborating. We know all about it." He deliberately gave the impression he was speaking on behalf of the Agency rather than embarked on a solo run.

"That's all bullshit … Don't try to put me on the defensive, Limon. You're the criminal here not me. Someone should put you out of your misery…" Robert felt the floor move beneath his feet and grasped the back of a chair for support. He would have preferred if his adversary were less composed.

"If you're not guilty why are you holding on to the tape?" Limon asked with only the barest challenge in his voice. "And don't ask, what tape. It's the one you've been trying to foist on the networks. At least they have enough savvy not to touch it. Even KNYBS got the message." He stood up, pushing the chair back, a mineral glitter of hatred in his eyes. "You're guilty, Lynskey. You're as dirty as a pile of coal. Did you really think you and your pal Khaled Hassan could free Jallud Fahd? You never had a chance. I can tell you now that Fahd is dead."

"You tortured him to death, didn't you?" Robert held his head, wondering what had happened to this country which once was an exemplar for the rest of the world. How had it mutated so much in just one generation?

"You betrayed your country."

Robert met his look. Where had he encountered such conviction before? Of such certainties are wars made. He wondered if Limon had any awareness. Could he not realize that he was the opposite side of the terrorist coin? Had he any qualms at all about shooting Khaled dead or killing Jallud Fahd? No, because blindness was the corollary of such conviction.

"I don't know what kind of power trip you're on, Limon, but I'm going to make you accountable for your actions, and for that accusation. Yes, I have the tape and I have my reasons for keeping it. Very good reasons." For a few seconds he was tempted to tell Limon about the bin Laden footage, and the devastation it would cause him and his beloved agency, but he couldn't, not yet. "That treason crap doesn't wash with me. You'd be laughed out of court."

"We're going to nail you one way or another." Limon again sheltered behind the plural. "You can't hide." He gave a sharp laugh. "A high profile isn't always an advantage." His eyes had almost disappeared in the suffused face. He knew he had revealed most of his hand but that would help flush Lynskey out. "People like you think you can sell out the country that gave them everything. I'm here to tell you it doesn't work like that. And don't think your connections will help. There are other ways of dealing with your sort. We don't always have to go by the book." It gave him some satisfaction to see the startled reaction in Lynskey's face.

"I don't … believe this…" Robert's stomach began to heave. "Go and fuck yourself, Limon." It took him all his remaining strength to get out of the office. In the elevator he popped a beta-blocker to slow his heart. On reaching the street he gasped for air. He felt idiotic and out of his depth, as if he had been sheltered all his life from this world of intrigue and dangerous infantilism which must have existed right on his doorstep; he had been safer in the cellar.

CHAPTER 26

HELPED BY BETH, his housekeeper managed to tidy the apartment and make it reasonably habitable. Robert thanked them and made a mental note to send flowers. He took a sleeping pill and crawled into the remnants of his bed.

Despite the pill, he had a troubled night and dreamt of the time he'd flown to Montana as a cub reporter to do a story about the Plains Indians, especially the Blackfeet, who were suing the Federal Government for the return of Glacier Park and for the rights to recently discovered oil on the reservation. He sat in the inside seat. Beside him was a young marine going home on leave, and in the aisle seat was a retired naval captain who made a point of involving Robert in the conversation. At one point, for no reason other than politeness, Robert asked the marine about Quantico and the kind of training he'd received, whereupon the old sea dog snapped, "Don't tell him anything, he's not an American. You don't know who he is."

The young marine turned ruefully to Robert and said, "You heard it from a captain." Robert clammed up for the rest of the flight, concentrating on the green and saffron patchwork of the Mid West which gradually turned into an astounding pattern of jagged earth tones as they approached the foothills of the Rockies. He had always loved America.

He woke refreshed and his mind was clearer than it had been for some time; gone was the climacteric and he had a plan of sorts which, on this occasion, would not wait until tomorrow. He showered quickly and brought his coffee into the study where he stood for a while gazing out at the sky, a lightly whisked soufflé that breathed over the cubist city; the contrast between cloud and concrete, curves and angles, never lost its appeal.

Sitting at his desk, he went methodically through an accumulated pile of mail which he had not handed over to Beth for sorting. As he'd anticipated there were several invitations to give addresses and to appear on talk shows, but none quite suited his purpose. Although he hadn't used a creative agency for years, he called one and outlined what he had in mind. The senior partner bent over backwards to accommodate him and made light of the specific conditions Robert laid down, even though they were, to say the least, unusual.

Thus it was that Robert appeared the next morning on a live breakfast show of a rival network, in breach of his contract with KNYBS. Before air time he chatted briefly with his host, Frank Redding, a genial man in an angora sweater who did not disguise the fact that this was the biggest coup of his career.

"I don't know why you chose our little breakfast show," he said, "but we don't look gift horses in the mouth. We ran promos all day yesterday and expect upwards of sixty million viewers. I guess I'm more nervous than you are. Hell, even the riggers are on valium this morning." He discussed a line of questioning which Robert readily agreed to. After a brief conference with the producer they took their places on the set, a bright butter-colored kitchen that suggested morning could be fun, especially if accompanied by a light and fluffy show.

When the cue came Frank introduced his guest in reverential tones and welcomed him to the studio. He asked Robert about the kidnapping, how he coped in captivity, what his abductors were like. Robert answered crisply and to the point, disguising feelings behind facts, keeping opinion to a minimum. The discussion followed a strict chronology and was so evenly divided between the two talking heads it could have been guided by a metronome or a chess clock.

"Try to draw him out more," the producer suggested to Frank during the commercial break. "He makes it sound as if it happened to someone else. This is Lynskey for god's sake. When're we going to have this chance again?"

When they came back on air Frank asked about the rescue.

"It was professional," Robert said. "Although in my view they didn't have to kill Khaled Hassan. As a matter of fact, I wasn't in any danger. And he had emptied his gun before going out…"

"I don't follow. The official account said he came out firing."

"That's not true. The fact is he wanted to die to prove a point and knew the authorities would be happy to oblige. They did oblige by shooting him."

"What point did he want to prove?"

"That Americans are not sufficiently aware of the Arab, especially the Palestinian, cause." Robert's voice was low, wrapped in tissue; he didn't have to force the pace. The facts would speak for themselves.

"But how would dying help?" Frank knew he was departing from his producer's instruction but he had to follow it up. He had too much respect for Lynskey to try to sidetrack him. Besides, it was heavy-duty material and it was his chance to play Hamlet.

"There's another tape which would explain it better than I can. But because of pressure from the CIA, the networks are not prepared to show it."

"Pressure? You're certain of this…?"

"Oh yes. The tape is in my possession as it happens. The CIA has been tailing me ever since the rescue and two days ago ransacked my apartment."

"But you were the victim…" Frank couldn't believe his luck. It was one in the eye for the 'serious' news guys who always regarded him as a lightweight. Through his ear-piece he heard the producer, "Frank, this is getting too heavy. Change the line of questioning…"

"Well, I bet you're glad it's all behind you now." Frank refilled both coffee mugs.

"Unfortunately it's not. Captain Limon of the CIA recently accused me of treason. They're desperate to seize and destroy the tape. And I know why ... I'm afraid the Intelligence community of this country has become paranoid ... The Patriot Act gives them far too much power..."

"Frank," the producer yelled, "Get him off this or we're going to have to pull the plug."

"You ... em ... seem to have lost a lot of weight ... in captivity..." Frank somehow knew that Robert wouldn't follow this lead, and was glad.

"And I'll probably lose more being hounded by the CIA. However, I've put the tape in a safety deposit box and have instructed my attorney to open it in the event of any 'accident' that might happen to me..."

"Jesus Christ, Frank, do something ... two and a half minutes left ... We're in deep shit..."

"Can I ask you about your personal plans for the future?" The question was a dual purpose one; it covered Frank and gave Robert all the running room he needed.

"To stay alive and hope that some network will have the guts to show this tape which happens to be most revealing..."

"Cut it now" the producer wailed. "Go into the break early..."

"Thank you so much for coming in and sharing your experiences with us." Frank shook Robert by the hand and, when they went off air, winked. "Thanks, man."

As Robert walked off the set he was met by the producer whose face was flushed behind the designer stubble. "Thanks a lot." His brindled forearms made a votive gesture. "Now I know why you wanted a live show."

"You're in the clear." Robert smiled at him. "They can hardly prove pre-meditation, now can they? And I believe you've just had a scoop. Anyway it had to be said." He quoted Robert Frost, "The best way out is always through."

He walked out wondering how long his triumph would last, and whether he had 'sold' the tape properly. He had at least insured himself and wiped Limon's eye into the bargain. And he wasn't finished yet. He was almost prepared to believe that Hassan was pulling the strings from his Seventh Heaven.

When he got home he typed out his letter of resignation which he addressed to the president of KNYBS. He didn't attempt to explain his reasons, which were not fully clear to him. All he knew was that the decision made sense. His life had been one long series of compromises and tradeoffs in a profession that prided itself on honesty and fair-dealing. He considered sending a note to Drew but decided to let him sweat. Instead, he wrote to Chaim, thanking him for his help, both personal and professional, in the past and offering to provide him with contacts and references should he choose to leave KNYBS. He sent a similar note to Peggy.

He checked his texts and emails, and set his phone to voicemail. There were as many pointless messages as usual, though Sarah's voice was conspicuously absent. It saddened him and he wondered why it was he couldn't live up to her image of him. He seemed to be disengaging from everything, an old merchant selling off his damaged stock without any clear idea of what to do with the proceeds. All that mattered was to clean out the shelves and closets that had groaned and bulged with the acquisitions of an inconsequential life. Or maybe, the thought insinuated itself, he was putting his affairs in order.

Gary found him hunched over his desk, an old gray-bearded pirate studying his charts for a safe haven.

"I watched the program. Boy, you've done it now." Gary flung his hat on a chair and sat on the edge of the desk. "At least you didn't mention bin Laden, but that's cold comfort … Christ only knows what's going to happen now."

"Yeah well, the die was cast a long time ago."

"So what now?"

"I'm going to the bank to get the tape. I'm going to make copies." He would conceal the copies all over town if need be, like botanists of old who planted rare species in as many different countries and climes as possible to increase their chances of survival. Hedging, Simkin would call it. Diversification of risk.

With a groan of resignation Gary decided to

go with him, and helped to shepherd him through the crowd of reporters which had reformed outside his door since the breakfast show. It was like walking through seaweed. Journalists skipped beside him, firing off questions, shoving mikes under his nose to catch the hoped-for replies. Snap-happy photographers ran backwards in front of him, crouching and clicking. They were all so young and vibrant, Robert noted; it was a pity he had nothing to give them. They followed him down the street to the corner and didn't give up until the cab doors closed. Then they sloped off consoling each other, the competitive zest dying with the mutual loss of a story.

"You know, I can't really believe this," Gary said as the driver followed Robert's instructions to go by a circuitous route in case of a tail.

Robert slapped him on the back. "Exciting though, 'aint it? All this cloak and dagger. Take the next left, driver."

"Jesus, Bob, it's not that funny. You've just taken on the CIA. What're you going to do for an encore?"

"Air the tape. Then we'll see. Come on, lighten up, Gary. I don't really think they're going to put me in cement pajamas, do you?" Outside, an atomized drizzle hung in the air, a bleak mist that heralded autumn. The incessant traffic took on a new swishing sound from the wet asphalt.

"I don't know," Gary said in a voice that matched the turn in the weather. "How many times did they try to kill Castro over the years?

Seven or eight – exploding cigars, poisoned thumbtacks in his shoes … It would be funny if it weren't so serious. You're charging into heavy artillery. And you're going to lose Sarah too, if you ask me."

"I may have already."

"You don't seem very concerned." Gary gave him a sharp look which Robert caught reflected in the glass partition protecting the driver.

"I know my limitations, Gary. I've never been good with women, not since Nita…" Robert caught hold of the strap to maintain his balance as the cab took a sharp right turn into the financial district.

"Stop looking for sympathy, you old fraud. You never worked at the relationship."

"Too selfish, I guess," Robert said in a small voice. The frank admission might have invited sympathy from anyone other than Gary.

"Absolutely," he concurred. "self-centered anyway."

The cab dropped them at the bank in Exchange Street. They were ushered in through the brass and marble lobby and met the manager in the doorway of his office.

"I'm so sorry, Mr. Lynskey. But we had no choice in the matter…" The manager's face was a sad mess of oatmeal from which the fiber had been extracted.

"What're you talking about…?" Robert asked, though a bad intimation had already taken root.

"I tried calling you. The authorities served us

with a distraint order … approved by the Fed, and the Justice Department, under the Patriot Act … It's against the policy of this bank I assure you … but we had to let them…"

Robert pushed his way through to the customer vaults and went straight to his box. It was empty. The small metal cavern shone with emptiness, as it had once before when Nita removed her jewelry on the day they'd agreed to separate.

"Christ Almighty, they can't do this." His voice echoed in the vault, a trapped tomb-like sound.

"I'm really sorry, Mr. Lynskey…" The manager followed him out. "It was out of our hands. If there's anything we can do…"

"You've done enough." The sepulcher was empty and there would be no resurrection. He was beaten. After all he'd been through only to fall at the last fence. God in Heaven, not even banks were safe from the tentacles of this Stalinist Administration.

Later, in a bar on fifty-seventh street Gary eventually broke the maimed silence. "Maybe it's for the best, Bob. You tried. Whatever it was all about, you tried and now it's over." While he sympathized with his brother he couldn't deny his own profound sense of relief. Now that the CIA had what they wanted he felt sure they would drop all that treason nonsense.

"Those bastards." Robert sat grim-faced. "I should have known they'd try something like that.

I should have made copies while I had the chance." He stared glumly at the polished marble counter on which his untouched drink rested. The exercise of raw power hacked at his senses. He felt as helpless as when he'd first arrived in the country. What use was the clout and influence he'd systematically acquired since that time if he could still be so easily toppled by an unconstitutional legal code and by operators who were trained like deliberately-starved Alsatian dogs?

This was what turned people into subversives. And now he too, coming full circle, had his first taste of impossible odds and the certainty of defeat. This is what the Palestinians must feel every hour of every day.

"Give it time," Gary said gently. It was difficult to give more precise advice without knowing the exact nature of his brother's dismay.

"I don't have time." It dawned on Robert that he'd spent his sixtieth birthday in captivity. It must have been the day he decided to cultivate constipation. Now that he had started his own conception at the ridiculous age of sixty, it was infuriating to be so helpless. Keeping the tape, he saw now, had something to do with recovering an early state of grace, if he ever had any, in those selfless times before that saurian inner eye developed. Now there was nothing, no guiding star, except for Gary who had that line to their father, ancestral integrity. Thank Christ for that.

"Of course you have time," Gary contradicted

him. "Plenty of time to do whatever it is you want to do. I can't pretend to know what that dumb tape meant to you. But you'll find something else, another way. You were always good at that." He called the bartender and waved his hand over the glasses. The same again.

"Another way," Robert mused, bleary-eyed, then sat bolt upright. "Another way!" He jumped off the barstool. "I'm so dumb it's not funny." Back in his brownstone there were all the facilities he needed for publishing, and a kind and loyal staff just waiting for a project. His face brightened and the bar-room gloom couldn't hide the determined glint in his eyes. He didn't have to *show* the tape; he could write it up. "I remember it all," he said, starting to laugh. "It's in here, all of it." He pounded the side of his forehead. "They can't confiscate what's in there … Memories not memoirs … I was so used to cardboard, don't you see… ? Memories!"

"Oh god, what now?" Gary held his head. The rogue elephant, his brother, was up and running again. He just refused to be put out of his misery.

"You'll see." Robert touched his glass to his and drank deeply. "Consciousness-raising; that's what Khaled wanted all along. Don't you see?" Of course, the book would make him more famous than ever, but he now knew how to use that double-edged attribute. Like Simkin's money, fame, he realized, had to be shared and spent most liberally or it would burn a hole in the heart. "You'll see the purpose in time. You will…"

"That's what I'm afraid of." Gary nevertheless accepted the arm that went around his narrow shoulders.